Books By Luke Smitherd:

Full-Length Novels:

The Physics Of The Dead

The Stone Man

A Head Full Of Knives

Weird. Dark.

How To Be A Vigilante: A Diary

Kill Someone. Anyone. (Coming late 2016)

Novellas

The Man On Table Ten

Hold On Until Your Fingers Break

My Name Is Mister Grief

He Waits

Do Anything

For an up-to-date list of Luke Smitherd's other books, his blog, YouTube clips and more, visit www.lukesmitherd.com

For anyone in my corner

Acknowledgements

At the time of writing, the following people wrote a nice Amazon.com or co.uk review of my last book, or sent a kind e-mail. Thank you so, so much. As someone fairly new to this game, those meant everything. I'm only using the names you put on your Amazon reviews, as these will be ones you're happy to have associated with my work ... I hope:

AJ hill, Adams family, Adrian Rasburn, Allison Travis - AC, alyson sylva - AC, amazonian goddess, Angela Wallis, Angie Hackett, Aunt Shish, Barbra, BigDog, bladerunner, Blanchepadgett, BoneyD, Book Thief, chananya, chrisbobs, Cinderiffic, David Plank, Dawnzilla, Dedicated Book Lover, Derek Cooper, Don, drac, Elliot Brown, FrCl, Glennccc, Gwendelyn Turensky, Ian Rendall, J Kinder, J. Vaughn, Jacque Ledoux, Jamie Greenwood, Jason goldsmid, Jason Jones, Jayme Erickson, Jinny, JMM52, Jo Cranford, JoanneG, Jon Perry, Karen Austin, katrina, Kelli Tristan, Kelly Jobes, Lady R, Leslie Young, LouiseTheFox, Lynda, M. Iddon, Maggie Anson, Mark3, MarkDA, MarnaKangas, Merlnich, Metalhead, Michelle Kennedy, Miss C A Evans, Missus.Robinson, Mr, Mr Matt Norgrove, Mr&MrsW, Mrs Kindle, Nabbo, Nick, Nita V. Jester-Frantz, P. Conde, P. Hughes, Paul Korhonen, Pooly4, R. Gaylor, R. GILL, Rachel James, Rachel Jane, Richard Hustwit, Rk, Rob Cantelo, Ron, S. Leach - AC, Sarah H, saultrue, Silversmith, Simon Abrahall, simon211175, Steph in Nottingham, Steve Gatehouse, Suzanne Sime, swebby, T J Wilks, tejadab, TerryHeth, the_goddess_isis, The Dogs Mum, The Fro, Thomas Mccann, Toni Boyle - AC, TonyM, trev, Vacman, Wellheld, YvonneHampshire5, and Zia Tiger.

Current list of Smithereens with Titles (see afterword on how to get yours):

Emil: King of the Macedonian Smithereens; Neil Novita: Chief Smithereen of Brooklyn; Jay McTyier: Derby City Smithereen; Ashfaq Jilani: Nawab of the South East London Smithereens; Jason Jones: Archduke of lower Alabama; Betty Morgan: President of Massachusetts Smithereens; Malinda Quartel Qoupe: Queen of the Sandbox (Saudi Arabia); Marty Brastow: Grand Poobah of the LA Smithereens; John Osmond: Captain Toronto; Nita Jester Franz: Goddess of the Olympian Smithereens; Angie Hackett: Keeper of Du; Colleen Cassidy: The Tax Queen Smithereen; Jo Cranford: The Cajun Queen Smithereen; Gary Johnayak: Captain of the Yellow Smithereen; Matt Bryant: the High Lord Dominator of South Southeast San Jose; Rich Gill: Chief Executive Smithereen - Plymouth Branch; Sheryl: Shish the Completely Sane Cat Lady of Silver Lake; Charlie Gold: Smithereen In Chief Of Barnet.

How To Be A Vigilante: A Diary

By
Luke Smitherd

" You SAW, and seeing, dared to DO. "
- Alan Moore, *V For Vendetta*

"...I knew that I had to be the second. I'd found my vocation."
- Alan Moore, *Watchmen*

"...with filthy body/ matted hair, and unwiped nose, Ralph wept for the end of innocence."
- William Golding, *Lord of the Flies*

"Everyone wants to save the world, but no one wants to help Mom do the dishes."
- PJ O'Rourke

"Let no man in the world live in delusion. Without a Guru none can cross over to the other shore."
-    Guru Nanak

"Everybody's got a plan 'till they get punched in the mouth."
- Mike Tyson

On September 28th[th] 1998, a laptop was found on top of a pump at a petrol station just outside of Manchester, England. It had been cleared of all files except a single folder on the Desktop entitled:

"TO THE FINDER: OPEN NOW TO CHANGE YOUR LIFE!"

It was subsequently handed in to the authorities, who have now given us permission – twenty years after the events herein occurred - to finally reprint the contents of that folder in their entirety.

The investigation remains open and unresolved. Nigel Carmelite's whereabouts are still unknown.

First Entry: Thursday August 6th 1998, 1:27 AM

I've decided to stop pissing around and get on with it. My problem has always been dithering, and after the last couple of years I'd say it's worse now than it's ever been. The dithering, I mean, but actually the same comment applies to my life in general. You'd think it would feel bad to write that, but it doesn't. After the decision I've made today, it feels liberating. It feels *good* to be starting. If I'd just been a bit more DECISIVE throughout my life, I'd probably have started to write this *years* ago. As it is I'm putting pen to paper, here and now, on day one of a new journey. I thought it'd be a good idea to keep a log of the whole thing, starting with the initial ideas and following them to their execution and beyond. That way, people in the future can look back and see how an influential mind worked; how the first man to do it *for real* got the ball rolling. (I just read that last bit over and it's not quite true, the whole 'pen to paper' bit. I'm writing this on my mum's laptop!)

Obviously, if you're coming to read this in - for wont of a less dramatic word - the future, you know who I am and what I've done (the precise details of the latter, obviously, I am not *totally* certain of yet, but I've got a wonderful idea). However, if I get the time or the inclination later on I may add some autobiographical notes. However, that isn't why you're reading this, are you? No doubt by now – you, dear reader, in whatever future lies ahead, knowing things as *history* that, to me, are things that *will be* – there are already several biographies about me. You'd be reading one of those if you wanted to know about my past. *This*, the account that you hold in your hands, is the progress chart, the ideas manual, the guide for anyone who wants to follow the path that I have blazed (will blaze, I mean). Well, it will be when it's finished. You want to know how to get started. Well, don't worry about that. I'm in exactly the same position as you right now, so in a funny sort of time-spanning way, we're really starting together. Except you have a big advantage that I don't. You have my diary.

This will be your blueprint.

The plan then. Something like this I shall obviously have to take in stages. As much as I would love to get straight out there and get started

NO, that's far too lame - how much I BURN to get out there and get started, how much it keeps me up at night with delicious visions that pump the adrenaline around my body and make sleep impossible... that really wouldn't be a good idea. I'd be stopped before I started, perhaps permanently, and I know I need to break this whole thing down into priorities.

By the way, did you see what I did in the above paragraph? How the previous sentence just cut off like that? Why would I leave that in? Because I want to show you how I think. This is real. This is an account of my thoughts so that you can know that I was an ordinary person like you. That I thought something – TYPED something – and halfway through the sentence, I realized I was writing the wrong thing, and then wrote something else. I'll leave *everything* in. Even the mistakes. Anyone who says I just didn't spot them is a goddamn liar and an idiot and a sheep.

I'm too juiced to think. Will hopefully be able to plan properly tomorrow.

Even so ...are you excited? I hope so. I am totally and utterly fucking excited.

Second Entry: Saturday August 8th 1998, 12:34 PM

Would have written yesterday, but got back from work shattered. That bastard Lawrence had me doing nothing but lug crates of beer around all afternoon. I should have been on tills, but he said that Lombard hadn't turned up and so I had to take *his* shift because I was the latest to arrive, which is bullshit logic as far as I'm concerned. I'm sure there's some sort of anti-discriminatory/anti-exploitation law or something about this sort of thing (I would like to point out to any possibly disillusioned future enthusiasts of mine that this break in writing doesn't mean any lack of commitment. I've started my route now and any days of dithering are long gone. I am on this 100% now, don't think otherwise. You will know by now how my belief in rigid self-discipline allowed me to follow through on my dream, and I hope you don't take this as a betrayal of that. I literally just fell asleep when I finally got home.).

However, on the positive side, this has pointed out the initial phase of my plan: that of honing my body to the peak of its ability. Any other planning is irrelevant until this is achieved, as this will literally be the spine of my new career. Everything else has to wait, and that is only sensible.

As I sit, I have Rage Against The Machine playing on the stereo, getting me in the mood for a workout. I'd like to take this opportunity to point out a key belief of mine to any people thinking of pursuing a similar career; that of the importance of MUSIC as a motivational source. The old me would have never thought about going to the gym. Only a couple of days ago I would have happily sat in a chair watching the Simpsons and eating oven chips, but the new regimen is this:

whenever I begin to think of sitting and doing anything nonproductive, I throw on something powerful, something that makes me want to BE powerful - anything by Bon Jovi being an excellent choice, Livin' On A Prayer in particular – and then suddenly it's so much easier to get yourself into action.

Also, in times when the mind needs to be exercised, a bit of opera in the background to help you think is wonderful, not to mention the fact that it helps to expand your cultural knowledge and improves you as a person. I bought three CDs of it today. I now have the best choices of opera in my living room, and I never appreciated it before. Motivation!

I have just come back from a small shopping spree, during which I purchased some new Nike Air Max, a workout vest, gym shorts, and - after some deliberation - some weightlifting gloves, a weightlifting belt, and some wristbands. It wasn't cheap, but there was a wonderful thrill about it. As I stood at the counter, holding my selections, the cashier smiled at me. The fact of my embarking upon a new regimen of fitness was obviously clear to her (of course, she couldn't possibly know the actual awesome depths of my plan!). I have to say, it was quite a profound moment for me. I had such a fantastic sensation of EXCITEMENT, a thrilling sense of preparation for something. I was proud and exhilarated as I handed over the extortionate amount of money, excited precisely because the amount I was spending *was* extortionate. I was committing myself to it. I had begun.

I rang round all the local gyms when I got home, and eventually found one with a halfway reasonable rate. I am slightly worried that I'm not going to be able to afford all this, but I've started now and I can always get overtime. A plan like this - as I'm sure those who are keen enough to read this now will agree - is *bigger* than money. As any bodybuilder will tell you, sometimes if you want it bad enough, you just have to make whatever sacrifices to your lifestyle that are necessary. I do wonder how easy it is for me to say that now rather than later, when it comes to actually making those changes. I shall simply have to cross that bridge when I come to it.

I'm supposed to have some sort of induction there in about an hour, which is particularly useful for me as I wouldn't have a clue where to start. Someone called Rob is supposed to show me around. I have a picture in my head of him and me becoming almost a team, although he will obviously never know what the team's goal is. No one will (until now, my friend! In your time, I mean.). In my somewhat fanciful head, I see Rob becoming Mr. Myagi to my Daniel-San, honing me towards my goal. Will write later and let you know how I get on.

Third Entry: Saturday August 8th 1998, 6:12 PM

It would not be unfair to Rob to say that any comparisons to Mr. Myagi would be a tad far-fetched. A short but trim white middle-class looking fellow, only a few years older than myself (obviously making it a little difficult for me to see him as any sort of, I don't know, guru), he came striding over and shook my hand in a very friendly way, which I have to admit I found likeable despite my normal reservations towards such over-familiar behaviour. I asked if I should go and get changed, but he sat me down in the canteen instead and began to ask me about me about my general fitness levels and what I wanted to achieve.

I wasn't happy about this, and told Rob so in no uncertain terms. He seemed a little taken aback by my reaction, but explained that this was so he could work out a personal program that would allow me to get the most out of my sessions. That seemed reasonable. He then asked me again what I wanted to achieve, so I said, and I quote:

"I want to be able to operate at the maximum levels of fitness and strength capable for someone of my genetic make-up." I told you I was committed! I expected him to look impressed, but he just sort of stared at me for a second. I assume he had never dealt with such a high level of commitment before for a beginner, and that is to be understood.

"Ok," Rob said, talking slightly differently now, seeing me in a new light (!) and leading me over to a set of scales. After taking my weight, he produced a set of calipers and proceeded to - as he put it - 'determine your body type.' Apparently, there are three basic body types: ectomorph, naturally slim and light; endomorph, larger but mainly consisting of fat; and mesomorph, naturally muscular. I am disappointed to find that I am an ectomorph, apparently. I asked Rob what body type he is. Rob is a mesomorph.

Rob then proceeded to take me around the gym, pointing out which machine works which body type and how each could be of benefit. This was all very exciting, and the buzz I experienced in the gym shop came back to me a little. Along every wall there was a row of mirrors, and I kept catching my reflection in them (currently 5'9" and about 140 pounds, should anyone be wondering what my original, normal weight was before I hit my legendary potential). I looked at Rob who was staring at me as I stared at myself in the mirror. He suddenly smiled.

"Miles away then, were you?" he asked. I caught my reflection again, and I was a little shocked to see the huge grin plastered on my face. I looked back at Rob. He'd stopped smiling. He caught me looking at him and smiled again. I wondered what's wrong with the man.

Anyway, once we'd finished our little tour, Rob asked me if I'd like to get started. I was surprised by this, and asked him about my 'precise personal plan'. He said he'd complete that fully later, but that we could get a very light workout in that day in order to get familiar with the machines. This was perfect, so I rushed off and got changed into the shorts, vest, gloves, belt and wristbands I'd brought with me. I was a little disappointed when Rob told me I wouldn't really need the belt today. I reminded Rob again that I wasn't there to mess about. He went silent again for a second and looked at me again in that funny way. Looking back, I find myself wondering now if the man might be a bit of a simpleton.

Apparently you only need the belt for the free weight stuff, and Rob said that we weren't really going to be doing any of that today. I must admit, I was this close to telling Rob to fuck off at that point and just get busy with my personal program; he could leave me to get on with the real stuff, thank you very much. However, this was just supposed to be my induction and even though he seemed prepared to keep me pissing about even longer than I already had been (and God knows I don't need any help in doing that), I'm sure that this was only for today. I thought (at the time) that it would perhaps be unwise to get rid of him just yet, as I would no doubt need him to temper my fiery enthusiasm later on.

We started off on what Rob called the 'Pec-Deck' (good lord I hate these yuppie colloquialisms for ANYTHING) and Rob set the weight at an annoyingly low level. I bit my lip instead of expressing my annoyance and got started. I completed fifteen 'repetitions' with a frustrating amount of ease. Rob congratulated me. I felt like telling him to piss off. I went again, and Rob still hadn't upped the weight.

"One more set, then," he said, "and we move on. Just getting acquainted here, remember." I looked at Rob.

"Well, let's move the weight up then," I said. Rob smiled and gave a little chuckle.

"Oh, we've got to go easy on your first time," he said. "Trust me, we'll get a little tougher as we go on, but for now it's best to go steady. You can really slow up your progress if you're not careful." This was highly annoying.

"Fair enough," I said, "but this is just silly. Can't we just put it up a bit?" Rob's smile faltered a little.

"No, really, this is best," he said. "I do this for a living, man."

That was when I had one of my insights. They don't happen very often, but I've had them ever since I was a kid. When I just KNOW. I felt the tension creep into my chest like always.

I realised that he was taking the piss. Looking back, as I write this, I don't know why I didn't realise before. Whether it was because he's the big shot mesomorph and enjoys secretly mocking less-fortunate ectomorphs like myself, it was clear that this man needed to be shown that he couldn't get away with that shit around *me*. I took a deep breath.

"Well, be that as it may Rob," I said, loudly, "I'm afraid that you're wrong in this case. I'm not having that." He said something then, but I wasn't listening as I leaned over and put the pin in the weight stack about 5 plates higher than where Rob had put it.

Before he could say anything, I was off, pulling the pads inwards. The extra effort involved was really quite shocking, but this was much better as now I was actually *working*. By the third repetition, however, I was aware of an uncomfortable, almost painful feeling in my chest and shoulders, but I'd started now and had to show Rob that he was wrong to try and dick me about.

Out of nowhere, the pads suddenly seemed to become twice as hard to move than they had for the first rep, and I was only four reps in, but Rob was standing there silently with that same gormless expression on his face, and I realised that he was finally getting the message so if I stopped now I'd blow it, so I kept going and I was on the sixth rep and starting the seventh when I could hear puffing and blowing and I realized that it was me as I felt the blood start to run to my head, and the pads felt like they were chained to the bumpers of two cars, but I was on the seventh rep and had to do at LEAST ONE MORE to reach a respectable eight, and I was squeezing and squeezing and they were going nowhere until Rob took a step forward, hesitated, and then put his hands on the pads and moved them together with me for the last rep and I was done. I flopped back in the chair and gasped air into my lungs, my shoulders feeling completely drained and my chest spasming. I looked at Rob who was still staring dumbly at me. I realized he just couldn't let me do it on my own. He had to make his point, had to try and prove that I needed his help. Rage began to build inside me.

'That was stupid, you know," said Rob. "You've probably strained all the muscles in your chest. I only helped on that last one as I could tell you wouldn't have stopped otherwise. You should listen to me if we're going to be working together...". He trailed off. He almost looked angry. HE almost looked angry? It was all I could do to just sit and gasp for air, but I still managed to say:

"Bollocks."

He stared at me. He clearly didn't know how to respond. I wondered how long he'd been doing this job. I just sat, panting, and stared back at him until he broke the silence.

"I can't work with you if you won't listen to what I say. I can't. You'll do yourself an injury and I'll get the blame. You really have to listen." He didn't sound quite so cocky now. Message received, I thought. Time to finish this off.

"Fine, Rob" I said, "To be honest, I think I've pretty much got it by now anyway. Thank you for your time." I continued to stare at him. He didn't look like a man confident enough to take the piss anymore. He looked like a whipped puppy. I'd won!

"Fine," he finally said. "Fine. I'll tell Marcus that I'll not be working with you. Go ahead and do what the hell you like. But I do warn you, this sort of antisocial behaviour will not be tolerated if you direct it towards any of the other gym-users. I was only trying to help you, but if you want to do it on your own, fine." Too late now to be pally, Rob, I thought. Shouldn't have had your little fucking joke. I waited for him to say something else, but he didn't. He nodded as if he'd made some sort of point, stopped as if he was about to say something else, then shook his head and walked away. I took a deep breath and continued with my workout. Rob returned briefly to make me sign some sort of waiver or some corporate tick box sheet that let him off the hook. Whatever. I signed it.

All this may sound as if perhaps I have lost a valuable asset. Not at all. In many ways, I feel that I have gained a lot here. Let me explain. I now have even more motivation to do well because:

1. **I must not let Rob see me fail.** For then he will win, as it were. I don't have to spend weeks and weeks 'taking it easy' because Rob is too scared of me hurting myself and suing him; and can get on with it as quickly as possible.

2. **Rob is clearly an idiot.** I don't need someone like that associated with the big picture, as he'll only drag me down.

All in all, I ended up having an extremely successful workout, and I believe today was a great start. I really FELT THE BURN, and as I drove home my limbs were so tired that I could barely drive! I feel I have made a major step today.

Fourth Entry: Sunday August 9th 1998, 1:22 PM

I can't raise my arms above my head. I can't fully extend them either, but even if I could do both of these things I wouldn't because my chest hurts so much that the thought of moving my arms at all is extremely unpleasant. All of this was enhanced by the horrible torn feeling in my shoulders. My legs ache wildly if I try and climb the stairs, and my stomach feels as if I've been punched in the gut all night.

I'm currently sitting in the living room with the laptop, practically immobilised in the armchair while watching the EastEnders Omnibus, and listening to my mum vacuuming upstairs. She thinks I'm just being lazy. If she'd done half the workout I have, she'd think twice before saying such stupid things. But then I stopped listening to her many years ago, so who cares?

I should imagine that one or two of you are thinking maybe I should have listened to Rob. Quite the contrary. It would be clear to the less cynical mind that this means one thing only; clearly, I actually got something done yesterday. The old adage, 'No Pain, No Gain', really is true. Yes, I'm in a large amount of PAIN right now, which can only mean a large of amount of GAIN. The point remains that I fully expected this too, as I am far from being naive enough to think I could retune my body – switch it from a life of softness to its peak athletic potential - without a small modicum of discomfort.

Regardless, I shall return to the gym tomorrow, and I shall give Rob - if he's there - a hearty smile as I walk in the door. Technically, according to my original gym plan, I should be going today, but I have decided that today is a day for planning, and that is what I am about to do.

As I said, I am going to tackle this in a series of stages. **Stage One** was entered into yesterday, obviously. **Stage Two** must now be addressed.

It is now half an hour since I finished that last paragraph, during which I gave much deliberation as to what **Stage Two** will be. For those of you who may be thinking that I am some sort of idiot that can't think of even the second stage of a plan in less than half an hour, I would like to point out that I was coerced into some of the vacuuming. This was time which I utilised wisely, I might add, by thinking while working. I just had to make this clear, as this *is* being recorded for posterity. I have come to the conclusion that **Stage Two** will involve taking up some form of martial art, running in conjunction with the gym sessions.

I had originally intended to have a much longer period in the gym, extending over many months, in order to ensure a far more healthy body before commencing any martial art. This was in order to facilitate easier learning of said martial art, but given more time to ponder the subject I believe that it would probably be best to just get on with it. The longer I wait, the worse things will get.

I now have with me *The Collins' Book Of Martial Arts*, which apparently is the most comprehensive general guide to martial arts around. This is lucky, because it is also the only book about martial arts we have in the house. I think I got it for Christmas many years ago, but I can't really remember that time anymore. After lengthy perusal, I have managed to whittle the choices down to five 'disciplines' (DISCIPLINE again, see? It's everything.):

Aikido: Basically grappling and throwing, utilising your opponents body weight, etc. Very cool, real stand-there-and-take-it stuff.

Tae-kwon-do: High, leaping kicks and striking moves. Jumping about a lot. Pretty spectacular.

Ju-jitsu: Apparently the composite martial art, incorporating striking, throwing, and blocking moves, but a little dull sounding.

Jeet-kune-do: What Bruce Lee did. Speaks for itself.

Capoeira: (I assume this is how you spell it, as for some reason this isn't in *The Collins' Book Of Martial Arts*, but I saw a guy on TV doing it.) Apparently a VERY spectacular looking martial art, with moves that flow into each other requiring a lot of acrobatic ability. Looks a lot like breakdancing.

I think it's very clear that the two obvious choices here are Jeet-kune-do and Capoeira, but it will really come down to which of the five are taught within this city (Derby). Two that almost made the list were Kendo (swords etc., particularly good because hardly anyone does it) and Muay Thai, but these were ultimately scratched. Kendo lost out because of the potentially lethal effect of a sword (a jail sentence, meaning that the likelihood of me actually using one on someone is quite low, plus a bloody *sword* is going to be rather hard to conceal) and Muay Thai was nixed because apparently it is bare knuckle, full-bore fighting. I think the chances of an amateur like me entering straight into this world and getting paralysed are, therefore, probably quite high.

I've made several phone calls, and I am pleased to announce that I have found the Hill Lane Dojo (Ju-jitsu) and the Dave Sharpe AXA Dojo on Grove St (Aikido). Though I am disappointed at the options presented - I particularly liked the idea of being able to leap a dramatic six feet into the air and kick a man square in the head - I have decided to opt for the Dave Sharpe AXA Dojo. My first class is on Tuesday, and I am sure Dave and I will get on very well.

If it wasn't for the pain, I would be extremely excited. I hope it has faded some more by Tuesday.

Fifth Entry: Monday August 10th 1998, 7:20 PM

Unable to make it back to the gym. As much as it galls me to think that Rob is, no doubt, thinking smugly to himself that he was right, I can assure you that this is certainly not the case, and I would assure him of the same thing were he here. Work was sheer hell today - more heavy lifting - and the ache, if anything, seems to have worsened overnight. I certainly hope this is a case of things having to 'get worse before they get better.' Plus, by the time I got home, I would have only had time for about an hour's workout (once I'd had my dinner and actually *reached* the gym) as opposed to my planned two hours. Therefore, I decided against it. Once again, I would like to point out that this is in no way due to any laziness. It is merely a practical decision based on a number of factors: the just-mentioned time element, and the fact that I had probably used up most of my energy earlier today at work and would therefore be unable to reach my potential.

My mum had already made my dinner, and insisted that I eat it. Despite the fact that I am now old enough to eat when I choose, to dispute it would mean a debate/talking, and so I just ate the beef stew she had prepared. Working out so soon after *that* would, no doubt, have induced stomach cramps, which would have reduced my workout potential even further. While I am sure that it is now clear to any reader that I have made the wisest choice here, I still intend to make up for it by undergoing *three* hours in the gym tomorrow! That's alongside my first Aikido class later that evening! Any remaining doubters may now pack up their bags and leave!

With reference to the mother incident, I must not allow this sort of thing to occur again. Though, of course, she is my mother, I cannot allow anything to halt me in my course of duty. I have made a major decision, and I *must not* allow items such as beef stew - however enjoyable - to deter me.

Tomorrow is a big day. As my dad would say, sometimes you really have to *work* to get what you want. Not the truest of men to his word, my dad – God knows he wasn't - but he was right on *that* one at least.

Sixth Entry: Tuesday August 11th, 1998 8:55 PM

Got to the gym at five, bang on. I worked out that if I was efficient and fired straight through, I could be ready to walk out the gym door at 8:15, thus being at the Dave Sharpe AXA Dojo by 8:30. The pain had subsided a little when I started, but was still noticeably present. However, as I said yesterday, I had no choice but to get on with it. I opted for spending a little time stretching first, in order to be a little less susceptible to the morning after pain (not too long, I might add; I wasn't bottling it in any way, just trying to do things properly), but this was highly painful to perform. This suited me fine though, because I was so keen to get started.

I had decided to make the first two hours purely strength building, and leave the final hour for cardiovascular/fitness work. This, according to my exercise book that I purchased today - who needs Rob?? - burns a LOT of energy, so I worked out that the strength stuff should go first, when I'd really *need* all that energy. As you can see, it's all reasonably straightforward to a logical mind. I hadn't really had time today to read the book thoroughly, but there were charts on the wall of the gym describing various types of exercises with free weights that work separate parts of the body, and I decided that as long as I did every single one of those and used every machine, I would have a good all-round workout. I'm sure you are like me in my amazement that Rob gets *paid* for 'teaching' this. If you look around, it's all there for you.

One hour in, I did begin to feel a surprising amount of fatigue to go with the, admittedly, rather high amount of pain, even though I did my best to fire straight through this. Fortunately, (although I would have continued regardless, obviously) Rob arrived with a 'client', a rather large, overweight woman in her thirties. I immediately sprung to my feet from the bench upon which I had been gathering my energies, grabbed two dumbbells, and began to work (the precise exercise I was performing, I cannot be one hundred percent sure of at this moment in time).

Rob gave a wonderful performance of not having seen me, but I could tell that internally he was crushed at seeing me working harder than he could possibly comprehend. It made the following hour a lot more enjoyable, following Rob and his client around the gym, working at least one machine behind. At one point, Rob's thin veneer of composure broke and he actually looked at me, pretending to see me for the first time.

"Oh," he said, obviously flabbergasted at being caught out. "Back then, are you?" I grinned at him in response.

"Yes, working hard, feeling the burn!" I replied.

"Good. Good stuff." He smiled in a funny sort of way, trying to make himself feel better perhaps, or maybe trying to be pally again, but no dice, Rob. I gave a little salute and went on to the next machine, where the pain was now at almost intolerable levels, but I certainly wasn't going to let Rob see *that*.

At the start of hour three though, I came to a sensible decision: finish up, and get some rest before the AXA Dojo session. This made obvious sense, because the Aikido session will no doubt be – I am sitting in the car outside the dojo as I write this - very vigorous and cardiovascular in nature, and this will *equal* the hour of cardiovascular exercise I was going to do in the gym. Some might say that it would be better to have two hours of cardio rather than one, but the more intelligent mind will say that it makes sense to conserve my energy for the Aikido hour. It wouldn't do to simply rush at everything, after all.

So, after a long shower, I got dressed, bought four energy bars at the counter on the way out (I drank a protein shake at the juice bar!), and drove to the AXA Dojo. Guns N' Roses was blasting away on the stereo (important psych up tape; ready to rumble with Dave!) and got there with 35 minutes to kill before the session started. During which I wrote all this! I am currently feeling excited and pumped (thanks to G n' R), and I will conclude here by just saying that you, the reader, are perhaps by now joining your *own* martial arts class, or maybe even reading this in *your* car before you go inside!! Well, I give you my best wishes and hope it all goes well. What have you chosen for YOUR motivational tape?

I'm off to class now. Tell all later!

Seventh Entry: Tuesday August 11th 1998, 10:15 PM

I am now back in the car after the session. I never knew a martial art could be so awesome. I will master this and become unstoppable. Girls will love it too, I should think. A nice bonus. If anyone ever tries to grab my wrist in a bar brawl, he had better think twice before doing so. I must confess I was a little concerned at first, as I never got a chance to speak to Dave when I initially entered the dojo. I felt highly out of place with everyone else in proper kit, even though I was in my special sportswear. I even wore the wristbands.

The warm-up took FAR longer than I'd have liked (close to half an hour, even loosening up our TOES and FINGERS, for crying out loud), although I'm sure eventually I will be able to get Dave to reduce this and allow more time for training.

Today I learned to roll properly, and also to come out of the roll in the correct stance (I even managed to do it once. On my first lesson!). I also learned three moves, the names of which I can't spell and won't try. One was breaking a wrist-grab, one was breaking a forearm grab, and one was getting out of a headlock. I asked Dave if eventually we will be doing something about avoiding getting punched in the face, and he looked at me funny and said all this was just as important in a real fight. I nearly had one of my Moments, but it passed. Unlike Rob, I have faith in Dave (about 5'11", black, quite skinny) who looks like he's had enough fights to know about this sort of thing. We'll probably be doing all the punch-stopping stuff next week.

I was also a little annoyed at not getting to partner Dave today, if I'm honest. He seemed only to partner with the black belts, in-between walking round and pointing out how to do certain bits. All the non-black belts just partnered each other. I would have liked to have squared off with him. I have visions of Dave locking up with me for a bit, then saying something like *Hmm, you have potential I have never seen before. There's something different about you ...you get free private lessons.* That would have been cool.

Can't wait to go back, I feel like I have progressed a long way tonight.

Eighth Entry: Wednesday August 12th 1998, 11:46 AM

Couldn't go into work today, the pain was so bad. Even worse than last time. I haven't bothered to get out of bed, as I am trying out a theory that performing as little movement as possible will enable me to heal quicker. I am obviously making major leaps that my body is unable to keep up with. This is good though, as it means I will reach my goals quickly. Today, therefore, is another **Planning Day**.

Though **Stage Three** is not ready to be entered into yet, it would perhaps be of great use to at least plan for it.

Ok, the items I will be using must be:

1. **Light.** I will be carrying them around for anything up to, perhaps, six hours, and I must not have to stop an excursion because of exhaustion (although thanks to the gym sessions, this shouldn't be a problem).
2. **Simple.** Until my mind is honed or accustomed enough to the job, I must be able to use my equipment quickly and effectively. I can't be out there getting them stuck or having to fiddle about. Pull it out, use it, done.
3. **Relatively Compact**: For now, at least, I will be carrying them around on foot, so I will need them to be concealable and easy to carry. I don't want to get arrested here. See earlier remarks about swords.
4. **EFFECTIVE:** This is VERY important. They must not be lethal, but must get the job done.

This will need looking into further. I am going to have a bath to ease the ache and listen to some Oasis. This will hopefully keep me focused.

Ninth Entry: Wednesday August 12ᵗʰ 1998, 2:06 PM

A thought has just occurred to me. One or two of you may be wondering how I came to this point in the first place. What major upheaval made me decide to take this dramatic change of direction in my plans for the future? Well, the simple fact is this: there wasn't one. There was no moment of revelation, no blinding flash of truth. I simply came to this conclusion slowly, as the idea grew in my head over time. A sunrise of conception. I don't know where the seed came from or which surrounding factors planted it. My parents weren't murdered, I haven't failed to save anyone's life, I haven't invented a weapon of mass destruction which murdered millions that I feel I must atone for, and I haven't taken a ruthless kicking which opened my eyes to the truth.

This just seems like the honest direction my life has taken me, the events of my eighteen years shaping me towards this decision. (I have always been different to everyone else. Why should my life be the same?) You may have experienced any of the above and that's fine. Your reasons are your own and your motivation belongs to you. As long as you ARE motivated, then you are righteous, and that is that.

What do you know? What have your unique experiences taught you, however mundane? What brought *you* here?

Tenth Entry: Thursday August 13th 1998, 6:43 PM

Went back to work today, even through the pain. Though the job is no longer (and indeed, perhaps never has been) that important, it IS necessary for the time being at least, if only to provide me with the necessary financial support for my plans. The gym sessions and the Aikido alone aren't cheap, let alone the equipment that I will eventually have to purchase. I must keep my job, and so I have returned to work.

As much as I hate to risk boring you with irrelevant details about my life, I mention this because having to go through such soul-sapping drudgery combined with the current physical challenge is, to be honest, a test of my commitment. So I mention this as an opportunity for you to see how I balance day-to-day factors with the actual important elements of my development.

Plus, there was a minor change in the workplace; the new girl, Chloe, is now on tills. That was a surprise. I wouldn't normally notice, or care – I don't really talk to my co-workers, to tell you the truth – but it changed my working pattern, and this was a concern. I found myself continually passing by her till, and lingering nearby for seemingly longer amounts of time than is normally required when checking if there is enough Windolene in aisle sixteen. I even noticed this, wondering why everything was taking longer today.

She's been there for perhaps three months (so her presence wasn't news or anything, as well as the fact that I have MUCH bigger things to worry about!), but I did notice myself hovering (sometimes I feel like I'm dreaming, the way I sleepwalk through the days at work). It's not that I find her attractive or anything because she's a little bit short and a little bit tubby. Not really my type. That being said, looking back – and if

I can't be honest with you, Future Fan, who can I be honest with?? – in my life I have had fairly little experience with the opposite sex, not having been the captain of the football team or Johnny Rich Kid (and I wouldn't want to be those guys anyway!). I would perhaps only succeed in embarrassing myself if I DID find her attractive, so staying out of her way is perhaps for the best. I doubt she'll even still be here soon. The churn levels at work are very high. Head office sent a man over twice to find out why. I blame the unreasonable demands on staff, but the head honchos don't bother to ask *me*.

I have, due to matters outside of my control, had to enter the pub across the road from the supermarket. I never come in here, but I have to admit that it's actually quite nice, I'm pleased to say. I'm sat at the back of the lounge with a lovely cold glass of Fanta, with the laptop sat on the table in front of me. The reason for the change of scene is that my mum has the decorators in to renovate the living room and the noise will be ridiculous. Difficult circumstances to think in, let alone write, so I've decided to utilise the relatively quiet scene of The Horse And Hound until the workmen have gone. Despite the level o

It's later. Apologies for not finishing the last sentence. Something terrible has happened. I am at home now but I will write soon.

Eleventh Entry: Thursday August 13th 1998, 8:30 PM

I apologise for the abrupt sign-off earlier. I needed to calm down before I could write about what happened. I just took a beating in the pub.

I don't want to go into it at length, but I can say that physically, at least, I am relatively uninjured. All of the training that I received on Tuesday flew from my mind. It's still weak. It's not quick enough to dip into the resources of my memory banks to retrieve the relevant moves.

I did nothing but cover up whilst they laid about me with kicks and punches.

Two drunken idiots took exception to me having a computer in the pub. They pushed it off the table (to my surprise, it is unbroken, as far as I can tell, though you probably know this by the fact that I am still writing), and then proceeded to shout in my face for about five minutes. I remember looking around the pub as they did so, looking for help. These were men, big men, fully-grown men, shouting in my face in a quiet room full of people.

I am eighteen years old, and these were men.

The one thing I remember most clearly - confirming what I already know - was that nobody did anything. About thirty adult men and six women were standing or sitting just feet away, and nobody did or said anything. Not a thing. They just stared dumbly, vacantly, somewhere between worried sheep and frozen hedgehogs.

When the two drunks pushed me off my chair, the people did nothing. When I tried to speak, and my assailants started to kick me in the ribs in response, the people did nothing. Even when the two men finished and poured the remainders of their drinks over me, they did nothing. Absolutely fucking NOTHING. I knew this, I always knew this,

28

and that is the reason for this whole thing, for the plan and this fucking journal and everything, because there are too many CUNTS in the world and too many that refuse to do anything about it.

FUCKFUCKFUCKFUCKFUCKFUCKFUCK

Worst of all, when they finished, they went and sat back down at their table on the other side of the room. They knew I wasn't going to do anything, even though I wanted them to die, even though I wanted them to be stabbed to death and raped in front of me. They knew, and they just sat there and stared at me. They knew I wasn't a threat, and they watched as I stood up with beer on my face and in my hair and soaking into my clothes. My hands were shaking as I recovered my laptop.

I left the pub without saying anything to anyone. When I got to the car, my lip was bleeding where I'd chewed it. That hasn't happened for a long time.

The pain isn't that bad. I have sixteen bruises around my ribs and chest, but fortunately none on my face that would bring a line of questioning from my mum. It hurt so much when they were kicking me, not just because of the force, but also because of the tenderness and soreness of my already-broken-down muscles.

The rage is gone. I feel totally pathetic.

Fine, there were two of them, and fine, I probably couldn't have done anything anyway, but I lay there and cried out like they were BREAKING my ribs. Do you understand? I made more noise than the pain justified. I think maybe I thought in some strange way that, if I made enough noise, they would get their kicks (for wont of a better phrase) and leave, feeling they'd done enough. I lay there and cried out for them, literally rolled over for them. I feel fucking useless, fucking useless. I wish I could cut them. Cut them all over. They deserve it.

I'm going to the gym now and fuck the pain. I don't need any music tonight, just this memory. I have more motivation, and that is what I will take from this. They haven't won. They have helped me out. They have given me more drive to do what I've known for some time MUST be done. They haven't taken from me, they have GIVEN to me. I have taken from THEM.

I was proved right, I was proved right, I was right.

Twelfth Entry: Friday August 14th 1998, 11:34 PM

I apologise for the disgraceful display of language in my last entry. After very careful deliberation I have decided to leave it in. My reasons for this are numerous:

1. **Empathy.** No doubt there are one or two of you who are perhaps feeling frustration, anger, or disappointment at setbacks, or perhaps incidents such as this yourselves. I put this in to let you know that even I became emotional when I was starting out. We're only human, no matter what we strive to be, but it is the struggle that makes us noble ...you might want to write that down and put it on your wall or something.

2. **Comparison.** I thought it might be interesting for you to see my development mentally, to see the way my self-control progresses. By the later stages of my journal, I intend to be so focused and sharpened that I will not become so over-emotional, and even have total control over myself.

3. **Encouragement.** The struggle can be hard and daunting. You must know that you can go on and bounce back from bad experiences (note: This is not the same as the Empathy one, if anybody is thinking this).

The pain is still excruciating, especially after last night when I lifted like a man possessed for two hours, but I am sleeping better with it now. Pain is weakness leaving the body and therefore is your friend!

Ironically, despite my earlier entry with regards to there being no 'moment' that set me on this path, I believe that yesterday's encounter was a 'moment' of great significance to the plan itself. This has therefore made my mind up over a matter with which I have been, admittedly, secretly preoccupied.

Waiting to complete my gym and Aikido training is wrong.

I have been thinking about this all week, and was strongly considering choosing this option anyway - choosing not to wait any more and to START NOW - but the pub incident has now given me the definitive answer that I needed. It has also told me, incidentally, that pubs should be avoided. Logically, I should have realised this before I even started; men, drinking lots of alcohol, are a powder keg of violence. In a way, I was lucky on Thursday night for that slight beating warned me off before a more serious beating could occur.

People do nothing to help other people. I have seen this many times, but not so strongly as the other night. While I wait, another woman is being raped; another homeless person is being beaten; another home being broken into. It would be safer for ME to start in, say, another year perhaps, certainly. But my conscience - that which keeps me awake at night - says that by even beginning on this journey I have accepted that my own safety is secondary. No one ever said this WOULD be safe. This whole thing is about OTHER PEOPLE'S safety. But don't worry! I have not turned my back on my belief in preparation. I will continue in the gym. I will continue in my Aikido training. Yes, I am starting my actual career now, and a lot earlier than expected, but I will simply start in a very SAFE way ...perhaps merely keeping watch on stuff, that sort of thing.

Let's be honest here. The world around me is letting so many things go wrong, and it needs someone to be an inspiration. People need it NOW. This was always the plan, right from day one, and I need to be active in some way NOW, even if it IS only day ten or whatever. I can do SOMETHING, even if it's just driving around at night with a pair of binoculars. WHATEVER! The end game will come in time, my TRUE calling. Eventually, I will be not just a vigilante, but a symbol.

I will be The Punisher. Daredevil. Captain America. Batman.

I will be a superhero.

I've always known it could be done. For real. That someone could be a REAL LIFE superhero. Then slowly, over time ...I realised that it SHOULD be done, that someone should stand up and do it properly.

Well, last Thursday, as you know, I started. And now things will MOVE. Yes, you've seen Guardian Angels, you've heard of vigilantes, but they were never a SYMBOL, never something for people to believe in or turn to or fear. Not anything to inspire. Not anything to give faith in the human spirit; a faith with the weight of an urban legend, grounded in a truth that they can touch.

I have made my role in life to become that symbol, to be the first. You will be one yourself. That's why you're reading this!

I know you all have faith in me. And I'm sure by now you know I was right, so what do I have to worry about? I have made a commitment to this, and I can stand idly by no longer. Things are going to move now, and fast. I am finally started for REAL. I will continue this entry tomorrow, for Mum is making me go to the petrol station to pick up some aspirin and tea bags.

Thirteenth Entry: Saturday August 15th 1998, 2:22 PM

Pulling in extra weekend shifts now, as I will need more money for all the start-up purchases I require. The extra work is especially difficult due to the constant physical pain. I dropped a bottle of Ribena and a jar of pickles today, as the ache is sometimes making me come over weak and spoils my concentration. I MUST get used to this soon.

I have drawn up a shortlist of what I will need after brainstorming well into the small hours last night. Most of it has made its way onto the final list (said final list being based upon my earlier list of priorities for items chosen), but obviously, some of it had to be cut. (When brainstorming, as most of you will know, one throws as many ideas down as possible, and so obviously, stuff like handguns and knives came up. Obviously, these had to be removed as options. I don't want to kill anyone.) The practicalities will be worked out later - how I will conceal them, how will they tie in with the costume, how will I conceal the costume, and get in and out of it quickly etc. - but for now, here's what I would be able to use in an ideal world:

Rucksack: To transport the more difficult to carry items around with me until I design some form of utility belt. This is fairly straightforward. I already have one of these.

2 x Nightsticks: American police officer style nightsticks, one for each hand. I can probably get hold of these through some specialist magazines.

Pepper Spray/Mace: To subdue an assailant quickly. Haven't got a clue where to get hold of this, and I'm not even sure if I can do that legally in this country yet.

2 x Shin Pads (pairs of): Simple enough to buy from a sports shop. Will buy two pairs, one for my shins and one for my thighs. Good for blocking attacks in a fight.

Steel Toe-Capped Boots: I don't think these need any explaining.

2 x Steel Baking Trays: Bullet-proof vests probably cost a fortune, but this is ENGLAND, and the Midlands at that, so I imagine the worst I will have to deal with would be a knife. I will strap one tray to my back (probably with gaffa tape or equivalent) and one to my chest, and this will suffice until I can buy some proper torso protection.

Something Throwable: Not sure about this one yet. Shuriken/throwing stars are too deadly, but maybe if I blunted them a bit. Maybe a couple of cricket balls would do nicely.

Crash Helmet: Obviously, for head protection. Will have to have a clear visor, as I will be working mainly at night.

That's it so far; don't want to get too crazy until I have designed the costume. I think these will probably be the essentials, so I will design it with these in mind. Anything else I can think of that ties in with the costume - or that can be transported easily - will go in. I have to get going now, as the gym is shutting early today for decorating.

Fourteenth Entry: Saturday August 15ᵗʰ 1998, 8:11 PM

During dinner, I had some revelatory ideas for the costume. My brother, David, had recently returned from his week-long camp, and was babbling about it. This is natural for young kids to do (he is eleven). I must admit to missing his presence around the house. Him not being here made me realise just how much his nature cheers me and saddens me at the same time. Innocence is a sweet and endearing commodity, such a rare, rare beauty in this world. I'm sure the rest of his peers are probably smoking and doing kiddie crack by now. Sometimes I have to suppress the urge to grab him up and hold him safe. A regular 'Catcher in the Rye' ...yet it's sad, isn't it? It's IMPOSSIBLE to be that. One day he will probably begin to grow into one of the little pricks that sit around in the park swigging cheap cider, talking about sex, nicking what he can and picking fights.

He was excited by a film he had seen for the first time that week, one they had been allowed to sneak in with some of the older kids to watch: 'The Crow', starring the late Brandon Lee. A supernatural superhero flick in which - to cut a long story short - the dead lead character is resurrected (his spirit contained within the crow of the title) and then proceeds to daub his face with black and white 'evil harlequin'-style makeup. He dons a long black leather coat and proceeds to dish out his own unique brand of Kung-Fu-laden justice to his and his girlfriend's murderers. An enjoyable film for sure, but it was David's mention of the leather jacket idea that set the cogs turning in my mind.

You see, one of the problems is that I REALLY WANT a proper costume. One can hardly become a symbol if one just looks like another vigilante with a baseball bat. The problem here, however, is that if you knock yourself up a lycra costume along with cloak and the works, you are going to look like a bit of a prick. It all looks so acceptable in comics BECAUSE of the quality of the artwork - it looks so awe-inspiring on the page that we suspend our disbelief and say yeah, I'd be impressed by that if I saw it in person. But the simple fact is that isn't going to happen because costumes don't look that good in real life.

Yes, in Hollywood, they can pull it off (one only has to look as far as Michael Keaton's costume in the first BATMAN film to see that it can be done very well ...although I felt the costume changes they made in the following three films were unnecessary and unsubtle), but they have a multi-million-dollar budget that they can dip into. The simple fact remains that in comics, a character can throw together a cool-looking costume for a budget of next to nothing - perhaps out of bin liners and some old bras - and end up looking the business. Look no further than both Peter Parker's and Ben Reilly's creations of their respective Spider-Man costumes for examples of this.

However, if you try this in real life, you will look a prize tit.

UNFORTUNATELY, I feel a cloak is a really effective way of striking fear into assailants at night time; something about the way it flows and flies out behind you lends an air of power and authority. It makes you larger than life. But I think appearing out of the shadows wearing one of them on the streets of Derby is a good way of getting mistaken for a rapist.

The long leather coat idea seemed like a good compromise on this subject. Brandon Lee certainly looked very cool wearing his, and it did seem to have the flowy effect desired. Yes, I know what you are thinking. It's the item of clothing NUMERO UNO amongst depressed teenagers and over eye-shadowed Goths, but they get the idea completely wrong and wear it in the DAY, even when it's sunny. It's all about context. You can't wear heavy eye make-up and a long black leather coat and expect people to think you're scary.

You have to wear it in the dark.

I think I will have to get hold of one. I think the costume will definitely have to have a long black coat. Perhaps with a symbol on the back and another one on my chest. That sounds good.

Fifteenth Entry: Sunday August 16th 1998, 6:53 PM

Was surprised to see Chloe is now working weekends as well.

She smiled at me this morning. I smiled back, then realised I was stacking the shelves with tampons and dropped several packets. She came over and helped me pick them up. I could barely look at her, like a total goose. She sounded like she was giggling as she walked off, but I might have imagined that.

I started taking painkillers today, and they seem to be helping a fair bit as I don't seem to notice the terrible aches and strains ALL of the time ...just most of it instead.

I am quite excited though, as I have made myself a deadline for what I am starting to think of as the **First Sighting**. Quite a cool name I think, coming from the day the papers will talk about the '**First Sighting of** ... who? Must think of a name soon! Obviously, I try to do this constantly, but can never settle on anything. It always sounds too over-the-top or too dull. Currently it's a toss-up between 'The Walking Shadow' or 'Wrath'. Not too happy with either of those, though, really.

I have given myself a maximum of two weeks to get the following done, in this order:

1. Design The Costume: After much careful deliberation, I decided to make this come before buying the equipment, as the equipment must tie in with the costume. You can't become a legend if there is no STYLE involved, for wont of a better word.

2. Buy The Equipment: What I can get hold of from the list, where to get it from, buy it.

3. Practice: How fast can I get in and out of the costume? Is it quick enough?

4. Venture Out To Fight Crime: Finally, finally, finally.

I found myself outside work today, watching the world go by, sitting on a bench. I had a funny revelation, as I sat there eating a small packet of raisins (little bombs of energy, my dad used to say). I used to go to school not too far from there, and I wondered what that young version of me thought would happen in his future. It's funny to think there was no way he'd know what it'd be, or what I'd be thinking now. It occurred to me then, that there'd also be another Nigel in about ten years' time, thinking perhaps about today, and he'd know stuff I didn't know now, and *he* will be thinking how it's funny he knows stuff that *I* didn't. It THEN occurred to me that there will be another me in just another *hour's* time who will know stuff that I don't know, or who will be thinking of me right now. I sat there for quite some time thinking about all this.

Sixteenth Entry: Monday August 17th 1998, 6:34 PM

Discovered a great new motivational game in the gym last night, which I call 'Smiling At Rob'. It works like this, if anyone would like to play anything similar:

1. **Enter gym**, and select your 'Rob'. Make sure he's not too big, or that there's any possibility of landing in physical danger.
2. **Start your workout**, continually observing him, and whenever he looks in your direction, give him the biggest, jaw stretching, wide-eyed grin possible.
3. **If he smiles back**, continue as normal.
4. **If he looks uncomfortable**, you have won, and reward yourself with an extra set of whatever exercise you are doing.
5. **Repeat throughout workout**.

Today's score, at the end of the workout, was Rob: 2, Me: 9. The extra amount of physical pain therefore was quite excruciating (the whole smiling bit has, however, an added effect of slightly convincing me that I am enjoying the experience), but I'm sure my painkillers will manage to keep it to a tolerable level. I only dropped a jar of mustard today.

I CAME UP WITH THE INITIAL COSTUME DESIGNS!! Here they are, reproduced in all their glory (excuse their crudeness, as I had to do it on Paint on the laptop, in order to be able to put them in this journal; the original hand-drawn versions look a lot better, believe me).

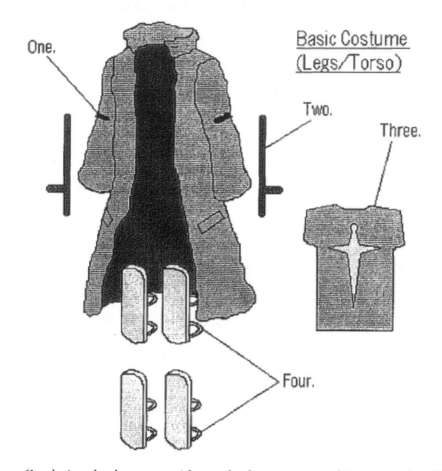

(I obviously have no idea whether or not this journal will eventually be published in colour or in black and white, so let me clear any confusion over the colour schemes I have chosen for this diagram. The coat is grey here, but it will, in real life, be black. Grey merely looks better on the diagram. Same goes for the background of the chest emblem. Both the shin pads and symbol are a bright, eye-catching yellow, as to be easily recognizable as part of a costume.)

Let me take you through it:

1. Holes In Elbows: A particularly neat little touch here, I feel, that will enable me to tape the long ends of the nightsticks to my forearms (for a better, more solid fit), yet still be able to bend my arms inside the jacket. Smart (the jacket will, of course, also have the emblem on the back of it).

2. Nightsticks: These, as stated, will be taped to my forearms, with my hands obviously grasping the handles. The added bonus of having them taped to my arms is so that I can release the handles and still be able to manipulate objects with my hands without dropping the nightsticks.

3. Logo/Emblem: Now I am particularly proud of THIS. After many various designs, I chose this one: it's a sword, it's an angel rising, it's a star, a shining light. All things that people will come to associate with me. I really like this. (Obviously I will have to buy a black top and sew this on myself, so no dressmaker will have a link to my identity. It'd be a shame to have everything ruined now by a mouthy t- shirt printer or someone)

4. Shin Pads: Yes, I know that shin pads don't really look like this, and don't often come in that colour ...but SHUT UP! Ha ha. The plan is to get the most simple pair of shin pads possible and spray-paint them yellow. The simpler the better; they won't look any good with 'UMBRO' visible across the front. Perhaps I will also - if I can build a good enough stencil - spray the emblem on the front of each one. As an afterthought (so it's not shown on the diagram), I have also added a cricket box to the costume, obviously for groinal protection.

I did think of merely putting the pepper spray (when/if I get hold of it) and the throwing stars/cricket balls in the pockets, but I decided that it would be far cooler if I could have my own utility belt (perhaps taking a workman's utility belt and spraying it yellow, to tie in with the rest of the ensemble).

The only things missing from the diagram are the steel toe-capped boots, but I should imagine you all know what they look like, the baking trays (which will not be visible, merely strapped to my chest and therefore, I decided, not needed in the picture) and the motorbike helmet, but you also know what THEY look like - I will buy a black one and spray the emblem on the forehead part.

However, having given it some more thought, I think a mask would look far, far better than a helmet. HEAR ME OUT! Ha ha. I will need maximum protection when I first start, so I will start OFF with the motorbike helmet, but eventually when I have settled into the role, and mastered Aikido, I will begin to wear a mask. I have thought a little ahead and produced two possible designs:

Basic Mask Design No.1

This I like, and I imagine it with the skin around my eyes blacked out to complete the effect (note the emblem on the forehead here as well - this really must look like a COSTUME). Although I am also very taken with this one:

Basic Mask Design No.2

The designs are very close, but this strikes me as being a little more ninja-like. For those who are interested, these are adapted from Ben Reilly's bandage mask that he created during 'Spider-Man: The Lost Years' limited series, and Matt Murdock's mask in Frank Miller's 'Daredevil: The Man Without Fear'. Interestingly enough, both stories were drawn by the talented John Romita Jr. A bit of history for the students there.

Either way, on only the second day of the **First Sighting** countdown (!) I have done even better by figuring out how to integrate the rucksack into the plan. I reckon that when I'm 'on patrol', I can walk around with the baking trays on under my clothes, and the emblem shirt on under my jumper/coat etc. When needed:

1. **Pull out of the rucksack and slip on the shin pads**
2. **Pull out and tape on the nightsticks.**
3. **Take out long coat and take off jumper/jacket and put in the rucksack.**
4. **Slip on mask halves (already tied).**
5. **Tie on utility belt.**
6. **Go!**

This is the system I will work with when running the 'getting ready' trials. I am going to have a muscle soak bath now, as I have bought some specialist stuff from the pharmacist. Combined with the Deep Heat rub and the painkillers, I'm sure I will hardly feel a thing come tomorrow. I hope I can sleep after today, I'm so excited!!

Seventeenth Entry: Tuesday August 18ᵗʰ 1998, 11:22 PM

Found Aikido a little frustrating today. Not only did we undergo yet ANOTHER lengthy warm-up, but then proceeded to WASTE twenty-five minutes going over the moves we learned last week. THEN, we learned how to put someone off-balance (useful), but followed it by learning how to get out of yet another wrist grab!! I don't know about you, but I can hardly see gangs of thugs on the streets of Derby shouting, 'Fuck me! It's The Dark Man (current favourite name)! Go for his wrists boys!!'

I took it upon myself to wait until the end of the session to have a quiet word with Dave. He didn't seem to recognise me at first. I introduced myself properly.

"Nigel Carmelite," I said.

"Oh, yes, you started last week, didn't you mate?" he said. "Nice to meet you properly." He was smiling. I was pleased to see someone so undoubtedly badass choosing to be friendly.

"Dave," I said, "I really don't wish to insult your skills as a teacher, I'm sure you're first class and I've enjoyed the sessions so far immensely, but ...I can't help wondering when we'll be looking at some of the more ...dynamic moves, for wont of a better word. "

Surprisingly, Dave broke out in a huge grin. He seemed to look me up and down, and then replied, still smiling.

"Nige, you have to start off small. These moves are explaining the fundamental principles of the discipline: balance, manipulation of weight, pressure points, etc. It makes the learning of the more ...dynamic stuff easier to master." That's exactly how he said it, with a little laugh. "I understand you want to get good, but sometimes you

47

have to take your time mate, know what I mean?" I knew what HE meant, but I decided to press my point.

"Dave, I know what you're saying, but I think I already have all this down. I think, if you look, you'll see I probably have a bit of a gift for this." I was pleased with that. Dave gave some sort of a funny cough into his hand, and carried on smiling hugely.

"I'm sure, ah, I'm sure you do, but you still need to follow it my way. This is the way people have been doing it for centuries, after all. It's good to see you so motivated, though." At this, I started smiling too. I knew we would have a connection, I told you so, didn't I??

"I appreciate you saying so, but ..." And then he cut me off!

"Listen, Nigel, my wife's just arrived," he said. "I've got to go. See you next week mate, yes? We'll, ah, see how you're doing, yeah?" He said all this as he was walking towards the door, smiling all the way.

"Ok, Dave," I said. I then saw he was holding the door open for me, realising he had to be the last out so he could lock up. I grabbed my Nikes and jogged over to where he was standing.

"It's just ...this is important," I said. "That I learn fast. You know."

"I'm sure it is," he said.

"No ...really important. Not just to me."

"I can imagine," he said, not getting it. In hindsight, that was probably for the best.

Chloe came and said hello today. I said hi back.

"Not dropped anything today?" she said with a smile.

"A packet of Daz and two boxes of ice lollies," I said. There was silence. Her smile disappeared, and then she laughed.

"It's surprising they're letting you stay here, butterfingers!" she laughed. I actually laughed back, maybe a little too loudly. She seemed to be waiting for me to say something, and my mind raced. I didn't think of anything. I started to become very aware of how much I was sweating. It WAS hot today, to be fair. She gave another little smile.

"I'd best be off anyway," she said. I smiled and nodded. She looked at the floor and then walked away, leaving me holding a packet of Smash while sweating. I could have handled it better I'm sure, but once again, it was probably for the best.

The bath soak and deep heat haven't worked, so the only relief I have at the moment is the painkillers. Not good.

Looked into buying some long leather coats today. Currently we're looking at about £300. That's just crazy. I will have to try some charity shops. Bought a black sleeveless vest (£15, sleeveless so it's easier to put on in a hurry) and for the chest emblem I bought a length of thick yellow cloth (£10). I also bought a length of thick black cloth (£10) - both from the fabric shop - for the logo itself and bandana/mask material respectively.

I've surprised myself with my skills as a seamstress! Fortunately, Mum was out most of the evening, so I had enough time to cut the cloth and use the sewing machine undisturbed.

I made a rough stencil out of cardboard, and drew round it onto the yellow cloth. I repeated this with a smaller stencil for the mask logos. After several practice runs on the sewing machine with the spare scraps of cloth, I used the stencil to cut the yellow material into shape and attached the chest logo onto the vest. It looked fantastic! I can't describe the thrill I felt creating my costume. I really felt, for the first time, like a comic book character. It was wonderful.

The mask proved a little more difficult, as I had no idea how big a bandana should be.
I decided, in the end, that Basic Mask Design No.2 was the disguise of choice, as it just seemed far cooler. I managed eventually to get the size right, and despite several mistakes I still had enough cloth left over for the second piece

Believe me, it took a superhuman effort of will not to try it all on there and then, but I have made a promise to myself not to do so until the 'trial runs'. That way I'll get the full effect. I have hidden all of my livery in my old rucksack, stuffed at the very back recesses of my bedroom cupboard so as to prevent discovery. I finally have the beginnings of a secret identity; I can't believe it!!

I am way ahead of schedule as far as the deadline's concerned, I reckon. Now I need:

The Shin Pads
The Nightsticks
The Baking trays (easy)
The Steel toe-caps (easy)
The Pepper Spray (difficult)
The Cricket Balls? (possibly)
Rucksack (already have)

David just came in to show me a page in one of his X-Men - where Wolverine gets his adamantium claws back - wanting to share it with me.

"You like comics a lot, don't you David?" I asked him. He looked at me.

"Yeah," he replied, confused, "You do too, don't you?"

"Of course," I assured him, "They're a lot of fun. It'd be cool to be a superhero, wouldn't it? Leading a double life, beating the bad guys." He grinned at me in response.

"Yeah, but it'd be really dangerous ...I don't know if it'd be fun all of the time. In the comics, they never get scared or anything. I think I'd get scared sometimes. But I bet all the girls love them." There was a wistful note in his voice, and I was surprised. David was growing up more than I'd realised. "But yeah, it'd be cool to be a superhero, obviously," he said, the 'obviously' said as if I were being an idiot. "Well, it'd be cool in comics anyway," he added with a shrug.

"What about being Batman, specifically, David?" I asked him, "Would that be cool as well?"

He looked at me in that fantastically exasperated way that only kids seem to manage.

"Well, of COURSE it would, Nigel," he said again. "I mean, BATMAN ...Apart from, you know, the parents thing." I nearly blurted out something about our dad probably being dead, but that would have spoiled the moment. Instead I ruffled his hair, and laughed as he batted me away.

"Well, you never know, Dave, he MIGHT turn up one day," I was teasing him, the way you would do a five-year old, and therefore David wouldn't have any of it. Once he would have gone all wide-eyed (*Really Nige? You think so?*), but now he laughed, as I knew he would.

"No one with that much money would bother!" he laughed. "They'd be off ..." he trailed off, trying to think what adults with that much money would do. "Eating! Getting fat!" He swung his arms out to show an impossibly fat belly, puffing out his cheeks. Then he left, shaking his head at his brother's silliness, amused.

Just like a young Peter Parker - for the first time in my life, just like a comic - I could smile and think internally, IF ONLY HE KNEW! Cheesy but true. I love having a double identity, especially a cool one.

P.S. Current favourite, 'The Dark.' As in 'afraid of The Dark.' Pretty clever, I thought.

Eighteenth Entry: Wednesday August 19th 1998 4:33 PM

I have a date tonight. This is very unnerving for three reasons.

1. **It's My First Proper Date.** Eighteen years old, and I've never properly taken a girl out for a drink. I just never got round to it, that's all.
2. **I'm Not Actually Sure If It's A Date Or Not.** I will explain this in a second.
3. **This Is A Crucial Time.**

Ok, I think the most important of these points to clear up is number three. I know I stated earlier that it would be a bad idea to get involved in any distractions at the moment, but this is not a contradiction of that, as I shall explain now.

As anyone with a basic understanding of psychology knows, one of the best ways to encourage success is with MOTIVATIONAL REWARDS. I have been working exceptionally hard towards my goal over the last two weeks, and therefore I have now earned a reward. The prospect of earning further self-rewards in the future will make me work harder still. It's all a process.

That is what this date is. Not a complication, but a reward. I am actually, if one cares to look, improving my capacity for work.

Ok, point two. The girl in question here is called Marie (works in the tobacconist's section of the supermarket), who I know to say hello to from time-to-time. She's okay-looking – well, not really if I'm honest, but she's friendly - but I never really thought about her like that until today. However, this morning when I got to work, she called me over and mentioned a concert that was on in town tonight and how a lot of people from work were going. She asked me if I was going too.

Now, I certainly wasn't – I hadn't even heard it mentioned, but then I don't really socialize with work people much, or at all - but I said yes anyway. (this was, I point out again, due to the previously mentioned motivational theory. My mind is becoming more and more focused.) She seemed very pleased, and told me to meet everyone at 7:00pm in The Highwayman. This does mean a shorter gym session, but I will just have to work extra hard in the time given. Fortunately, I have an earlier finish time today.

So is it a date or not? I simply have no idea. How should I dress? Do I want to look good, or should I go casual in case it's not? How do you dress to go to a concert these days? It's been a long time since I went to one. Are flowers too cheesy for a date? Will I look stupid if I DO take flowers, especially if it's not a date, or will she think it's a nice gesture anyway? As far as rewards go, I think a night in with some beer and a few videos would be a lot less hassle and more fun.

They don't teach this stuff in school. They really should. Maths and Chemistry are all well and good but these grey areas are the things that glue life together.

Anyway, I have to dash in order to get to the gym and get ready and everything. I merely hope I get through this with my pride intact.

P.S. I apologise if this is all irrelevant to you, and I can certainly see how it would be, but really, tonight may also be completely confidence-shattering, and so I include this to display how I deal with obstacles and possible setbacks on the path. I think you will find it useful.

Nineteenth Entry: Thursday August 20th, 1998 6:34 PM

Ok. It's the day after, obviously, and last night was ...unusual. After the gym, I dashed - sweating profusely myself and completely removing the effects of the shower - over to The Highwayman.

I had opted for a pair of smart black jeans and a dark blue shirt. I wasn't sure if this was a good balance or not, so I rolled the sleeves up. That seemed better; more suitable for any way that the evening might go. When I got there - ten minutes late - I was surprised to find Marie dressed far more casually then I was. It was almost as if she hadn't made any effort at all. This seemed to suggest that I'd been wrong to believe that this was a date of sorts ...although not for certain. To be honest, I found myself not being particularly disappointed by this. She's not really my type. I'm not exactly sure what my type definitely is, but I don't think it's Marie, to be honest. That's not a criticism; it's just my personal taste.

I apologised for being late, but she seemed fine about it, and I asked what she wanted to drink. She asked for a pint of lager; I bought the same, so as not to look bad.

Conversationally, it actually went ok. From the little I knew of her, she'd always struck me as quite the outgoing sort, and this was proved correct by the way she instigated most of the banter. I must admit to still struggling a little, striving to find something more interesting to say than 'yes' or 'no' to her questions. As I am sure you all realise by now, I am FAR from being a boring person, but something tends to happen to me when I talk to one person for too long. I start to get this hot feeling in my neck and feel a little bit sick. I have had to actually disappear and BE sick in the past, on occasion. This all makes me go a bit quiet really, but that's okay because then the conversation ends and I feel a lot better. So despite Marie's genial nature, in this particular one-on-one situation, I did seem to feel a rather large amount of pressure. This stilted the flow of ideas to my brain somehow, which is perhaps a good thing, as if I come across as quiet and, as they say, mild-mannered, she will never suspect me of being Night Master - CURRENT FAVOURITE - in the days to come.

I asked her where everyone else from work was, and she said they'd all be arriving shortly. This DEFINITELY wasn't a date then. I did feel disappointed then, but this was because of having to spend an evening with people I really didn't know very well at all. Dealing with Marie had seemed difficult enough up to this point, but having to handle ten or fifteen individuals in a similar way made me feel distinctly downhearted.

One thing did strike me after a while though, and that was how she kept seeming to somehow steer every subject towards the new girl, Chloe. I wondered if, perhaps, she was a little resentful or jealous towards Chloe (goodness knows the reason why; women have always seemed to me, at least, to be able to get wildly jealous at each other over nothing), and that this was the reason why Chloe seems to play on Marie's mind so much. I wondered whether or not Marie was aware of how much she talked about Chloe. She probably didn't even realise.

I asked Marie if Chloe was, in fact, coming. Marie then leaned forward and asked me if I'd spoken to Chloe at all since she started working at our place It was a very conspiratorial gesture. I told her yes. She asked me what I thought of her. This was clearly dodgy ground. What if my theory was wrong and they were best friends? I was feeling the hotness on my neck again and made a snap decision to go with my guess anyway. I said what I thought Marie would want to hear; that I didn't think there was that much to Chloe. I didn't mean it, but I thought the correct social move would be to agree with what I assumed Marie thought.

"Really?" she asked me. Uncertain, but already committed, I responded in the affirmative. She looked at me quizzically. "Why do you say that?" I was stumped now. I could hardly tell her that I'd only said it to try and keep the evening going smoothly. She'd think I was an idiot. THIS is exactly the reason why I don't talk to people.

"That's ...that's just the impression I get, that's all," I said, wanting desperately for this confusing situation to end. "What do YOU think?" Marie paused, and then suddenly looked at her watch.

"Oh ...I have to make a phone call", she said, and quickly rose from the table and disappeared. Five minutes later she returned and sat down, sipping at her drink. She was silent for the first time all evening. Eventually, I asked if everything was okay.

"Hmm?" she replied, as if noticing me for the first time. Had she been doing drugs in the toilet? "Oh ...yes. Fine, everything's fine." Silence again. Long silence. I thought perhaps I should repeat my earlier question.

"Is ...IS Chloe coming tonight?" Marie put her drink down and shook her head.

"No ...not now," she said, absentmindedly.

For all intents and purposes, conversation practically stopped from that point on. When everybody else arrived, I found myself being almost ignored by Marie and was hardly spoken to by anyone. After an hour or so of this, they all finished up their drinks and left the pub to walk to the concert. I hung at the back of the group, walking by myself, and eventually slipped away. Nobody seemed to notice.

Saw Marie at work today. She smiled and waved hi. I did the same back. She clearly didn't notice my disappearance last night, then. Saw Chloe. Smiled and waved. She didn't wave back. I found myself deeply surprised by this.

However, though last night's encounter was not in any way a heartening or rewarding experience, once again I am able to turn things around for the good. This reminds me anew of my role in things; reminds me of how I am not meant for the foibles and trappings of the socialite circuit. I had forgotten this. I knew this in the playground, and I knew this when everyone else hurried to be a 'big' kid, trying to be the first to be drunk in their class, forgetting the importance of imagination and innocent fun. Now I know this to be a BLESSING. Then, I didn't.

Enough of this, which I include once again as an encouragement to any of you who may have experienced similar potentially disheartening experiences. For today I have taken more steps towards the costume.

Bought the baking trays (£2 from Everything's £1! Not £2 each, obviously ...) and the shin pads (slightly more expensive, let's put it that way) and some gaffa tape on my lunch break. However, when I still hadn't found a leather coat, I was beginning to doubt whether or not I'd ever find one for under £300. Obviously, if spending that much money is what it takes, then that's what it takes, but I'd like to check all my options first.

The big news today though, was that I finally found a way to get the pepper spray and the nightsticks! Well, only sort of on the Pepper

Spray front. I'll explain shortly, but either way, the idea was so obvious I was amazed I hadn't thought of it before. I've been using this laptop constantly for the last two weeks after all ...why not buy them over the internet? This is a new experience for me!

A quick 'search engine' use (those things are great) and I'd found the two 'websites' I needed: Police Defence.com, and Bodyguard Force.com. I also found HTG Defence, but there was a huge, huge problem: you can't buy Pepper Spray in the UK. It's illegal.

My equalizer was, therefore, gone. To say I was crestfallen would be an understatement.

But then I remembered: this is an OBSTACLE. And what do we do with obstacles? WE OVERCOME!

Back to the search engine: PEPPER SPRAY ALTERNATIVES. Bingo!

While not quite Pepper Spray, Gel Spray Criminal Identifier IS legal. What is it, you may ask? It's used identically to Pepper Spray – point and shoot – and while not an incapacitator, if you get it in your eyes you're going to know about it. Plus, it's so sticky and all-pervading that it will seriously disorient whoever is coming at you. That's all the time you need! The blast radius is huge, and the gel STICKS to your assailant – trying to wipe it off only makes it worse – and get this!! Unlike Pepper Spray, it leaves a bright red residue that only comes off after SEVEN DAYS! Do you see? Overcoming the obstacle has given me something even better! How much more effective is leaving my criminal victims marked? It's practically the equivalent of webbing them up and leaving them hanging outside the police station! A perfect calling card!

I plumped for the Man Marker spray, which has a range of over four meters! I bought two of these. I ordered these on my credit card (not often I get to use THAT) so I don't actually know the dollar-to-pound conversion. I hope it's not too much. The Man Marker is 15 dollars, so in UK money I shouldn't imagine that I'll be paying more than £80 to £90. Either way, it's worth it.

The nightsticks - from Police Defence - were surprisingly cheap compared to what I'd expected, cashing in at a respectable 60 dollars. They have rubber grip handles as well, apparently. Both companies claim to deliver within 7 days, and I am VERY excited. Just the leather coat left to buy now (and the utility belt, once I know how big the sprays are.)

Twentieth Entry: Friday August 21st 1998, 12:35 PM

Just a quick entry during my lunch break, as I have had another flash of brilliance. Idly flicking through one of the magazines in the staff room (and trying to drown out the babble from the loudmouths I have to share a lunch break with), I came across an advert for something called a 'Go-Ped.' Apparently, this is some sort of petrol-powered scooter that can go at 20 mph, top whack. By the looks of it, the throttle is on the handlebars and the engine on the back. It looks fantastic.

And suddenly I had this vision of me on night patrol, parking up the car somewhere in town, rucksack on shoulders, unloading the Go-Ped from the boot, and proceeding to patrol the streets on my Fury-Mobile (Fury: CURRENT FAVOURITE). How COOL!! When I go into action, I can quickly stash it somewhere, strike, and then I have an unmarked and nippy getaway vehicle (yes, a car would be faster, but one glance at the plate and I'd be busted in five minutes) that can get me out of trouble fast. FASTER THAN PEOPLE CHASING ON FOOT, is the point. I'd be able to strike like lightning and be gone before they knew what hit them! They have a website to check as well, apparently. I will check it later tonight.

Twenty-First Entry: Friday August 21st 1998, 11:04 PM

My bubble has been burst a little. The Go-Ped website had several different types of scooters, the obvious choice being the apparently whisper-quiet electric version – 'The Hoverboard' - but it is £699 pounds. It goes for 12 miles on a three-hour charge, has a top speed of 14 mph, and is fully collapsible. Dammit, I want one. The other version, the cheapest-but-still-decent petrol-powered version is around £500, and goes faster, but I've got to be all about stealth here. There are some notes about them not being exactly street legal in the UK, but I can't see the cops bothering to stop someone on a scooter.

I'm going to buy one. I've decided this. I want a Hoverboard, and more importantly, I *need* a Hoverboard. NEED tops WANT. This will, however, drastically remove a lot of my savings, and possibly jeopardise the future of my mission should I need any emergency cash for whatever.

I am very concerned about my future in the gym. The pain is literally becoming unavoidable, and I often find it is rendering me weaker during sets, making me falter. Even 'Smiling At Rob' is not aiding me at the moment.

Sod it. I'm going now to make an order for a Go-Ped Hoverboard over the internet. That will, at least, put a positive spin on the day as a whole.

Twenty-Second Entry: Saturday August 22nd 1998 12:19 PM

I am, I must admit, a little shaken up right now. I just had to endure a highly unexpected and embarrassing outburst from Chloe. I will explain (in case it is to have any relevance to future events. If not, I will remove this entry at a later date. So you won't know about it anyway if it doesn't, so

FUCK IT I DON'T KNOW

She had literally been hanging round me all morning. Every time I turned around, she would be within visual range, always seeming to turn the other way when I looked at her. It was like she was waiting for something, and she didn't look in the slightest bit happy.

Later (well about five minutes ago actually), I was in the staff room, sat at my usual spot in the corner, when I saw her walk past the staff room window. She then stopped by the door, paused, and walked off again. About two seconds later, she strode past AGAIN, only to stop just before she cleared the last window. She suddenly turned around and strode back to the door, flinging it open.

"Can I have a word with you Nigel?" she said in a very loud voice, and then turned around and slammed the door behind her.

For the first time, all twenty people in the staff room were looking at me. There was a horrible, long, drawn out silence. My neck felt like someone had set in on fire. I nearly had one of my Moments, but I held it in. I've become a lot better at it in the last five years or so.

I slowly put down my pickled egg as I felt forty eyes burning into me, the unquenchable human thirst for fucking gossip sensing a new drip-feed.

"I'd better go and see what she wants," I said with a little chuckle, pretending that I thought it was funny. I think I convinced them, but no one said anything in reply. I stood up, greatly disappointed to realise that my fly was unzipped, and subtly placing a hand over it to retain at least a grain of dignity. Slowly and calmly, I walked over to the door and opened it to discover Chloe standing outside.

She had her arms folded, facing away from me, but spun around when I opened the door. Her lips were pursed, and she didn't speak until she heard the staff room door close behind me.

"Why did you say that?" she snapped, petulantly. "Why did you say such a horrible thing about me?" I just stood there, an unusual sweating sensation beginning to wash over my lower back and forming a perfect accompaniment to the fire in my neck. Chloe took my silence for an admission of guilt. "I've never been anything but nice to you," she said. "Some people here say horrible things about you, and I've never listened to any of them. Really sick made up stories. D'you know, sometimes I've even defended you, or told them to shut up. And I'm new here!"

"I should be doing all I can to make friends here. God knows I've never had that many, and now I've probably got people saying nasty things about me instead. Because of you! And you go and say something like that!"

Her lip was beginning to tremble. I had to fight a sudden and overwhelming urge to take her face in my hands, just to hold it.

"I can't believe you. You're such a ...such a bastard! I should have just let them slag you off and have nothing to do with you. Even Marie says you're weird! Well, I may not have much about me as you put it, but at least I'm nice to people, or don't pretend to be and then slate them behind their backs. You're a bastard, a weird fucking bastard, Nigel. No wonder people take the piss out of you!"

She was on the verge of tears now, and I still hadn't said a word. I couldn't. She opened her mouth to say something else, but the tears were starting. She turned on her heel and stormed away, crying. I stood watching her go, feeling sad and strangely detached at the same time.

After what seemed like a long time, I turned around and went back into the staff room to get my lunch and my laptop. Forty eyes followed me back to my seat. I gathered it all together in my arms. Forty eyes followed me back to the door. I wondered what they had all said. I realised, with a conflicting amount of sadness at the thought, that I didn't care. I must be numb to all this by now.

I am currently sitting in the toilet cubicle, finishing my lunch and typing this. No one has come in. Everyone must be busy. I perhaps should have started my shift by now, but I'm going to finish my lunch and sit here, maybe type, maybe just sit.

Twenty-Third Entry, Saturday August 22nd 1998, 6:36 PM

Spray-painted shin pads. Checked baking trays against my chest and back. They fit nicely. Man Marker and nightsticks haven't arrived yet. I'm in a lot of physical pain today, worse than normal. I am still going back to the gym.

Twenty-Fourth Entry, Sunday August 23rd 1998, 1:22 PM

Fortunately, I have the day off today. The pain is so bad that I have told my Mum that I'm sick and have lain in bed all day. No mail will come on a Sunday, so certainly no chance of my purchases arriving in the post either.

Nothing to report, really. Just playing the waiting game today, but perhaps I can use this opportunity to encourage those of you who may be in a similar situation. The upcoming hero is only human, whatever we may strive to be, and despite his best intentions, may not always be capable of driving his quest further. He feels dead in the water. He feels that time is racing away from him. He (or she) feels useless, lazy.

It is entirely natural to feel this way when we are reminded that we are not omnipotent and cannot control matters as we'd like. There is no easy solution to days such as these, but there IS one way to at least make it better, and that is to simply STOP for a second. Use these days to gather your energies, but still contribute in some small, active way, one that will keep you happy and keep you 'moving', however small that movement may be.

So here for you today is a story that you might find interesting, one that will explain a little about who I am. Why not sit for five minutes and enjoy it?

When I was eleven, I decided to customise my bike during one day of the summer break. I thought it'd be cool if it looked like it could fly, like some hover-bike or something from a sci-fi program; as if I could press a switch on it and then take off into the blue expanse above. Plus, I had nothing better to do, and I liked to build things.

I got up early that morning and scoured the house and shed for discarded bits and pieces that could go onto the bike: old circuit boards and cables, broken toaster innards, tissue boxes, toilet rolls, cassette holders and plugs. Anything that could be cobbled together to look like the workings of a futuristic mode of transport. I took cardboard, felt tip pens, glue, sellotape and scissors, and disappeared into the front garage for the morning.

I taped all the junk to the frame, in relevant places where it looked like it could serve some function. The circuit boards went on the main frame of the bike (the engine parts, the INTERNAL workings of the thing), with decorated tissue boxes and toilet rolls sticking out from the back (rocket boosters, to fire the beast along). I was even lucky enough to find an old switch I could tape to the handlebars (ignition - what else?). I was lost in it for hours.

I drew bright letters on the cardboard, cut them out, and stuck them on the side (ROCKETBIKE), added colour here and there, and found hours of pleasure creating my little fantasy in that garage. In the end, it looked as if it could blast straight through the garage doors and soar down the street, skimming a few beautiful feet off the ground so everyone could see, then soaring upwards into the sky to leave them staring.

Eventually, bursting with pride and pleasure and desire to RIDE, I opened the garage doors and wheeled my bike out onto the street. Mounting up and scanning the road, I made a big show of flicking the ignition switch. Then I started to make a rumbling sound in my throat as I slowly began to roll. Pedalling nice and steadily, I moved at a taxiing pace now, almost feeling the throb of the engines, eyes narrowed for the oncoming surge. Halfway up the street, I reckoned I'd covered enough distance to be clear of the hangar. I pulled my wrist downward on the handlebars.

I screamed an engine's roar as my legs blurred into life and was then rocketing up the street at seemingly a hundred miles an hour. As the houses flew by, my legs working, I looked down at the machine I had created and laughed out loud. I then gritted my teeth and screeched a 'nyyyeeeewwwww' noise as my engines pumped and my bike soared higher.

I circled the block, but then in my invincibility, I decided to bomb out onto the main road and set off into the main part of the village, driving my steed onwards and needing new challenges. I blurred past an old couple who seemed to smile, but I couldn't be sure as they went by in a flash. Then I was flying up the hill, rising like a phoenix towards the village green, preparing to slingshot around it for greater velocity as I shot back toward home. I felt like I could go from there to anywhere I wanted.

I crested the hill like a sunrise and hurtled towards the village green, where a group of five or six lads - around my age - were sitting in the glass bus shelter. They were all dressed in trendy clothes, as if they were about to go somewhere special ...but it was still mid-afternoon, so it couldn't have been that. Although I was still going at warp speed, I could see one of them poking the boy nearest to him and pointing at me. Some realisation passed down their line, and they all started smiling at me. As I passed along their flank, one of them beckoned. They didn't look rough, so I assumed it wouldn't hurt to stop for a moment. I even thought I might have a laugh with them. I didn't have many kids to hang around with in the village, and those that were there didn't really share my interests. That was what made it so weird. I'd never seen any of these kids before.

I managed to slam on the air brakes in enough time to bring the engines to a standstill, and maneuvered the craft over to where they were sitting. I smiled, sitting proud and upright on my vehicle.

"Nice bike mate," one of them said, the others grinning. I'll never forget his face: blonde, cropped hair and freckles, loads of freckles, and an almost snout-like nose. He was wearing a polo shirt and his hair was neatly gelled; again, a bit much for a random afternoon, but some kids liked to dress older than they were. Although I found myself feeling a little uncomfortable already, I didn't think I should just ride off. That would have been rude.

"Thanks," I replied, "I did it all this morning." I patted the handlebars. I remember that. I actually patted the handlebars. The kid who'd spoken looked at his mates, grinning some more.

"What's that say on the side?" he said. "'RocketBike.' Yeah, that's cool." One of his friends made a snorting noise and covered his face. Another one snickered, and I wanted to leave now, but I didn't.

"Mate ...how old are you mate?" one of the others said.

"11," I told him. They all snickered now, openly. I wondered why. They had to be the same age as me no matter how they dressed. I felt my face get hot, and my neck especially. That was relatively new back then.

"That's good that, mate. I think I'll do that as well. I'll call it 'SuperBike.'" They all snickered loudly now, one or two of them jostling one another, boys together. I remembered wishing they'd stop calling me 'mate', seeing as it was now clear they didn't want to be my mate. I became very aware of my Batman t-shirt and Bermuda shorts, which were totally at odds with their much cooler clothes. "Fuckin' SuperBike!' he repeated to his mates, laughing at his own joke.

"How old are you?" I asked, trying to turn things round somehow, feeling small, embarrassed by my bike covered in bits of junk and cardboard, embarrassed to be sitting on it.

"What's that mate?" the first one asked, stopping laughing. He was talking in a funny way, brightly, too bright, fake pleasantness.

"How old are you?" I repeated. I tried to sound calm.

"11 as well mate. Though we're just about to go and play fuckin' hide and seek, are you coming?" All of them ROARED at this. I will never forget thinking, in a very clear and confused voice: What's wrong with hide and seek?

I had to get out of there.

I straightened up on my stupid-looking bike, covered in a kid's coloured cardboard and machine innards, and pedalled away, hearing one of them shout:

"Nice fuckin' bike mate!" It made me go faster, wanting to be away from there and safe, wanting my silly-looking bike out-of-sight, wanting it home before anyone else could see it so I could strip it down and make it normal again, wanting to strip it bare so no one could laugh at me for it, wanting no one to see that I had been childish enough to try such flights of fancy. I was ELEVEN.

I flung the garage door open and almost threw the bike inside. Shutting the door behind me, I began to cry. Crying because I would have to destroy what I'd spent all morning proudly creating. I didn't want to destroy it. I thought it was cool, I liked what I had made. It was my little creation, my little bit of fun.

Weeping gently, I peeled off the tape, and piece-by-piece I took RocketBike away. I slowly realised, as I sat there in my garage removing circuit boards and toilet rolls from my bike, that I was an idiot. I wasn't allowed to DO this sort of thing anymore. I was supposed to have grown beyond this now, and yet I couldn't think why. Worse, I didn't want to.

Why was I not allowed to be like this? Why wasn't I allowed to have a little bit of a fantasy in my head, to pretend and enjoy myself? I wasn't harming anyone, so why did I have to leave this part of myself behind in childhood? It was FUN. Why did they laugh at me for that? I came to a major realisation in our garage that day, which perhaps, looking back, maybe began at least to sow the initial seeds of what would become **The Plan**.

If I wanted to do things that people thought were weird, or laughable, or childish, or not accepted, I would have to keep them secret. I would KEEP my childish pleasures - the ones everybody thinks are stupid and ridiculous, that I was not allowed to indulge in - secret. I would not give them up.

The power of imagination gets ridiculed. You express flair and you get hurt. You try something different and you feel a fool. So don't let them see. Only share it with those who understand it. Gather together. Maybe one day, even express yourselves together, but never do so alone. When you're alone, if they see you, they will eat you alive because they know you can't defend yourself.

Perhaps this is why I grew to love comics so much, why I loved this world of secret identities, of double lives, of those who were mild-mannered and unassuming by day yet dangerous and exciting by night. Why I loved to see 'Puny' Peter Parker – outcast at school - pushed around by Flash Thompson, and yet having adventures as The Amazing Spider-Man ...only to have the idiot Thompson worship his alter-ego! I would have loved it if Flash had ever found out while they were at school. The look on his smug face ...

You see, my friends, your imagination is a wonderful thing. It's what sets us apart from the idiots, the losers, those who can see no further than their next paycheck and the next session in the pub. We are the few, and we are the righteous, and this is why you are here. You have had the imagination; the vision of making a difference. You can do it, like me, and you WILL do it. I have proved it. I was (will be) the first. I KNOW we can do it.

Twenty-Fifth Entry: Monday August 24th 1998, 9:12 AM

Man Marker spray arrived!!! I was expecting to have to wait at least a couple more days, but here it is! Great news.

Twenty-Sixth Entry: Monday August 24th 1998, 6:26 PM

Dropped a crate of Pepsi today. Cans ended up strewn all over the aisle. Chloe walked past and saw me scrabbling after them. She didn't stop. Like I say, probably for the best. However, I won't have a job anymore if I keep this up. Got to get the pain under control.

I am sitting and typing with the Man Marker spray on the bedside table, and have just finished a little target practice against the back of the shed. The canisters are really small, fitting right into the palm of my hand. To be honest I could do with someone to test its effectiveness on, but that wouldn't be right. Maybe I could slip David a fiver so he'll volunteer. I doubt it!!

The nightsticks better get here soon, as I have now just six days left before the **First Sighting**. It will be terrible if I don't make my own deadline, a real failure. If I have to, I will chop up a broom handle or something and use that instead. It's all about being adaptable, my friends.

Twenty-Seventh Entry: Tuesday August 25th 1998, 11:12 PM

Something incredible has just happened. Even I can scarcely believe it, but it's true. On arriving home this evening, my mum must have noticed my despondency (today I had AGAIN failed to procure for myself a long black coat) as she asked what was wrong. I normally avoid this kind of thing – we haven't had a relationship since Dad, to be honest, so it's a little late now to try and care – but for some reason I openly told her (seeing no harm in telling her that I wanted that kind of coat) of my search to obtain one and subsequent failure to do so.

She put down her magazine and sat up in the new leather armchair, perhaps eager for an opportunity to talk. She looked older than she was and frazzled. Again, she had for years.

"Sort of a trench coat, like that?" she asked. I nodded, wondering why she was suddenly so interested. She paused, thinking. "I'm sure we've got one in the attic," she announced.

I froze.

"Are - you sure?"

"Yes ...yes, your dad used to wear it years ago. Never took it off when we were first courting ...it'd probably be in a right state now, but I'm sure he never threw it away." I was already off up the stairs before she finished, grabbing the thin metal pole from the airing cupboard and unhooking the loft's hatch. This was incredible. A SIGN. Not only was the coat I'd been after in the house all along ...but my FATHER'S COAT. I would be going into my war wearing my FATHER'S COAT. The costume, the garb of my mission belonged to my father before me! It was so much like fate that I felt like I was touching something much bigger than I was.

The loft steps almost hit me in the face as they fell towards the floor on their runners, which brought me sharply out of my trance-like state. Making sure they were resting sturdily on the floor, I began to ascend the steps on shaking limbs. To be totally honest with you, this was only partly due to excitement, with the rest due to a long-standing childhood fear; when mounting the steps, you hang right over the stairwell in our house. The fear of plummeting into that pit haunts me still, but today I didn't look. I gritted my teeth and went ever upward.

The loft is very small, with a frighteningly low roof. The only light in there comes from the hatch you will just have entered through, and everywhere are the little landmines of fibreglass, those 2-foot squares that since I was a child I had been warned to avoid, lest your foot went straight through and you found yourself smashing through the bedroom ceiling. In the gloom there were several boxes, some clearly more recent than others; I could still see the pages of David's copies of Shoot! Magazine. Eventually, finding a safe space large enough to kneel in, I dragged a box over to me, surprised by its weight, and began to rummage.

It was full of old crockery, the chintzy kind that you'd come across in elderly relatives' living rooms. I could only assume that this box contained the property of one of my long-gone grandparents. I began to push this box aside, but my eye fell upon the collection of black and white photographs stuffed down one side of the crate. Pulling them out, I saw they were some very old photos of my parents, perhaps taken by an approving grandma or granddad. My mother, still dumpy even then, but with that winning smile that seemed to stretch across the whole bottom half of her face. My father, tall, not the best-looking man in the world, but strong looking, thick set ...he was an imposing man, my dad. However, I felt I was perhaps travelling down an avenue (as I am doing now, I realise!) that I had long since bricked up, and moved on.

A few boxes later, I tried an old tea chest that was covered with what appeared to be a sheet of tarpaulin. On further inspection, this proved to be incorrect; it wasn't covered with it, the open top of the box was merely FILLED with tarpaulin, as if it had been stuffed with it. Putting my fingers on either side of it, I realised that it was in fact some sort of bundle, and whatever was inside wrapped in the protective tarp. I squeezed. It was soft, as if filled with some sort of cloth or material. My heart leapt.

I began to notice the ridiculous amount of sweat I was producing, but ignored it as I pried the bundle out of its tight enclosure. It came free, and I laid it reverently on the floor of the attic. The thick black bundle sat there, pregnant with hope and tightly rolled.

I felt a little faint. My fingers trembled as I opened the bundle like a Christmas present that would determine my future. Inside, intact, was a long, faded, black leather trench coat. My father's.

I held it for a while – a long while, I think – and then took it downstairs and hid it in my cupboard.

Later, I went to Aikido.

"Dave? Could I have another word?"

Dave seemed to remember who I was and grinned. "Hold on a sec, mate, stay there," he said, and jogged over to where one of the black belts was standing. Dave had a brief word with this other person came back with him in tow. The black belt was grinning, almost expectantly.

"Nigel, this is Keith."

I looked at Keith, who held his hand out. Keith was tall, also skinny, wore glasses, and was surprisingly stupid looking, to be honest. He didn't look in the slightest bit hard. He probably wasn't. I shook his hand.

"What's the problem mate, anyway?" said Dave, grinning at Keith, then back at me. I decided to ignore him.

"Well, it's about the warm-ups," I said. Another grin exchange between the two.

"Uh-huh."

"Well, they do seem to go on a bit? I was thinking, maybe, the time would be better spent actually getting on with the class, rather than maybe being a bit over-cautious with the warm-up. Obviously, you know, safety's important and all, and I'm sure you know what you're doing, of course, but I have been feeling a little concerned about this."

Dave's grin widened. I didn't bother looking at Keith.

"Sorry Nige, I know you want to progress, but we HAVE to do it this way. It's my responsibility to my students to both ensure they don't get hurt and also get the best physical workout from these sessions. As much as we'd all love to dive in at things straight- away, we have to warm-up properly and make sure you're ready to start, then you'll get the best out of it. You have to prepare, or people get hurt. Every instructor knows this."

For some reason, I began to sense a feeling of guilt creeping into my mind. I pushed it away, eager to make my point.

"Don't you think perhaps you're being, maybe, just a little ...you know ...picky? Over cautious?" Dave chuckled and patted me on the shoulder, and Keith was suddenly very interested in his feet for some reason. I honestly didn't know how to take all this.

"Trust me mate," he said. "I know what I'm doing. I AM qualified. I'll see you next week mate, all right?" He and Keith then turned and walked off together, discussing something that had amused them. I didn't feel reassured at all. I felt like I'd been ignored, to be honest. I'm sure Dave means well.

Twenty-Eighth Entry, Wednesday August 26th 1998 9:12 AM

I'm so excited I can barely write properly. The nightsticks have arrived!!! I haven't got the steel toe-capped boots but I'm not going to worry about those. They're only going to be too heavy to walk in on a long patrol. Anyway, that means that all I have to do is get the utility belt (I can do that at LUNCHTIME), and I will have everything I need to begin running the 'time trials', so to speak. To *finally* don the costume for the first time. Today is going to DRAG by, I know it. Wednesday, August 26th will go down as the second most important day of my life. This Sunday will be, of course, the first.

Twenty-Ninth Entry, Wednesday August 26th 1998 9:22 PM

I am not going to be able to sleep tonight. I know this for a fact. I have seen what the costume looks like when worn. I have seen what my criminal victims will see, justice embodied before them.

It looks fucking awesome.

Found a utility belt today, after testing how a Man Marker canister fit into one of the pouches. It goes in easy, they're tiny. The belt cost about £20. I have spray-painted that yellow too, now, although this will no doubt need reapplying over time. But enough of that.

After giving David a fiver to go to the cinema and renting mum a video to keep her in the living room (anything with Sean Connery has her pretty much sorted), I delved into the cupboard where I had hidden the chest emblem and headgear and gently removed them with trembling hands. I felt an incredible feeling of PRESENCE. The time was very close now. This meant it. Somewhere in the back of my head I could hear orchestral film music, imagining this scene being panned around by a moving camera, zooming in to focus on the symbol. Crash of chords.

Pan back. Close up of hands taking the rucksack down from the back of the top shelf, hidden at the top of the cupboard containing the weapons of war.

The rucksack opens, and I feel that there should be a hissing sound, accompanied by a huge cloud of mist rising from the opening, as if there was some sort of coolant hidden within to prevent the volatile nature of the equipment from exploding on the spot. I take the equipment out, and lay it all on the floor in front of me. I am already wearing my black combat trousers, regular boots, and sweater. I gingerly pick up the utility belt. I feel fantastic. I am tooling up for the first time.

I slowly fasten the utility belt around my waist. The shin pads go on next, the tearing Velcro sounding so professional. They are slowly, reverently secured in place. Hands shaking, I pick up the chest piece, the black tank top/vest bearing the symbol. I stand for an immeasurable amount of time staring at it, then pull it over my head.

As yet, I hadn't looked in the mirror. That stands out in the hallway, and I was saving that. I pick up one of the nightsticks and the roll of gaffa tape that is lying on the bed. I tape the nightstick to my forearm, tearing the strip free from the roll with my teeth. I repeat this with the other arm.

I pick up the leather coat. With a surprisingly small amount of difficulty, I put my nightstick-clad arms through the sleeves. It broke my heart to put those slits in the elbows of my dad's coat so that I can bend my arms, but it was a regrettable necessity.

The masks. For ease, I should have put these on first, but I wanted to put them on last. It felt right. First the skullcap/bandana/eye mask half, then the mouth half.

I was done.

I worked my arms around slowly, watching my knuckles whiten around the handle of the nightstick as I held it. The bottom few inches of the nightstick protruded out from the sleeve, blunt and hard looking. I liked that. Plus, I could cover it with my hand if I needed to. I looked down at my chest, seeing the symbol sitting there, bright and proud, the bright protection on my legs, the bright belt on my waist, contrasting with the black of the trousers and coat. Darkness and light, straight out of a book. I walked out into the hallway, to where the mirror hung.

My heart was racing faster than it had ever done since the inception of this plan, pounding like a huge piston in my chest that threatened to burst. It was becoming REAL; childhood dream coming true. How many people can say that? Not the childhood dreams of becoming a racing driver, a millionaire, a footballer, I'm talking about the DEEPER dreams, the DREAMER'S dreams. The dreams you indulge in at the age of five but that are so impossible you know even then they are just that, so impossible that even at the age when anything is possible you see them as just a bit of fantasy. Well, mine was coming true.

I savoured the anticipation for a moment more ... then I stepped out.

I saw a figure round the wall; a flowing coat, patches of light here and there about his person, his face masked but bearing a bright, bright symbol on his forehead, a strip of flesh in the centre of his face revealing dark eyes that stared intensely. I started laughing with a desperate joy, an excitement, a satisfaction so intense that I was actually crying. I looked fucking amazing, fucking amazing.

About an hour later, when I had calmed down, I indulged myself for a little while trying out a few poses, a few dramatic moves that would add to my overall effect. These also looked incredible. An idea suddenly struck me however; what about my voice? I would have to change it a great deal just to ensure that no one would ever recognise me. This was an interesting aspect I hadn't covered in my plans. This was rather a foolish oversight, but I am only human.

I leaned forward into the mirror, assuming that I would be this close if I ever had to actually talk to someone (in my experience, superheroes always talk up close and personal).

I didn't have a clue what type of voice I would be going for, or what I was going to say. Anything would do. The ceremony was over now, and I simply had to rehearse. I decided that a gruff voice would be the best choice for a number of factors:

1. **Easy To Put On**. In the middle of a stressful situation, the last thing I would need to be doing would be having to remember all the right inflections of the voice. A gruff voice would be simple, and more importantly, would disguise my own tones.

2. **Effect**. It sounds harder, scarier. You sound like someone who is used to fighting, has maybe been scarred so badly by constant involvement in the world of violence that your very voice has been affected, that you ooze danger and aggression.

3. **It Sounds Cooler**. Sorry, but it does.

This decided, I looked into my own eyes in the mirror, seeing the pupils expand.

"You ..." Not gruff enough. No, not DEEP enough.

"YOU ..." Better, but not quite there. Should be breathier, heavier.

"You ..." That was it. That was the voice that they would remember in their nightmares. I adjusted my stance, anchoring myself better to the floor, sturdier, wider, menacing.

"Next time you think about stealing from the post office ..."

Not dramatic enough. I must remember that I am to be a symbol. My speech must be dramatic, as well as my movements, or I shall seem ordinary. How can I inspire respect and fear if I still talk like mild-mannered Nigel Carmelite, shelf-stacker and sometime till operator? Try again.

"The next time you feel like picking on those weaker than you on the bus, like the scavenger that you are ..." Good stuff. "Remember me. Not everybody on the streets at night are victims. The victims are rising up. And soon, punk, there won't be any left. No more easy pickings for you and your kind. Because I'll be there. Because I am ...THE NIGHT MAN."

I saw my eyes blink and widen. I stepped away from the mirror, stumbling slightly as I lost my composure, as I fell out of character. I had it. I had the name. Out of NOWHERE. Fate surely intervening once more. First my father's coat, now this. I saw the muscles under my eyes raise upwards as I smiled beneath the mask. My mask. I swished the nightsticks upwards, then arced them down and crouched. I started laughing.

Thirtieth Entry, Thursday August 27th 1998 6:22 PM

Three more days. That's all that has been running through my head for the last 24 hours. This Sunday, when dark has fallen, The Night Man will take to the mean streets of Derby city centre. The Night Man. I have an alter ego. I have a secret identity. How incredible is that?

I wonder if I will eventually become someone else when I put the costume on, whether the essence of my character will change when hidden under the mask and symbol? That would be interesting. The Shadow is like that. Dipping into his hidden dark side, ironically using it to fight the darkness.

Saw Chloe again. Haven't seen her for a few days. She was doing a stock check on tins of sweetcorn in aisle F and hadn't seen me. I said a casual hello as I walked past, merely to clear the unpleasant working environment that may possibly be affecting my capabilities. Personal differences are not conducive to a good day's work. She turned round, looking a little surprised. I suddenly stopped, and when I try and remember I don't particularly recall why I did. It had been my sole intention to stroll straight past and get on with loading aisle H with boxes of Coco Pops and, of course, our own brand of Choco Pops. There was a brief silence.

"How are you?" she said, her face expressionless.

"Yeah, fine ...you?" A pause.

"Yeah ..." she said, looking at the floor, then over my shoulder. I didn't turn around to see what she was looking at.

"How's it going?" I asked after another pause, gesturing at the clipboard in her hand. She looked down at it like she had forgotten it was there.

"Oh ...yeah, easy." I looked at her, then for some reason I had an irrepressible urge to get out of there. I suddenly saw her standing in front of me in her blue uniform, clipboard grasped in one hand, long dark hair tied up on her head with her blue eyes staring at me, and simply couldn't be stood there. I was sweating again, and the urge to run was so strong that I simply nodded, spun on one heel, and briskly walked away. I would have said goodbye, but I couldn't speak. It was like the ABILITY to speak was there, hidden behind some paper thin invisible membrane, but I couldn't find the extra tiny but vital amount of effort to break through it. I put this down to the pressure I have been putting myself under. I haven't seen Chloe since, so I don't know how she reacted to me walking away. Hopefully, however, I will have at least cleared up any unpleasant feeling in the workplace, and in so doing, my job was done.

After last night's entry – after I tried the COSTUME on for the first time - I ran the Quick Change Time Trials. Problem number one displayed itself almost straightaway: the nightstick-securing gaffa tape that was then stuck to all of my arm hairs. The age-old debate of whether to do it slowly or rip it all off in one big go presented itself. Looking at my reflection, I decided that The Night Man doesn't mess about. It was going to have to be the Big Rip. Keeping my eyes focused squarely on the mirror, I gripped the end of the first strap of tape on my wrist. It was about three inches wide. I squinted, then yanked it free.

There was a split second of nothing, and for a brief instant I thought I'd got away with it. Then the burning kicked in with a vengeance. My eyes began to water as the intense fiery soreness settled slowly into my wrist. Knowing that it was only going to get worse as I went further up the arm, I reached for the middle strip. Although I didn't exactly hesitate, I gingerly pinched the end of the tape free and tugged it away without giving myself time to realize what was happening. As there were so many more hairs up there, the pain was far worse and my eyes began to stream. The third one was pulled away quickly, as by then my arm hurt so much I just thought it was best to get it over with. It was on fire as I reached over and started on my left arm.

When I was done I grabbed a tub of cold cream from the bathroom in an attempt to ease the burning, but this did nothing as my ever-forward-thinking mother had left it on the window sill during one of the hottest summers on record, meaning that instead of a sharp burning pain I now had a greasy, warm burning pain. It felt as if my flesh were made of it.

Fortunately, the tape I'd used to secure the baking trays had only actually stuck to my flesh along my ribs - where I am obviously hairless - and over my shoulders, so removing them was relatively painless. Still, the prospect of having to re-tape the nightsticks and rip them free several times whilst I practiced getting in and out of the costume was not a pleasant one.

Soon enough, my costume was off and lying on the floor. I went to my room to fetch the rucksack - as this was to be a proper, simulated test - and brought it back to the hallway, where I proceeded to place all the pieces of the costume inside the bag, including the gaffa tape. I had already tied the top half of the mask into the correct size for my head, in order to be able to just pull it on quickly.

Looking at my watch, I saw that I had just over an hour before David got home. Listening carefully, I heard Sean Connery's spit-filled drawl wafting up from the living room, and decided that Mum wouldn't be disturbing me anytime sooner than that. If she did, I could simply jump into the bathroom and lock the door before she mounted the stairs. Setting my watch to timer mode, I started the counter.

All reverence went out the window. This was to be all about speed and efficiency, and this was the mode in which I worked. The shin pads, baking trays, emblem-shirt and mask all went on surprisingly easily. The difficult part was the nightsticks, both in the attaching and getting the coat on over them. Finding the end of the bloody tape seemed like an impossibility. I realised that I was rushing, that this should be a case of MORE HASTE AND LESS SPEED, one of my mother's old adages finally being of some fucking use for once. I forced myself to relax. Soon after, the nightsticks were bound to my forearms, and I was bucking and jerking the coat, trying to get my wood-encased arms into the sleeves. Eventually, I was garbed once more, and The Night Man stood in our hallway. I looked at my watch. 4 Minutes 12 seconds. Not good enough. Somebody had just been raped while I was too busy playing dress up.

I took all the gear off slowly, breathing deeply and trying to force myself to relax and focus. This was a difficult thing to do when you know you are about to cause yourself intense physical pain for the second time within twenty minutes by ripping a pair of gaffa- taped nightsticks from your arms. I managed to console myself by reasoning that I had probably ripped most the hair out the first time, and therefore it couldn't be as bad. This turned out to be bullshit, as there was indeed plenty of hair to go round, and the burn in my arms doubled.

Sleep was a long time coming last night, I can tell you.

The second attempt was a slight improvement, 3 minutes 25 seconds, but I had decided the maximum amount of time to fly into action had to be under two minutes. In reality things are over so quickly, and I had to be quicker. I didn't bother with the cold cream this time, firstly because I only had about half an hour or so left before David's arrival, and secondly because the stuff was crap anyway. The third time I managed 2 minutes 7 seconds, which was close enough, but I had to know I could do it again, just to be sure. My forearms were now a bright, startling red, and were screaming out at me to stop, both visually and from the pain, but I HAD to be sure. Wearily, I opened the bag again.

1 minutes 53 seconds. That's how long it takes for Nigel Carmelite to transform into the scourge of Derby's criminal element: The Night Man. Not super-fast, but a great start, and I'm sure this will improve tenfold as the weeks and months go by. Possibly even down to about a minute, I reckon.

Once the rucksack was full and stashed in the cupboard once more, I was able to have a more thorough search through the back of my Mum's bedroom cabinet. I blessedly found a bottle of after-sun that had been kept relatively cool by, shock horror, actually being kept in a cool dry place. It eased the intense burn only slightly however, and it took a long time in the shower to remove the surprisingly thick residue of gluey adhesive that the repeated application of gaffa tape had left on my forearms.

My only worry now then, is if the Go-Ped will get here by Sunday. Or rather if it will be here by Saturday, as there's no post on Sunday. I am beginning to doubt it. It would be a terrible shame if The Night

Man's first outing was without his trusty steed, but the failure and personal guilt I would feel if I missed my own deadline would be far worse, so I will go without if need be. Commitments are commitments, and if you fail yourself, how can you have any self-respect? Tomorrow is Friday. Then there will only two days to go. I doubt I will get any sleep tonight either, despite the exhausting workout I am about to put myself through this evening. Even though my arms are still rather tender, I am going to anyway. Onwards and upwards. Sunday is the day.

Thirty-First Entry, Friday August 28th 1998, 6:35 PM

Arms better. Soreness reduced. Redness reduced. Muscles feel like broken glass. Still no Go-Ped. Chloe got picked up after work today by some bloke. Like I say, probably for the best. Nothing else happened today, really.

Is this it? Is this all I fucking have? Go to work, come home, go back? Surely I need more than this shit.

Back. It's later.

Additional point. No. Of course this isn't all I have.

I have David. To a much lesser extent, I have Mum. But more importantly, I have the quest, the mission, the vision. That is more noble, more important than any other stuff that I could be filling my head with right now. My life isn't empty; it couldn't be farther from being empty. I am the first human being to attempt what I am doing. When I get to the end of my life, I will be able to say I have done this, I have done that, this is the life I have lived, and I will dedicate my life to that death-bed moment, the final moment of satisfaction.

I am purged now. I shouldn't be thinking like I was above. It's the pressure. I really don't know what's up with me tonight. These doubts are bullshit, and in a way I am glad they have happened because they have reaffirmed me, solidified me. Remember my friends, take your obstacles and turn them around, turn them over, climb on them to get you onto higher ground.

Thirty-Second Entry, Saturday August 29th 1998, 5:46 PM

Once again, I have deliberated over whether or not to leave an entry in (re: the previous entry). This time it was far easier, given the upbeat ending of it along with its strengthening nature, and I have decided to include it.

Although I am highly embarrassed by the way it starts, these feelings may apply to YOU at one time or another. Remember, this is not just a historical account. It is a guide, a self-help book (that should confuse the staff at Waterstones – which category are they going to put it in?), and so I hope that you may take solace from this. I am only human and therefore prone to such moments of confusion. Anyway, the past holds nothing and on we go to today's events.

Still no Go-Ped, and that is a terrible disappointment, but wasting time on such feelings is not a luxury The Night Man cares to afford. As I realised last night, the plan is all that matters, and there lays today's focus. Where to begin the hunt?

As I promised myself earlier, by not waiting to complete my Aikido and gym training - by holding the safety of innocents OVER MY OWN - I must start off in a little easier environment than the city centre itself. I do however want to do more than merely walk the streets for several hours and then go home while people are getting raped and mugged elsewhere. I decided that the best compromise would be the nearby town of Robinson. Not as big as the city centre, and certainly not as dangerous; Derby has many pubs and back alleys and drug dealers and fights. A Saturday night in Derby itself ...that will be the trial by fire. The prospect excites and terrifies me at the same time.

Robinson is a fairly unassuming place – nobody would ever call Robinson big - but it has been known, from time-to-time, to erupt in uncharacteristic bursts of violence, fights happening after kicking out time, burglaries, etc. Typical small-town stuff. Certainly everybody I've ever met from there seems to be unhealthily obsessed by fighting; indeed, they seem to talk about nothing else. Quite an idiotic town, really. Perhaps it will display more action than I anticipated.

The dodgier area of the place is widely regarded to be based around the Stanley Street/Horninglow Road area of town, so I will begin there, parking the car nearby and setting out on foot. Obviously. I should, however, be able to cover a lot of the quieter areas as well during the course of the evening, just in case.

Obviously, I would dearly love to see some action during the First Sighting, if only so there can actually BE a sighting, but it will go as it goes. There are places I can go in Derby where I could practically guarantee this, but the First Sighting is the warm-up, the start of the reputation. I have shown considerable restraint, I feel, of my more childish, overexcited whims throughout this whole plan, and it would be a shame to give in to them now.

My only REAL concern is about my physical form. I am still in my usual hellish amount of pain from the gym, and indeed, I have to go again tonight. I had hoped desperately that it would have begun to subside a little by now. No such luck. I worry if maybe, in the heat of a fight etc., that it would prove to be a distraction? Or would adrenaline carry me through? I certainly hope so, because said adrenaline has done a bang-up job of preventing me from getting any sleep the last few nights and tonight will no doubt be the worst of all: the anticipation. I certainly want to be at the height of my awareness tomorrow. Plenty of coffee, I think, throughout the day.

Tomorrow IS *The* First Sighting! It feels like all of the Christmas Eves of my life to the power of ten.

Saw Chloe get dropped off by the same guy today. I wonder if she stayed with him last night? If so, if she is that way inclined, then it really is for the best. I mean it would be anyway, but even more so if this is true. Especially now, as the action is about to begin.

Thirty-Third Entry, Sunday August 30th 1998 5:46 PM

It's not quite dark yet; not quite time for The Night Man. Everything is packed up and ready to go. As I sit typing - here in my room with only the lamp on to help me focus - the rucksack that contains the equipment of The Night Man sits beside me on the bed. I thought that it would be proper to record a few thoughts before I set out on this historic and ground-breaking night.

I feel an unusual sense of calm. Perhaps I am beginning to be as focused as I would like. This is a good thing.

I have told David and my Mother that I was going to a friend's house. They seemed quite surprised by this, but they seemed to believe me regardless. This is good. When the news reports start coming in, I don't want them to think of me as being anywhere but indoors. They may make a connection.

I am going to wait for another hour, then set off. Soon, I am sure, I will have much to tell.

Thirty-Fourth Entry, Monday August 31st 1998 1:22 AM THE FIRST SIGHTING

I am back. I'll get straight on with it, as you no doubt want to know what happened on my first night.

You will not be disappointed.

At around 7:00 PM I arrived in Robinson, leaving the car in the car park of the local pub, the Revill Arms. I decided that this would be the best place to start as I would be able to perform a nice round-trip route of the town from here, covering a large area within a few hours, and returning back to my starting point quite nicely. I checked the rucksack for the tenth time that night before I got out of the vehicle, and of course, everything was still in there.

I was dressed in the same black combats, boots, and black jumper that I had been wearing when I tried the costume on. Though I had been intending to leave my glasses at home (I don't need them that much; they merely make my vision a little easier, so they aren't essential), I decided they would be a more effective way of defusing any suspicion. Though I hate to pander to a stereotype, glasses do make you look less dangerous. Hell, Superman has gotten away with it for forty-odd years by this method, so I thought it was good enough for me.

I hefted the pack onto my shoulders. It was heavy, and my aching muscles cried out at me. I knew that by the time I got home, I would be in a lot of trouble, and it would only be worse the next morning.

Shutting these thoughts away, I set off walking. As I turned out of the car park I saw the main road stretch away before me. It rose up the hill, with rows of houses and the odd bus stop and shop flanking it on either side. It was quiet, and I could barely hear the sound of the motorway that I knew wasn't far from there. There must have been fewer cars out that night. Perhaps they somehow knew there was a new predator in town!

I could see the metal shutters - highly necessary security procedures - drawn down on the shop fronts of the Post Office and off-license. The town was battened down, locked up for the night, protecting itself. Now was the time for dangerous folk to be roaming, and I was one of them ...except I was on the side of the angels.

The night was clear and warm, and the breeze on my face made me feel wild even though I was in the middle of suburbia, although Robinson is hardly suburban, with nary a tree or shrub to be found except for those in pub beer gardens. But there was, of course, a reason for this. Tonight I wasn't just another fella out for a late night walk or someone staggering off to the pub.

I was hunting. I was on a mission, and I was doing it in secret.

As I walked past rows and rows of houses, sticking to the main road unless I saw any particularly dodgy-looking streets (where burglaries were perhaps more likely to occur, as both morals and security are notoriously low on these terraced lanes ...everybody knows it), every smell on the wind, every movement of the trees, every passing moment felt alive and full of potential, as if something could happen at any moment. I was aware, constantly, of the stars above my head, of the bigger picture above me. I felt alive. I grinned and grinned in the moonlight and began to hum Eye Of The Tiger under my breath.

However, I must admit, the boredom began to creep in a little after about an hour and a half.

Though I had now covered a great deal of ground, and found myself on the southern side of the town (over by the Valley Road area where the town's tiny cluster of shops was to be found), I had only seen maybe five people during my rounds so far. All of them had been old or middle-aged men and women either getting out of their cars or walking to/from the pub. While obviously this was an inherently good thing - no innocents had been in any trouble so far - I still couldn't help wishing that something would happen so that I could test myself and begin to break into my new role. Yes, I had managed to get in a little target practice with the Man Marker before all this, but I still hadn't encountered a MOVING target.

To be perfectly honest, I just wanted to get some hands-on practice, full stop. However, I would like to point out that under no circumstances did I want anybody to get in trouble just so I could save them. No, I was glad this was the case, very glad. I'm just saying that I would have liked some PRACTICE, but peace on the streets is of course infinitely preferable. Of course it is. I passed a bus stop where a couple of scruffily dressed fourteen-year-olds sat and smoked. They avoided my gaze, so I guessed they were harmless.

Two hours in, I kept thinking how much easier this would be if I had a Walkman with me. This was a mere flight of fancy, of course, as the music would be both a distraction and would remove my ability to hear any trouble. I began to cross the dark expanse of McGlone Park, favourite haunt of tramps, glue sniffers, and no doubt the occasional drug-dealer meeting up to hand over someone's 'hit'.

I entered from the northern end of the football field, behind the netless goalposts. The play area and climbing frame beyond the grass looked strangely distant. The view at night was actually quite eerie. Other than the moon in the pretty much cloudless sky, the only illumination was a single streetlamp, standing high in the middle of the play area. Everything else was black.

As I was strolling through the darkness, surrounded by trees and alone, I felt more than a little unnerved. I realised I had to do something about this and tried to shut these thoughts out of my mind, but it was all too easy to imagine something following just behind me, just out of earshot, moving when I moved and breathing when I breathed. Something low and creeping and loping and cunning, something made of wiry muscle and teeth.

I remembered the bag and what it contained. I was alone, but not unarmed. The Night Man could be called at any time, and I had to focus on this. Forcing myself to walk slowly, I set off again. I reached the light of the play area; it was abandoned, not a wino or drug dealer in sight. The plastic benches looked particularly inviting, and a rest seeming like a lovely idea ...but while I was resting, a mugging could be occurring. I wasn't there to rest. I had to complete a full sweep of the park (I really will have to get that Go-Ped soon, as it will ease the workload by a huge amount).

As I left the play area, I dropped back into darkness again and the air seemed colder. I considered taking the coat out of the rucksack and putting it on, but that was not going to happen. The coat was/is part of the costume, and the costume stays in the bag until action time. Even so, I balled my fists into the ends of my jumper sleeves, trying to conserve heat.

I came to the gap in the trees that took me back to the main road, as the streetlight poked its way slightly between them. I realised that by cutting my way through McGlone Park, I had pretty much made a full circle of the town and would soon be returning to the car park of the Revill Arms.

The night's work was almost over and nothing had happened. It had taken me two and a half hours. I had always been expecting a minimum of at least three.

Trudging along for the fifteen minutes it took me to get back to the car park, the rucksack slowly seemed to feel heavier and heavier. I was exhausted. A mere two cars rushed past me on the road as I walked the home straight, and not another person was seen either strolling the streets or even in the windows of their houses. It was as if everyone had gone to some enormous party that I didn't know about.

It was then that I heard the raised voices coming from the pub car park.

I stopped dead. I was about one hundred metres away, and I could hear shouting quite clearly, and it sounded like ...angry shouting. My heart rate suddenly tripled the speed at which it had been coasting along. A fight may be occurring. A fight that The Night Man would have to break up. The first time anyone would see him in action.

I looked at my watch. 10:35 PM. Of course. It was a Sunday night ...the pubs would be kicking out early. If drunken aggression was going to spill out into the street, now would be the time. Breathing in short little gasps - even though I was only creeping along - I made my way towards the car park, keeping close to the hedges that lined the fence leading up to it. Slipping the rucksack off my shoulders, I crouched down. I felt an intense rush crouching like this, like a spy in a film, waiting and listening to the enemy's plans to bomb London. Eventually, I managed to calm myself enough to sort of semi-stand up and peer over the top of the five-foot high fence. Normally I would have just strolled past, pretending not to notice and hoping I didn't get involved - just another pub fight - but now I was someone else and this was deadly serious. This might be my first act as a superhero.

I could see five blokes, standing in a very spread out circular pattern, about fifty metres away. Two of them were nearer to me, and three were further away, all standing roughly side on to my view. There were clearly two different groups. One of the group of three was the one doing the shouting. He was about thirty-five years old, crewcut, tall and skinny like Dave from Aikido but rougher-looking in the face. He wore a ratty expression and had reddish skin, either from shouting or sunburn. He was wearing black trousers and a blue button-up shirt, and was pointing aggressively at one of the two who stood side-by-side. They were wearing suits, and somehow I got the impression that this was the reason why Red-Face felt so aggrieved by them. They were young, not too much older than me, and looked nervous, yet still not wanting to back down. Red-Face's mates stood behind him with their arms folded, one smiling and the other one looking stern, with broad shoulders and a wide forehead. His smiling mate looked a lot like Red-Face, tall but even skinnier, with a pathetic slicked over haircut. He seemed to be enjoying the spectacle. It was quite clear to me that this was going to end in a fight. This could not be allowed to happen. It was time for action.

My breathing doubled and became more harsh and breathy as I began to hyperventilate. I was going to have to confront three, possibly five men on my own, armed with some nightsticks, a can of Man Marker spray and two baking trays.

I was going to fulfill my childhood dream.

All the weeks of planning and waiting and physical agony were about to be put to the test. My mind was whirling. I fell back against the fence and forced my breathing to slow and tried to push all unnecessary thoughts from my mind - to focus. Time was short, and I couldn't afford to mess around. I couldn't screw this up. I had to get changed.

However, I was in clear view of the road! Although I hadn't seen a single soul all night, it would be absolutely typical for me to discover - the instant I started to get changed - that the reason no one was around tonight was that it was the evening of the Robinson residents' annual parade, and that the entire town would come chanting round the corner and catch me pulling my shin pads on. Unlikely as this event would be - or anything even vaguely like it - I could not take the risk right there. My secret identity must be sacred at all times, and so I had to play it safe.

Unfortunately, the only cover available to me was now all the way back up the road, as the street leading up to the pub contained a row of terraced shops. There was nowhere near to duck into, certainly not anywhere safe at least. I then realized that if I was prepared to take a major risk, there WAS ... about ten metres further up the road, the beginning of a new row of houses. The first one - a large, white house that for some reason was rather dirty near the roof - had a fence running around the outside of the garden. The curtains were open and the lights were on in the living room, but I could see no one in there from where I stood.

I could change behind that fence.

Snatching up the rucksack and ducking low once more, I ran across the road, now level with the men in the car park. If they cared to look, or if I stood up to run, they would see me. However, I knew that my whole life was/is about danger now, and I was just going to have to get used to this kind of thing.

I reached the opposite fence - the border of the house – and dashed to the gate, quietly opening it and slipping through the gap. Continuing to crouch-run along the inside of the fence now, I moved into the corner where it was darkest and squatted there like a spider. There were no trees or bushes to conceal me from anyone inside the living room. The only things around the house were an immaculately mowed lawn and an ornamental fishpond. The comical looking gnome wasn't big enough to hide behind.

Keeping my eye on the living room window and listening to the sounds drifting over from the car park for signs of escalation, I dropped the rucksack to the ground and undid the straps with sopping wet fingers. I madly wondered why; then I realised it was sweat. I had become completely soaked in less than a minute. Pulling out the various articles from the bag and throwing them hurriedly onto the grass before me, I grabbed the nightsticks and the tape and began to strap one to my left arm. I stopped when my whirling mind realised it would be far easier to put the nightsticks on second-to-last, just before the coat. Throwing the nightsticks down, I pulled on the shin pads, desperately trying to remember the order in which everything went on from the trials. I took my glasses off – I'm only very slightly short-sighted anyway – put them in the bag and put on the masks and vest. I'd just started to work on the nightsticks when an old man entered the living room of the house, putting me in his plain sight, hiding – or trying to - in his garden.

I froze. If he saw me, he might call out of the window or come outside. He might even call the police, which would certainly prevent me from resolving the violence at the car park. He seemed to be looking for something inside the house as his eyes scanned the room. I waited for him to catch a glimpse of me out of the corner of his eye. The windows were very large and wide, and he would have no difficulty seeing me even in my relatively dark corner. I felt naked.

However, he didn't seem to find what he was looking for, so he turned around and left the room, shutting the door behind him. I let out a breath as gently as I dared and suddenly realised that I couldn't hear any more shouts from the car park. This terrified me even more than the man in the living room. I had begun to raise my head above the fence when the shouts began again. I realised that the other man must have been talking, the one in the suit, perhaps trying to calm down his would-be assailant. Obviously, his non-shouting voice wouldn't carry this far.

Then my fumbling fingers dropped the fucking tape.

I dived to the ground, searching like a parent who has lost his child. As the tape itself was black, the roll disappeared completely in the gloom and my frantic, trembling hands couldn't find it. I would have been stuck had my foot not bumped against it. Snatching it up, I finished off the second nightstick, stood up, and began to put the coat on. When it finally slid over my arms, I was caught for a minute as I saw my reflection in the living room window. The Night Man. Out at night. About to descend. This was a moment I had no time to savour however, because just as I was about to run, the living room door opened again on the other side of the glass and the homeowner strolled in once more. He saw me.

His mouth dropped. This was the first time anyone other than The Night Man himself had seen The Night Man. He froze, confused and surprised. I didn't know what to do. He just stood there, coffee mug in hand, holding his copy of the Radio Times under his arm.

Realising this man was seeing the world's first superhero, I felt such a wonderful rush, a surging of confidence and energy. I raised my arm and tipped him a sharp salute. I then grabbed the rucksack and threw it over the fence behind me without looking, followed by my whipping around dramatically. I then put my hands on the top of the fence, jumped over it (I just clipped it a little with my trailing foot), and, snatching up the rucksack, began my crouched return run across the road towards the car park. The car park and the fight.

For the first time that evening, conscious thought had properly left my mind, and I was running on a fuel of instinct, adrenaline and nerves. I hit the car park fence again and crouched against it. At about five feet in height it was a foot higher than the fence I'd just cleared – yet clipped - so this one was going to be more difficult to jump over. I strongly felt that I needed to do so though, as that was the way it SHOULD be done and would also give me a much better element of surprise. I thought if I really, *really* tried, really leapt at it, I would perhaps make it over with a minimum of difficulty. I was sweating so much now my eyes were stinging and my palms were literally dripping. My heart felt like it would literally thump its way out of my chest, like something out of Alien. I screwed up my eyes. It was one hell of a gamble, but if I started bottling it and compromising what I wanted to do now, then this entire project would be completely pointless. It was going to have to be the leap. I dropped the rucksack at the foot of the fence and stood up.

My head was now clearly visible over the top. I was behind the group, and fortunately, the way they were standing now meant they might not even see me as I jumped. The whole group had circled so that their backs were to me, with their eyes fixed on each other. This was extremely fortunate. Funny little noises emanating from my throat (goodness knows why, side-effect of adrenaline I should imagine, or something), I put my hands on top of the fence, bent my legs, and sprung.

Unfortunately, halfway through the leap I realized that I wasn't going to be able to pull it off. My muscles suddenly spasmed (again, because of adrenaline, no doubt), and I only just managed to sort of catch myself. I'd got the upper half of my body raised above the fence, supported by my arms; my waist was just below the top of the fence. This meant that swinging my legs over would be incredibly difficult. I snapped a furtive glance over at the arguing men who miraculously hadn't seen me yet. It would only take one of them to look this way, and I would be finished.

I began to scrape my feet against the outside of the fence, but the noise my boots made on the wood made me freeze, certain I had been noticed. They hadn't noticed. I then saw that the only logical way forward from this position would be to bend over the fence from the waist until my front half was hanging over the inside, my backside above the level of the fence. I did so, the blood rushing to my head, but it meant that I could, if a little ungraciously, drag first one leg, then the other, over the top of the fence and drop down.

As I hit the ground, my knees bent and the bottom of my long coat followed a split-second behind with a satisfying sounding FLUMPH. One of the suit men noticed the movement and turned slightly. He then immediately turned all the way around. The others followed – literally – suit.

Looking back, I now realize the look on their faces must have been fear. At the time, I didn't know what to make of their expressions at all. Open-mouthed, stopped dead in their tracks, Red-Face with his pointing finger frozen in mid-air. My mind went - of course due to the physical exertion I had just performed - completely blank. Nobody moved. I could tell they just didn't know what to do. Unfortunately, whatever animal impulse had propelled me through the night and over the fence, whatever charge I had felt in the opposite garden, had now vanished. I must have used it all upcoming over the fence. I stared at them; they stared back. I realised that I had to get it back, had to psych myself up, had to break this frozen moment.

But how?

Fortunately – and this was the most uncanny feeling – my body seemed to take over.

With no conscious thought behind it, I fumbled open the utility belt, grabbed the Man Marker, and surprised myself utterly by starting to scream, perhaps taken by some primal memory. It was like one of my Moments, but very, very loud. I should point out that this was not fear, but a mental strategy. I was making myself work on instinct. I saw Red-Face turn to look at his friends, who stared dumbly back.

Then, to my own amazement, I started to run toward them.

I ran towards Red-Face, still screaming so hard that my throat hurt, and his expression changed from shock to confusion. I think he began to say 'what the fuck' but I couldn't be sure as I pulled the trigger on the Man Marker and sprayed him right in the face. I wasn't far away and the shot was fairly easy, especially as I was running towards him, but I still felt an incredible amount of relief when I actually got him precisely where I wanted. Unfortunately, this relief was instantly replaced by fear when, initially, nothing happened.

A sliver of a second later though, Red-Face realized what had happened and cried out in surprise. He went UH! Then put his hands to his face and started frantically trying to wipe it off, gasping as he did so, blinking and blinded. The marketing was true, it seemed; trying to wipe it off DID make it worse, as his hands very quickly began to move faster and faster. He began to hyperventilate, either from the spray or from panic. His two friends must also have been shocked and fascinated by all of this, as they were just staring at Red-Face's frantic wiping as well.

As I ran right up to him I saw that Red-Face still hadn't dropped however, and I must admit, for a moment I didn't have a clue what to do. I was going to have to hit him, but I couldn't seem to make my arms move to do it. I was dimly aware through the haze of adrenaline and fear that at any second his associates would wake up from their shock and attack me, and that would be very bad. I must admit, in that moment I deeply regretted getting involved here, and desperately wanted to be in my bed at home, wrapped up tightly in my violence-proof duvet. I had to make myself get a grip and sweating even more, I managed it.

I made myself scream again, this time with an effort, and it worked. Thoughts went away. That was good. I'd distanced myself from the action I was about to perform.

Wide-eyed, heart racing, unable to believe what I was doing, I raised the right nightstick-arm and brought it down on his head. There was a dull thunking sound. Red-Face shouted louder, but didn't fall. SHIT. This was bad. Panicking a little and feeling sick, a strong copper taste in my mouth, I did it again. THUNK. It was pretty horrible. Red-Face shouted and blindly backed away a step, holding his head with one hand and wiping at his face with the other. I was about to give him another one, to really put some effort into it because he HAD to fall, when I felt a huge crack in my jaw and was knocked backwards. His stocky mate had hit me in the face, and was advancing for another one, shouting something about fucking Halloween. The pain was excruciating. I have never been properly hit in the face in my entire life and it was deeply unpleasant. I tried to get the world to swim back into focus as he kicked me in the groin and the pain level trebled, my insides seeming to ball up into a fist inside my stomach. I was scared, very scared, and everything seemed to be going horribly wrong. Panic was starting to settle in as I saw visions of me being beaten to a bloody mess with my own nightsticks, and worse still, being unmasked.

I blindly brought the Man Marker up and fired. I heard a bellow, and managed to get myself together enough to see the big guy holding his eyes and now doing the same frantic wiping as Red-Face (well, very Red-Face now I guess). The third guy hadn't moved, still staring, bug-eyed. I realised, with a hope I hardly dared to believe, that I now could actually win this, but it had to be NOW. Doing my damndest to shut away the pain in my balls - which now felt like two ruptured zeppelins in my pants – and all the while wishing I'd brought the damn cricket box, I blinked my eyes back into focus, and saw my second attacker moaning and staggering further away, wiping at his face and making it worse for himself. On unstable legs, I walked over to the first guy. I briefly felt a twang of regret and fear as I brought the nightstick up, feeling terribly bad about hitting him like this, but also fearful that he wouldn't go down at all. Then I remembered who I was and who he was and that he HAD to go down, fear or no fear. The scream did its magic again, operating my limbs, and I brought the nightstick cracking down onto his head. This time he went out, falling utterly limp and almost dead-looking. I had just knocked a man out. This was a very, very unusual feeling, but my spasming testicles reminded me - with a surprising sickening feeling - that I had to do it again to my other assailant.

For some reason, doing it the second time required a lot more effort than the first, and it was nothing to do with the pain in my jaw and crotch. It was really, truly knowing - having done it once - that I had to hit a man in the head with a length of solid wood just above his brain. It was very, very difficult, breaking a lifetime's habit, but I made my screaming way over and focused on doing so. I had to hit him four times before he was rendered unconscious; two of those performed while he was lying on the ground. I did my best not to think about it. I will have to get used to this.

I stood there, panting, looking down at the men on the ground. My mind was still completely blank for some inexplicable reason. I looked up at the third man: Slick-Hair. He still hadn't moved. The initial rush had been over so quickly and yet the whole job wasn't over yet.

I HAD knocked two men out, though. I couldn't believe it. It wasn't good or bad, it just WAS, and that WAS stunned me to the core.

Slick-Hair looked at me. His mouth was working but no words came out.

He was clearly wondering what to say, yet incapable of saying anything. I turned my head to look at the two suited men. They were much the same. I think they had ascertained that I was on their side, but it was far from being a certainty in their minds. I turned back to Slick-Hair, and to be perfectly honest, I was at a bit of a loss for words myself. I was still calming down after being in a primal state, and I couldn't get my head together. I think we actually ended up standing there for about five minutes, nobody saying anything. It truly was what they call a STUNNED SILENCE.

Eventually I realised that it was probably up to me to say something. It was especially difficult, because even in this state of mind some unconscious part of me knew that I had to say something effective, something confident, in order for the name to spread. I had run over scenes like this in my mind for a large part of my life, in bed or on a bus or bored at the back of a classroom, and when it came down to it - with two thugs lying on the ground and a third standing in front of me – and I was coming back to myself, I actually found myself feeling a little embarrassed.

You're The Night Man, I thought. What would The Night Man say?

You see, my friends, whenever we are shaken, the thinking man can dip into mental reserves to gather his strength. Learn from this.

I stared straight back at Slick-Hair. The pain in my nuts was incredible, and my jaw felt like it had been fractured, but I couldn't let any of them see this. I was The Night Man, and they had to think I had just laughed off the blow to my balls or I would lose any possible psychological leverage that I currently had. My heart was still about to rupture from the incredible effort it was going through, however. Gathering my nerves as best I could - I could hardly keep my hands from trembling like leaves – I remembered the voice that I'd been working on. Keeping that in my mind, I said hoarsely:

"What the hell was that all about?" Pretty good, I felt. Slick-Hair's mouth continued to work silently, then eventually he found his own voice.

"It ...these two ...John was ...". Seeing him stammer made me feel more in control. I still had this inescapable feeling of pushing my luck, as if the spell would be broken at any minute and Slick-Hair would decide to start throwing a few punches himself. The best way to keep control was to cut his gibberish off.

"Shut up, punk, or you'll get some of what they got!" I hissed, hoping against hope that he listened. Wonderfully, beautifully, fantastically, Slick-Hair did exactly as I commanded. I began to feel another rush, this time of satisfaction as the realisation of what had just happened began to sink into me. I resisted the urge to walk right up to him, as he was taller than me and I didn't want to lose the status I had earned. I felt the giggles begin to come up, threatening to burst, freeing a stream of excited euphoric laughter, but I swallowed them back. It was time for a speech. Time to lay some foundations.

"Now you listen to me, you greasy ...little shit! I want you to tell people what you saw tonight, got it? Tell them what happened to people who felt like a bit of violence. Tell the people who want to break the law. You understand me?" Slick-Hair nodded rapidly. He was fishbelly pale by now. I had clearly impressed him. I came up with a great line and literally had to bite my bottom lip under the mask to stop myself from laughing like a loon. "Tell them you saw The Night Man ...and that he let you go. That he DIDN'T scar you for life. You understand THAT? YOU TELL THEM THAT THE REVILL ARMS, I MEAN ALL OF DERBY, IS UNDER MY PROTECTION!" Slick-Hair nodded some more, much faster.

However, I suddenly realised that I had a rather large problem on my hands, one I had not foreseen. This cannot be blamed on a lack of good planning on my part, far from it, as no one could have seen this coming.

Due to not having a Go-Ped stashed nearby, if I now ran off into the night as I intended, it would be incredibly easy for them all to follow me if they chose; perhaps even to run, get some mates and then catch up with me. Slick-Hair might do so for revenge, and the two I'd saved might follow me out of curiosity. I would also be running down the main road in full costume as, having now been seen, it would probably be a very bad idea to run back into the garden in which I had previously changed. My heart fell as I remembered the old man in the house, who had probably by now called the police. This meant that I had little time and had to find a way around this undesirable state of affairs as quickly as possible. Plus, someone could come out of the pub at any moment.

I looked at Slick-Hair. He really did look scared and kept glancing from the can of Man Marker in my hand to his unconscious mates on the ground. I had initially suspected that seeing me get knocked around - despite the fact that I had won - would make him fancy his chances a little, but it had become clear that he was not a fighter. It made sense. If his two, far harder friends were lying on the ground unconscious, all memory of how they had got there was irrelevant; the ease with which it happened, or lack thereof, didn't matter.

"Now, you listen to me, cuntface!" I barked. I grimaced under my mask when I said that. I don't like to say the C-word; it just came out. The Night Man shouldn't use words like that. "You're gonna walk to the other side of the car park, and you're gonna stand and face the fence. And you aren't gonna turn around for ...five minutes, got it? If you turn around before then, I'll shoot you in the face! You understand me?" I thought I'd better add to this: "And I don't mean with spray either!" I wasn't sure he had understood. "I mean with a gun! With a Magnum, in fact!" He looked terrified. He clearly believed me. After all, if I was 'crazy' enough to be wearing a costume and brandishing weaponry, I was 'crazy' enough to have a gun. "Get moving then! Before I do it anyway! It's got a silencer too, so no one will hear it!" He nodded frantically and walked rapidly to the far side of the car park. You could tell he didn't have a clue what was happening, that nothing remotely like this had happened to him before. Of course not. There had never been The Night Man before, had there?

I waited till he was out of earshot and well across the wide expanse of the car park. Then I started slowly to back away. I was actually starting to believe that I might get away with it. Then I noticed the two suits staring at me, wide-eyed.

I couldn't really talk to them in the way I'd spoken to Slick-Hair. They were the good guys. I wanted these two to talk about me to their mates as their saviour, a hero, not as a psycho. I didn't want to be feared by the GOOD guys. However, I couldn't be all pally either ...I had to maintain their sense of awe. I had to hide the dull throb in my nether regions. I tried to find a balance.

"Listen!" I hissed, then thought I'd better soften it. "Listen. You two are gonna have to do that as well, but don't worry, I won't shoot you or anything." They nodded quickly, just like Slick-Hair had. This was good in one way, but bad in another. They clearly thought I might turn on them. I had to dampen that. "Are you both ok? Did they hurt you at all?"

Good stuff. They shook their heads, sweat flying from one of their foreheads.

"No ...no they didn't," one stammered.

"Ok! Get going!" I said. Screw it, I gave up. I had to get out of there. "And you'd better not turn around either!" They didn't hesitate, turning quickly to walk hurriedly away. I waited until they too were out of earshot. Slick-Hair standing by the far fence, looking rigidly forward. I started to back away again, finally being able to hold my aching balls and massage my jaw.

I suddenly wondered if they - the suits - had heard the name of The Night Man when I was speaking to Slick-Hair. This was really important, as they needed to spread the name too. However, I couldn't exactly just run over and say excuse me, you did catch the name, yes? I decided to do it like a battle cry.

"I AM ...THE NIGHT MAAANN!!" I shouted in a booming, powerful, dramatic voice. Even from here, I could see the two suits visibly freeze for a second, as if they feared a shot, and Slick-Hair actually jumped a little. I decided that in the morning, the suits would realise that I was not to be feared by the good of heart. It was time to move.

Running towards the gate, wincing with every step as my legs crossed in strides and my genitals were squidged, I realised that my car was parked in the middle of the same bloody car park.

This was bad.

If I started the car up, they would know I was leaving, and though Slick-Hair probably wouldn't turn around all night (I expected him to still be there when the cleaners arrived to open up the pub), the two suits MIGHT turn around just as I was leaving and see the car's plate. They might expect me to have a Batmobile or something and want to see it. I'd hate for them to see my Mum's Micra instead. I had to do something.

"The Night Man says, make it ten minutes!" I screamed. "Or any of you gets shot!"

Ah well. So much for good public relations. I'm sure the suits would understand the next day that I was merely saying that to prevent them seeing my escape route. The car park was dark, so I would not be seen by anyone who was still in the pub, and the only people around were currently facing the fence. Screw it. I ducked into the shadows and whipped off the masks, coat, shin pads, gloves, and nightsticks to make sure I didn't look remotely odd if the police arrived. I could claim I had just come out of the pub. I dashed to my car and flung all my stuff into the well of the rear seats and took the handbrake off. Keeping my eye on the little assembly by the far fence - cursing the pain in my muscles all the while - I slowly wheeled the small car towards the car park exit and eventually out onto the street. I looked at the far fence. None of them showed any sign of looking around. I wonder what they were thinking.

Even if they ran towards me now, I would be too far away before they had a chance to see anything. I hopped into the driver's seat, started the engine, put my foot on the gas and I was AWAY.

I had completed my first night!

I had the stereo on full blast all the way home. As soon as I pulled away, I burst into mad, joyous laughter. Satisfaction and achievement and the sheer adrenaline rush were firing through me and making my soul soar, the pain temporarily forgotten. I pummeled the steering wheel. I had done it. I had done it! I was a superhero! And this was only the beginning!

This is the reward of the righteous, my friends. This is what we all can achieve if we have the guts to USE our imaginations. Wonderful, wonderful.

Good lord, I have been writing for hours! It's now half past three ...I apologise, my friends if this has been a lengthy entry, but I was just reliving it all. Reliving the most wonderful evening of my life. Despite the lump on my jaw which feels like a golf ball of pain (my testicles, mercifully, have ceased to ache a long time ago), I feel so charged that I don't think I will sleep at all tonight. I must try however, as my muscles are so sore and need to recuperate. My legs feel like water. I have so much more to tell you and have had so many fantastic ideas inspired by tonight, but I must TRY to sleep. I can't believe it, it's finally happened, it's finally begun!

When you become disheartened or disillusioned, take out this book and reread this entry and take your motivation from it. Make reality your reality. It's never been your friend, after all.

We are heroes. Wonderful.

Thirty-Fifth Entry: Monday August 31st 1998 12:42 PM

Lunchbreak.

I'm not going to bore you with this, but I will quickly say that I am in agony. I managed about an hour's sleep.

Ok, I have just re-read last night's entry. There's so much there! I felt the rush all over again. I still can't believe I have done it, that I managed it, but I did. What a start! The future feels full of opportunity and hope.

Mentally, at least, I feel great. There are a few takeaways to learn from last night, however; the end of the fight, having them stand against the fence, the car etc. That was messy. There are three things that I will implement to avoid this kind of thing happening again:

1. **Never Park In Pub Car Parks**. Obvious really. It is highly likely that there will be many fights outside of any pub that I park at. I will have to intervene when this happens, and will therefore end up in the same push-the-car-out-onto-the-road situation as last night. I shall have to find alternative places to park.

2. **Put Blindfolds And Rope In The Utility Belt:** If I had tied up Slick-Hair and blindfolded him, there would not have been any problem with potentially being followed. The same could be used on witnesses like the suits, as I could then make an anonymous phone call as The Night Man to the police (telling them where the witnesses are) so they could go and untie them. This is not only easier, it is

especially cool to be able to call the police and say, 'Hi, this is The Night Man'.

3.   **Use The Go-Ped:** After much difficult consideration, I have decided not to venture out again until it has arrived.

I will explain this last point. Not only will the Go-Ped make patrolling easier and save more energy (I would surely have cleared the carpark fence with ease had my energy not been so spent by the two and a half hour walk), it will also prevent the problem of getting away quickly. Stash it nearby, change into costume, strike, away, jump onto the Go-Ped, and it won't matter if they see you. You will be off to a hiding place before they can follow you and there will be no license plate to report to the police.

This means that the next mission occurs when the Go-Ped arrives. While this is incredibly galling - I have had a taste of the night and I desperately want more - it would be too dangerous to go out again without it. Goodness knows I haven't gotten this far without playing it safe all the way!

However, I can appease my desire to get out there with the knowledge that my next outing – when it happens - will be on a SATURDAY NIGHT in DERBY CITY CENTRE! That's right! I will plan the expedition when I have a definite date.

Checked all the local papers today for reports of my appearance. Was a little disappointed to not see any, but not entirely surprised. I had expected them to be in tomorrow's edition anyway. This is a very exciting feeling for me. Imagine it: MASKED FIGURE SIGHTED IN

ROBINSON. Or, MASKED HERO PREVENTS BRAWL. I mean, really imagine it! Straight out of a comic.

Obviously, initially the police will pursue me - perhaps even want to arrest me - but eventually they will come to see me as a figure for justice, a helping hand that they all secretly admire. They will bend the rules for me. They will appreciate my efforts and privately applaud them. Why, Chief of Police Jackson? Why do you still allow The Night Man to terrorise our streets? That's what the safe, unrealistic upper-middle-class moral majority will say. Well, he'll reply, we're doing the best we can, but when you're getting shot in a dark alley or stabbed in your eyes or your children are being raped and then He shows up to help you out ...I think maybe you'll be singing a different tune. And he'll probably be harangued for it, criticised in the papers, in the NATIONAL papers, because as the reputation spreads it will become a national obsession (a real superhero on the streets of Derbyshire, hoax or truth?). But nothing will actually be DONE, because secretly everybody will know that I am right. They will all secretly agree with Chief of Police Jackson and see me as a hero.

Incidentally, I must have cleared the air with Chloe, because I ran into her this morning. This is very good news because, as I say, it makes the work environment more pleasurable for everybody. She said hello as she walked past, hardly looking at me to be honest, but I felt that I really had to make sure everything was all right - for everyone else's working good - and so I stopped what I was doing and fell into step beside her.

"Hi," I said. She looked surprised to find me walking with her, but then quickly faced straight ahead and carried on forward. Neither of us said anything, and I thought I'd better explain my actions. "I'm just heading over to Beverages. Stock check." I said.

"I thought Chris was doing the stock check today," she said, still not looking at me. I think I handled the situation rather well by saying:

"Well, he asked me to do it." She didn't say anything in reply.

We kept on walking. It seemed like things maybe hadn't been cleared after all. I had to make the effort, then, or I would be letting my colleagues down.

"Are you finishing your shift now then?" I asked, finding a conversation source.

"No, I finish at six today, like most days," She replied. My next question, purely to continue the conversation, would also clear something up that I had been idly wondering about for the last couple of days.

"Oh ...and then your boyfriend picks you up, yes?"

She looked at me properly for the first time, still walking alongside me.

"I beg your pardon?" she asked. I felt suddenly guilty, like I had been caught. I don't know why. I said, sounding as casual as possible to not come across as nosey (this would have a negative effect, and I was trying to mend work ties):

"I saw you being picked up the other day by someone, your boyfriend I assume?" She looked at me curiously for a second and stopped walking. So did I.

"When was that?" she asked, staring at me.

"Oh ...a couple of days ago."

Her thick eyebrows knotted and she seemed to realise something.

"That was my brother. He was home for a couple of days. He was picking me up so I didn't have to get the bus. Not my boyfriend."

She started walking again, and so did I, still feeling a tension but somehow feeling better about the whole situation at the same time, even though I knew things weren't really cleared. I kept the conversation going as best I could.

"What bus do you normally get?' She looked at me again, like she was thinking about something, but eventually said:

"The 35." That meant she lived Burton way. I happened to live somewhere around that route myself, only about a twenty-five-minute drive or so.

"Oh, I live out that way," I said, keeping things bouncing along nicely. My next comment was my best effort of the morning to cement things back together nicely. "I could give you a lift if you like, if he's not here now." A friendly offer, one that should make things all right again. She looked at me, squinting, and did so for what seemed like a very long time.

"No," she said eventually, "No, it's all right, but thanks Nigel. The bus is fine, it's direct, it's no hassle." I felt a rather large feeling of failure. It was very strange to feel so despondent over something as trivial as work relations, but I suppose I'd had virtually no sleep the night before. I didn't express this, of course, and said:

"Oh. Well, never mind anyway."

"I've got to work now, Nigel. Thanks anyway. Bye." She then turned straight around and began to move cans around randomly on the shelf next to her. She must have been told to do this or something, but it seemed an unusual job to be given.

I stood behind her for a while, watching what she was doing, and then realised I should also be working. That strange, tiredness-induced feeling of depression settled in deeper, and I knew that I had to shake it off and get back to work.

"Goodbye," I said eventually and walked off. The feeling didn't shift for the rest of the morning to be honest. I must sleep well tonight. I'm sure th

Ok, sorry for the interruption. It's now a few minutes later and something surprising has just happened. Chloe just walked into the staff room - fortunately with far fewer people in it this time – then came straight up to me and asked quietly if she could have a lift home after all. Of course I agreed, and then she said thank you and walked straight out again. I was most surprised by her manner, but never mind. I am feeling particularly pleased with myself, as my diplomatic skills are clearly far more effective then I first realised. All in all, a surprisingly satisfying day so far.

Thirty-Sixth Entry: Monday August 31st 1998 6:48 PM

Feeling strangely tense. I want to write about this. Chloe came up to me just before six pm and asked me in a quiet way where she should meet me, and I said that the staff room would be fine. When six pm came and I walked in, she gave me a little half-smile, and we walked out without saying a word to each other. I don't know why I didn't say anything. I just didn't seem to want to talk. Still tired, I suspect.

Anyway, once we got into the car, we had driven along in continued silence for about five minutes, and I was really beginning to feel that I should say something. My tiredness was inducing quite a strong feeling of anxiety, and I was sweating again. I am beginning to wonder whether or not I have some problem with my pores. There seemed to be - and I really could not explain this - a kind of palpable tension in the air, and as the journey progressed, it seemed to get worse. It was most unusual. I chanced a sideways glance and she didn't seem to be sitting in an entirely relaxed way either. I was about to say something, anything to shatter this illusion of the mind that had me breathing heavily and sweating quite noticeably. However, I actually jumped a little in my seat when she said:

"Do you mind if I turn on the radio?" I felt a rush of relief.

"No! Not at all!" I said, more loudly than I meant. She leaned over and flicked the stereo on, the sound of Radiohead only coming out of one speaker as the other one has been broken for some time. She sat back, but I could feel that she hadn't relaxed into her seat.

"Do you like this sort of music?" I asked, after a while.

She jerked her head round and said quickly:

"Oh yes ...I really like this. I'm not a big fan of all this House and Garage stuff. I prefer, you know ...bands."

I looked at my knuckles on the steering wheel. They were white. The top of the wheel was slick with sweat. This was crazy.

"My brother's in a band," she said.

"Really?" I answered quickly. "Are they any good?"

"Oh yeah," she said emphatically, nodding and looking out of the window. "They're really good. They play in town a lot."

I don't have a clue how to talk to women, to be honest. Interacting with people has never been my strong point. My interests have often brought me ridicule and the interests of others normally strike me as moronic, so I have never really had the chance to talk to many members of the opposite sex. This has never saddened me, however; far from it, as it has meant I have had plenty of time to develop as a human being by pursuing said interests to the fullest and not have to suffer fools.

None of this, however, was any comfort to me now, knowing I was stuck in a car for another fifteen minutes and wondering what the hell to say because keeping the conversation going suddenly seemed very, very important. I just said the first thing that came to mind.

"Where was the last place they played?" I asked.

"The Snazell Bridge," she said, looking at me now, "they're playing there tonight actually. That's why he couldn't pick me up." There was a long, heavy pause, the only sound being that of Thom and the boys lilting woefully from the stereo. Then:

"Would you like to come along tonight?" she added, quietly.

Now this was the funny thing because here I could swear I felt my stomach turn a little and my skin went cold. I stared at the road straight ahead and heard myself say:

"Yes ...yeah, that'd be good. Whereabouts in town is it again?"

When she spoke next, she did it so quietly I could barely hear her over the stereo.

"Well, why don't you pick me up and I'll be able to tell you the way?"

"Ok. Cool. Yes. What time?" I asked, feeling the blood running to my head now, my temples pulsing.

"Um ...8:30?" she suggested.

"Yes. Yes, that's fine." I said, tongue dry and thick.

Silence then descended between us like thick syrup for the next ten minutes, the only words being Chloe saying directions quietly from time to time. When we reached her house, she said:

"Thanks a lot," then got out of the car and walked straight to her front door without looking back.

I turned the car around sharply and drove round the corner into the next street along, parked up, turned the engine off, and sat there with the windows open, trying to calm down.

I am still parked there now, typing this, and my breathing has only just returned to normal. I thought it best to write it now, whilst I was still in the moment, so to speak. I have my second proper date ever within two and once again I am not sure if it is actually a date. Is she just inviting me to boost the crowd for her brother's sake? As a friend? The dress code problem remains, so I shall try to have a similar balance as last time.

Also: is this wise? I have just started my career and this could prove a major distraction. However, in all fairness, the Go-Ped is yet to arrive, and this means - as I said earlier - that I can't do any more just yet.

In fact, thinking about it, this IS a good idea. The 'reward' system that I talked about earlier should be used here; a little free-time treat, as I successfully completed a major stage of the mission and should therefore reward myself. Motivation. And besides, my last little 'reward' was hardly a reward, was it? A highly uncomfortable evening out with a rather obsessed girl?

A drink and some live music would be good. Good fun. And I will get to know a work colleague, which can only be a good thing. All in all, a sensibly chosen reward.

Netry nighttime ocxc2333

had a drink so this may be short or it may be long I don't know which it is going to be but I am writing because I writing in the writing and that's what Ive been doing for ages

I picked the girl up at the time I was supposed to and was dressed myself in something cool yet smart so I couldn't be looking stupid in front of anyone. This was clever. She looked really GOOD and I was very surprised and she got in the car and smiled and I couldn't speak for ages because I didn't know what to say but then I was being polite and said you look really nice and she went red and I mean RED bright red all over her face and we drove to the pub. The car is still in town I couldn't drive when I went home because t=it is illegal and they take your licenseaway.

We got to the opub and we hadn't really said anything to each oteher but we got ther'e and we went in. She showed me her brother who was sitting at a table with the band he was a big bloke but weasnt nasty at all, and it was very busy and I bought her a drink at the bar she ahd a fosters and I had a fosters too. There were a lot of people but she found a table at the back of the room, and we sat down and we still ahdnt realy saod anything at all to each oter, until she said all red again in the face like she was embarrassed to say, you look realy nice as well you look a lot different without your glasses because id taken them off before we went in, I don't know hwy. Noone has ever said anyting like ths to me evr EVER and I didn't say anything I was so surprised and she said what like she thought I was angry and all I could say was that svery nice and then the band started.

It was so loud that she was saying something and I couldn't hear her so I just nodded but then I think she realised it weas too loud and then she didn't say anything else. So we had our drinks and I mimed did she want another and she nodded and I got some more, and then we sat and drank because there was no point talking s it was SO LOUD, I think she even mimed TOO LOUD at me and the nshe got some more and we just looked at each other no an then and smiled poikltely and then I got some more drinks and we drank them and then she was saying something finally and I couldn't hear so I mimed CANT hear and she shouted so I could hear why did I say that stuff to marie about her when I took marie out. I was drunk by then I am not a big rdirnj drinker pubs are dangerous to be in fights happen and then where is the night man hahaha so I just said because I thought marie didn't like you and I didn't want to annoy her. She said why did you lie to her or were you not lying did you really mean it and I ewas really embarrassed I remember thinking plaesse ground swallow me up but I still said I don't know but I was lying I do like you really and then she said Id really upset her about it and I said I didn't mean to I honestly don't know why I said it and she smiled and said I was weird, but then she looked worried and said she didn't mean it like that (I don't know now how she meant like that) and then she said she was really sorry for all the stuiff she said outside the staff room and that she felt bad afterwards but was still angry because iof what Id said, and I just said it was OK and then she smiled and went to the abr to get more drinks the band finished and she we talked and talked then, I was talking so much and she just sat there and smiled looking at me with her head sideways I never have talked so much to at anybody evr but I wjust kept going and she was asking questions and it felt lovely, listening ot her talk and I sat there for ages and we drank thn some girl came over to us

She said hello to Chloe but in a funny way, and Chlow went all white and just said Sandra like she was surprised and scared, and this girl who I suppose was called Sandra goes I thought you were going out with your mum and dad tonight and Chloe says nothing, just sit theer looking terrified and then the girl says and whos this looking at me and I say I'm Nigel and then she stares at Chloe for ages and then she says experimenting a ittle bit are we Chloe and I wonder what the hel shes on about theres noexperiment but then she says to Chloe can I have a word and Chloe gets up from the table and without saying anything and disappears off somewhere with this girl, and I don't have a clue what happening but about half an hour later the other girl goes storming out of the door and Chloe comes back crying. She sit there crying for ages and crying and crying and I don't know what to do and thn eventually I say what happened and she shakes her head and carries on crying and she says Im so stupid Im so embarrassed, Im an idiot just take me home please Nigel Im so sorry and I don't know what to make of it then I realize I can't drive now so I go and call a cab. We go outside and wait for the cab and shes still crying and its raining and we get in the cab when it turns up and she hasn't said a word to me she sits on the other side of the cab and then we get back to hers and she gets out saying Im so sorry Nigel and that makes her cry even more and so I get out of he cvab and say what happened what happened and she says all tears I shouldn't have done this, blah blah blah, I was just curious, I was just confused, I shouldn't have done this to you or her I was having doubts but I knew already and I'm an idiot Im so sorry Nigel please don't tell anyone Im so sorry, I do really like you but then shes crying far too much and then she sahkes her head and runs back inside the house. I got in the cab and found I only had enough money to get halfway home and so I had to wlak for half an hour and here I am writing this now.what the hell was all hat about I feel very strange very sad disappointed but no the hight man takes this and turns it around gets tright back up again never goers down he's ghj

fuck fuck FUCK

Thirty-Seventh Entry: Tuesday September 1st 1998 12:34 PM

Another day, another dollar, another month. The first thing I said this morning, of course, was 'white rabbits', which you can only do on the first day of a month with an 'R' in it, and that means it will be a lucky month. It is difficult to remember to do this when half asleep, but I have practiced this for years and so it comes pretty naturally.

I have left all that in to see if you can make any sense of last night. I don't know what happened to Chloe. Maybe it was nerves. I think perhaps she had cancelled an evening out with her friend and told her an excuse so she could come out with me and got caught. I know girls seem to take these things very seriously, and that would account for Chloe's behavior (that and being very drunk). Until then, everything had been fine, if a little weird. To be honest, time seemed to pass very quickly - we'd only been there about three hours, but it seemed like less than one - and after the first drink or two all of my usual palpitations etc. suddenly stopped. No bad Moments. Either way, it would have been a most satisfactory reward, which would have spurred me onwards, but then ...well, you can read.

However, despite excruciating, crinkling glass pain throughout my body, and generally feeling depressed (hangover symptoms, terrible, this is why I'm not a big drinker), today is a great day because the Go-Ped is here!!! When I think of this fact, I find myself lifted automatically out of the strange mood that is following me today. I will finally get to ride upon my steed, my hero's transport!

A knock on the door came during breakfast, and a man in a delivery uniform stood on the front doorstep. I couldn't w

Sorry. Chloe has just walked into the staff room and asked if she can have a word after work. She looked all funny - very pale and nervous – and kept looking at everyone in the staff room like she was afraid. I said yes and asked if she wanted another lift but she said no, she'd meet me in the pub across the road and that we should talk. I wondered why she was so serious and what she so desperately wanted to talk about (thinking on this brought another stomach roll, so I stopped doing so), but I said that I had to take my mum to hospital.

Obviously that wasn't true. Tonight was the Go-Ped test. Gym and Aikido first, too. I have to admit that all this seems suddenly less appealing then earlier today when I felt quite excited. I must cut out drinking altogether, it affects my moods too much. But it is still appealing, very appealing, but don't worry about THAT my friends. Negative feelings are no use to anyone. Keep it positive. Anyway, I didn't want to ever go in that pub again after what happened in there before.

She looked at her fingers, gently clasped together, arms hanging down.

"Oh," she said. I found myself suddenly blurting out:

"But we can talk after work tomorrow? But let's go to the Martin Arms instead." She looks up, eyes wide, and nods.

"Ok ..." she said. "I just want to explain ...last night. Tomorrow then. I have to work a bit later, until eight. Is that ok?" I nodded yes, and she then walked out the staff room quickly, and I found myself letting out a deep breath that I didn't even know I was holding in. That WAS weird. Have to get back to work. Write later.

Thirty-Eighth Entry: Tuesday September 1st 1998 9:34 PM

The first newspaper reports are in!!! After scouring the local papers before leaving work, there it was, page 9, News In Brief column no. 4. I've transcribed it here:

Elderly Man Catches Vandal

William Bricknell of Glover St. caught a masked man attempting to vandalise his garden on Sunday evening. Mr Bricknell, 82, spotted the individual from his living room window. The intruder was hiding in his garden.

"Once I turned on the light, he knew I'd spotted him," said Mr Bricknell. "then he scarpered." Police are investigating the incident.

I can hardly believe it! The first newspaper report of The Night Man! Fine, it is admittedly of a rather negative bent, and I was called a 'vandal', but I expected this. Every superhero is misunderstood when he first starts out. Look at Spider-Man, whose career has spanned a good thirty years or so and is still being branded a menace and a criminal by a surprising number of people in New York city. This only gives me another source of motivation: to start getting some good headlines (turn it around, make it work for YOU!). I feel on top of the world this evening, last night forgotten.

I have a little folder now marked 'cuttings' that I have placed this in, which I have stashed along with my costume bits, and I will continue to fill this with various news reports throughout my career.

At least the Aikido warm-up even seemed to be a little more brief this week. I wonder if Dave has taken on some of my suggestions after all. That is a gratifying thought.

Let me tell you: you want to buy one of these Go-Peds. When I finally got back today - after driving through some frankly ridiculous traffic - I knew it would be ready to go. I'd been charging the thing all day.

I know I will have to give it a good test – to get used to the weight and handling of it - before I even think about using it in a dangerous situation, so I will ride around for an hour or so before venturing into town. Just in time to catch the pub kickouts. That's right: I'm going in TONIGHT!

I know I said earlier that I would be going out on the Saturday night coming, but I didn't expect the Go-Ped to arrive before then. So tonight is The Night Man's SECOND MISSION!

The Go-Ped weighs about forty pounds at a guess, with a solid wood board to stand on and a small electric engine mounted at the back above the wheels. It has a metal steering column with the throttle mounted on the handlebars on one side and the brake on the other. The suspension system looks most impressive, and allegedly the sensation whilst riding is one of 'hovering.' I am very, very keen to try this out, as I have no doubt that it will make night missions a lot more enjoyable. I have made a note to myself to buy one of those T-bar things that mountain bikers use to lock up their wheels – or something like it at least - to prevent it from being stolen while I am busy elsewhere.

I had originally intended to hide the Go-Ped from Mum and David. This is for the simple reason that it would be a perhaps surprising coincidence should their son and brother purchase a new motorised scooter out of the blue, and then reports start coming via the papers of a masked crime fighter riding some sort of motorised skateboard. HMM! Obviously, perhaps the papers would not even mention The Night Man's mode of transport, but I wanted to play it safe. Either way, the debate was rendered academic as David came blundering into my room and saw me taking it off charge, despite the KEEP OUT notice on my bedroom door. The look on his face said it all.

"Wow! Is that yours??"

I thought of a response quickly.

"No. It's a friend's. I'm charging it up for him."

"Why can't he do it?"

"Because ...he' s not very good with electrics."

"But all you're doing is plugging it in."

I thought quickly.

"Yes. But ...he electrocuted himself once. He has a phobia about plug sockets. Silly but true."

He cocked his head.

"Come on Nige," he said with a smirk. "Who are you trying to fool?" The little fucker really was getting older. I decided to change tack.

"You tell Mum about this and I'll fucking kill you David."

He actually smiled. I'd screwed up by mentioning Mum, and I normally knew better not to even try and threaten him. Now it was moot anyway; a secret from Mum meaning he had me over a barrel.

"Why are you keeping it so secret?" His eyes narrowed. "You haven't STOLEN it, have you?"

"No, I bought it." There was a long silence.

"I'm telling Mum," he said, and began to walk out of the room. I love my little brother an enormous amount, but sometimes I really could quite literally murder the little bastard. I ran across the room and clapped one hand around his mouth, the other around his waist, and carried him back to the centre of the room. He was trying to shout, his small but wiry muscles working as he tried to break free, but my hand was on his mouth and he was saying nothing. I knew that violence wouldn't work, because I know David. He would just wait and then tell Mum later out of spite. I put him down in the middle of the room.

"Listen, it's mine, I bought it," I hissed. "I just don't want Mum to know because it cost a lot of money and she'll only complain about me wasting it, all right? Don't tell her and ..." The next words were like pulling my own teeth out. "...you can even have a go, ok?"

His head came up quickly. He backed away a few steps and looked at me petulantly, attempting to regain some of his dignity. His hair had been messed up.

"How fast does it go?" he asked eventually, his curiosity getting the better of his annoyance.

"Fast enough," I told him. His eyes drifted to the Go-Ped again, full of a child's hunger for any new gadget, especially one as cool as this. You can ride around on it. What child wouldn't love the idea of that?

"Can we use it now?" he asked eventually.

"Not now," I told him firmly, "I have to test it first. But if you tell Mum, you won't get to use it at all. Ok?" He nodded, still staring at the Go-Ped. "Ok then," I said, turning away from him, "Get out then. I've got to get ready."

"Where you going?"

"Out for the evening," I said, still with my back to him, starting to grin as I realised I was about to get into some typical superhero excuse-making banter. You'll like this, this is funny. I started to have a little fun. "I'm taking the Go-Ped out, in fact," I said, picking various pieces of my underwear up off the floor, pretending to tidy up.

"Can I come?"

I grinned again to myself.

"No, it'll be too dangerous tonight Davey. Tomorrow maybe." I could picture him huffing behind me as he said:

"That thing's not dangerous! What are you talking about?" I had to stifle a laugh as I said:

"No ...the Go-Ped's not dangerous Davey. I just said tonight will be too dangerous." He didn't say anything, and my cheeks flared as I gasped back a laugh. I had clearly bamboozled him. Then - in the way little kids often do - he tried to raise himself above it to try and win.

"Yeah right, Nige," he said. "I'm sure you're up to really exciting stuff. I'M sure. Ooh, I'm so dangerous. Ooh." I turned around, and looked at him with his hands on his hips and his little pot belly sticking out, smirking and mocking me. He can be a vindictive little git.

I felt that 'click' inside and then suddenly I was slapping him across the face with my open hand. I hit him hard, harder than I meant to, and several times.

It left a red handprint on his cheek. Sometimes I can lose my temper, and he knew this and he pushed the wrong button anyway. It was his fault, really, when you think about it. It was his fault. I've even tried to apologise since and everything, but he's still sulking. He made me do it, so I don't know why he's still being like that.

His eyes began to well up, and I knew I had to speak quickly.

He put his hand to his reddening cheek, surprised and physically hurt. I was equally surprised, I must admit. I didn't say anything, but I stared at him. I think he must have really known - inside - that he'd asked for it, because he didn't fully cry. Instead he screwed his face up and shouted:

"I'm telling Mum!" and ran out of the room. Unfortunately for him, Mum wasn't in at that moment, and I knew this, so I shouted after him:

"Tell her and you won't get a go, ever!!"

After saying that, I know he won't tell her now. If Mum had been in at the time, he would have done so anyway. Now that he's calmed down he'll think better of it.

Right, I'm off to try the Go-Ped out. And then I'm off to begin The Night Man's **Second Sighting**. My first night in town. In the danger zone. Write later.

Thirty-Ninth Entry: Wednesday September 2nd PROPAGANDA NIGHT 1:53 AM

I'm sure you're all wondering about the title. Read on.

After bombing around the local streets for an hour or so, I realised I should have bought a Go-Ped years ago. They are tremendous fun, and I realised instantly that it would make Night Man operations a hell of a lot more enjoyable, as well as more efficient. I can now cruise instead of walk. And that's not to mention all the practical applications! It really does have a feeling of hovering, thanks to the excellent suspension and reflexive throttle. I came off the thing twice initially (after taking a few early corners a bit too vigorously), but of course this is nothing like coming off a bike. You simply step off the thing in an awkward manner and feel stupid. But I soon learned how to prevent this from happening, and I was eventually gliding along, the electric engine whirring in a barely audible fashion. I was the embodiment of stealth.

Once I felt confident enough - and the thirst for some action had gripped me - I 'Pedded' (a verb of my own creation; to 'Ped.' This is to differentiate between when I am driving the car and driving the Go-Ped. I 'Ped' when I am on the Go-Ped. Clever, eh?) back to where I'd parked the car (some way from our house, as obviously I don't want Mum to come home and see me whipping around on the thing. She's nosy.), which contained The Night Man's rucksack. I collapsed the Go-Ped and placed it gently on the back seat. Heart racing, I started the Micra up and drove into town. It was about 11:00 PM. This was not QUITE the big one – that would have to be a Saturday night - but this was still The Night Man's first foray onto the streets of the City Centre and the charge that had whipped through me on Sunday night gripped me once more. The

Night Man wanted out, wanted to come out and hunt, and I was all too eager to let him.

Town was still relatively quiet when I got there, even for a Tuesday night (never the busiest night of the week in town), but I realised that the town pubs wouldn't be kicking out just yet. It hadn't passed eleven thirty and some of them had a one o'clock license. One o'clock licenses in the week ...just asking for trouble. Whichever genius thought it would be a good idea to ship that one in from the continent has a lot to answer for. It'd mean I wasn't sat typing this so late, for starters! Ha ha.

I chose to park in the easiest access car park: an outdoor, single level one as opposed to one of the multi-level ones, as this would be easiest to ride into if in a hurry. I would recommend this to any drivers who wish to become superheroes. I parked up and got out of the car.

Pack on back, costume inside, I set off on The Night Man's NightCycle (I just thought of that-what would you call YOUR steed? This is the fun stuff.) around town. I was relieved by the lack of attention the Go-Ped drew, as that way if anyone ever noticed that The Night Man also rode a Go-Ped - despite the fact that he dresses completely different to me – then my secret identity would be blown, poof. As I say though, no one seemed to notice me at all, as I assume the near-silent nature of the machine perhaps meant that people thought it was an ordinary, foot-propelled scooter.

An hour passed, and I circled the town centre with pleasing swiftness. 14 miles per hour may not sound like much, but it certainly feels fast on one of these things. It certainly hammers walking into the proverbial cocked hat. I scooted past the various pubs, from yuppie bar to local-style boozer, past the shuttered-up chain stores like Top Man and Boots, passing progressively greater amounts of people as the night went on and more and more people piled out of the pubs. The boredom factor was greatly reduced by the pleasure of riding along effortlessly, even though I had been doing it for some time.

I thought I saw a fight breaking out on the opposite side of the street, and slammed on the brakes ...only to realise that it was a couple of friends play fighting outside a chip-shop, making Bruce Lee style noises as they high kicked each other while trying to avoid spilling their chips. Idiots. I carried on.

A new dilemma was presented to me; one I had not hitherto encountered: at what level of crime should I intervene? For example, one young man was standing on top of a bus-stop, singing loudly. Not only is this vandalising public property – sort of - but it was also disturbing the peace. I considered getting into costume and dashing over there to give him a stern warning, but by the time I had changed he would probably be gone anyway, and for the amount of effort it would take to saddle up just to tell him to stop singing ...it hardly seemed worth it. Despite my admitted keenness to get into costume and get working (a highly necessary and admirable trait for any young superhero), I thought it best not to in this instance. If he had been vandalising the bus-stop in an outright manner then that would have been a much clearer case for some preventative violence.

The reason I mention this is because it kind of led to 'the big idea'. Later, when it had reached one o'clock (the time when everybody who was likely to be out on the streets causing trouble ...would be, well, out on the streets causing trouble), one thing became clear: no one was out on the streets causing trouble tonight. While this was good, it was also bad for one simple reason: once The Night Man's reputation for being someone YOU DO NOT WANT TO CROSS has spread, I should imagine it will make my work a lot easier as people will be more scared to try anything funny or whatever.

However, this would not happen unless The Night Man was actually SEEN riding into action at some point.

How could the papers know about him if there was nothing to report? No crimes being prevented because no crimes had even been attempted? How could the people have faith when there was nothing to believe in? It was a Catch-22. To become a deterrent, I first needed something to deter.

And that was when I had 'the big idea'. Think about it: technically, as far as the police are concerned, The Night Man doesn't exist. They obviously haven't heard of him yet, and therefore, they certainly don't know that he had committed the arrestable 'crime' of incapacitating two thugs who were about to hand out a beating to two innocent men outside The Revill Arms last Sunday night.

It came to me in a flash. Tonight could be very useful after all, in an inspired and dramatic way. Tonight could be PROPAGANDA NIGHT. I could disappear, get into costume, and ride about town. Not only would people look at the costume and be in awe, wondering who I was, but when the first reports started coming in they would say to their friends, 'HEY, I saw that guy on Tuesday night, the masked guy'. Nothing spreads an urban legend better than word-of-mouth. It's the only way. News reports would be often regarded as hoaxes, but if Bob down at the pub says with absolute sincerity that he saw the scary-looking masked guy himself, well ...you wouldn't think twice. And if anybody asked what

I'm doing dressed up like that, I could tell them ...I'm The Night Man. Spread the name. Let them know. The Night Man is here.

That was it then. My mind was made up. Now, I know what you're thinking. Surely the police will eventually come to know - when the reports come in and the muggers etc. are found incapacitated - that The Night Man rides a Go-Ped. And if they see me, out of costume, riding a Go-Ped, they would be most likely to question me.

I have already thought about this. If I see any police, I lose the bag quickly and then they can pin nothing on me. If they ask about the baking trays, I'll just say they are for protection in case I fall off. Even if they don't believe me, they'd have no evidence, so I'd get away with it. Let no one ever say I don't cover all the possibilities.

I Pedded up to the back of the warehouse at the top of McCrickard St. and found a sufficiently dark corner to change in. No one would be around here at this time of night, so I was safe. I couldn't believe the almost physical jolt of excitement I felt when I reached into the bag and touched the material of the mask.

Minutes later, people were seeing a masked, cloaked, speeding figure, zipping its way along the streets of Derby. Their faces! I could clearly see the awe there as I dashed past them, their mouths hanging open. Some people tapped each other on the shoulder as I went by. That look was RESPECT.

Occasionally I would drive past people and shout in my booming (but gruff) voice:

"THE NIGHT MAN IS HERE!!!" Then I'd speed off, leaving them to re-gather their shattered senses and pick their jaws up off the ground. I felt like I was flying, soaring over them all and spreading the good word, instilling hope. Perhaps there were a few criminal types out that night. Perhaps there were a few who had even managed to commit a few crimes that escaped the watchful eye of The Night Man and thanked their lucky stars. They wouldn't get away with it again, I can tell you!

After a while, I had another great idea: I should create a Confirmed Sighting. And how would be the best way to get that? I already knew the answer, and, grinning from ear-to-ear, charged with adrenaline, I made my way over to the HSBC bank on the corner of Pitchford Rd. and Samuels St.

I pulled up, making sure that no one was at least within visual range. Giggling in a low but almost uncontrollable way, I collapsed the NightCycle once more and stashed it behind a bin, then composed myself. I flattened my body against the wall. Two feet to my left was the corner of the bank, with me against the wall that led up Pitchford Rd., round the corner from Samuels St. I took a deep breath. I decided it would be a good idea to create a huge, dramatic comic-book image of The Night Man in my mind, seeing him the way other people saw him, reminding myself, psyching me up. Then I jumped around the corner, and into the path of the SECURITY CAMERA that hung over the wall-mounted cashpoint.

I struck a dramatic crouch as I landed, then slowly, powerfully, stood up and put my hands on my hips, my chest thrust out. I raised one arm and pointed to the sky, then dropped it into a salute. I then promptly launched myself back round the corner. Let them put that on CrimeWatch UK. What an irony.

I quickly re-erected the NightCycle, and set off for the next part of the evening's plan. What was that, you might ask?

A visual, human contact, in-person sighting.

One that would happen in a place where they would be likely to tell everyone they met afterwards. A place where people would be likely to ask: have YOU seen The Night Man, mate?

I was heading for the kebab shop.

As I expected - being quite late for a Tuesday night - there were no customers in the kebab shop, merely the owner and his skivvy. This was how I wanted it. The rush was burning in my head, and for the first time in my career as The Night Man so far, I felt afraid of no one. I will get on with the story, but I have to make it clear that I was very, very enthralled with this situation.

I collapsed the NightCycle, picked it up and entered the shop. I was greeted by the tinny sounds of Ram FM - the 'local' station where half the broadcasts are exactly the same shows played nationwide - playing out of the small speakers near the polished metal counter. It very nearly drowned out the sound of grease sizzling on the rotating elephant leg of garbage kebab meat. The lights were bright, the floor had just been mopped and the smell was unusual. No one had seemed to have noticed me yet.

Putting the NightCycle on the floor, I struck my hands onto my hips, proud and powerful, and said in my Night Man voice:

"Good evening."

The eldest fellow behind the counter, presumably the owner, turned around. He was short and Asian, with slight stubble and a squat head. He looked me up and down in quiet surprise. He was clearly taking in the costume. I must have impressed him, as his jaw became visibly tight. There was a pause. He obviously knew he had a serious customer here, because when he spoke next, he did so in a very wary voice, very slowly.

"What can I do for you mate?" he asked, but let me tell you, that might sound like a jolly phrase, but HE didn't say it like that. Hell, he almost looked scared. Looking back, he was definitely scared; in fact, wide-eyed and jaw set. It must have been the pose. I shall have to lose that when talking to innocents. It's all a learning experience.

I realised I hadn't actually prepared for this point. The other fellow behind the counter - a young lad but tall, with a thin bum-fluffy moustache - turned around as well, and clearly registered more surprise than the owner. He started to reach for something under the counter, staring at me, but the owner cut him off, saying something sharply but firmly in some Asian language. The boy stared to say something back, but he was cut off again. He seemed to stand up reluctantly. Perhaps he wasn't allowed to serve tonight or something, perhaps as a punishment. He'll get his chance. The owner looked back at me, and raised his chin slightly, bobbing it upwards quickly. Well? The gesture said. I found the words.

"Seen any trouble in here tonight?" I asked him. His gaze not changing, he shook his head slightly, jaw still set. I must admit, I had expected more of a reaction than this.

"Well, if you do, remember one thing: The Night Man will bring the perpetrators to justice." I felt incredible, invincible, daring to say things like this to people's faces, my mask, my role, setting me free, making me alive! He nodded, eyes still set. The poor fellow didn't know what to say. I started to say something like well, I'll be off, but then something rather surprising happened. I'll write it as it occurred to me.

The door opened and a large Asian fellow came in, tall and broad, young, with cropped hair. He clearly knew the owner, as he waved drunkenly when he came in.

"Evenin' Sham," he said, slurring his words a tad. He began to walk past me, but stopped dead when the owner suddenly started talking in Asian again. He was addressing this new guy using the same sharp tone he had used with the boy but louder, more urgent. The big fellow took a few steps backward and turned to look at me. I hadn't moved. My hands were still on my hips. He looked down at me.

"Is he now?" he said to me in English, advancing. I suddenly was aware dimly of a shift in atmosphere, and a feeling of danger. Was this big lad trouble? He kept on walking. "Well, you picked the wrong place, didn't you mate?" He was talking with his face completely straight, his jaw set now, too. I realised he was between me and the door. A funny feeling washed across my back. Looking at that moment in hindsight, I imagine it was probably instinct kicking in or something.

Suddenly, he shot a hand out and pushed me back into the wall, where my head connected hard. CRACK. The pain was surprisingly intense, exploding seemingly inside my brain, and my breathing suddenly doubled. I was about to get into another fight OUT OF NOWHERE, and the sweat suddenly began to sting my eyes as I realised what was happening. A guy twice my size was picking a fight with me and I couldn't get away, couldn't get out now the pain had started, didn't want to get smashed up. Panic was setting in, but I must point out to you all that I realised this - that was the important thing - and tried to think clearly, through the haze of urgent messages flooding to my brain. This is the mark of a true superhero.

However, it didn't work just then. He grabbed my collar and pinned me against the wall, smashing my head again so everything went white for a split second. I couldn't believe it. Everything actually went white.

He was saying something but all of my senses were temporarily offline, distracted by panic and disorientated by the blow to the head. I was fumbling for the Man Marker but couldn't get it, couldn't feel it, but then suddenly it was in my hand and I'd brought it up and fired into his mouth by chance.

I had meant to get it in his eyes, but this apparently worked just as well, if not better. The pressure on my neck went, and he was now on the floor choking and coughing. Breathing heavily, it suddenly came to me what had happened: these guys, the kebab people, were low-level CROOKS! They thought I had come to bust them and set big guy here on me to prevent that. I had to strike and move. I was too bleary now to do anything about the main operation they had going on, but I could still win the night. I stepped over him, trying to focus on the people behind the counter who were now shouting to the big guy and me in Asian, but I brought the Man Marker up and shot the owner in the face. I missed the boy. The owner cried out and started wiping.

The boy stared at me, wide-eyed, seeing the reaction of the owner and fearful of the spray, wondering what I was going to do. Normally I would feel charged by the criminal's fear, but for some reason I felt weak. I was breathing very heavily and standing up seemed like an effort. I think it was the blow to the head, but I managed to say:

"That's a warning. Clean up your act. The Night Man is in town now," or something like that. I can't quite remember, but either way, I was then staggering to the door. I don't know what happened to them next. I picked the collapsed Go-Ped up off the floor, managed to quickly erect it, and Pedded off back to the car. My limbs were like jelly, my heart was pounding, and I was amazed at what I'd discovered: crime was everywhere!

Something unusual happened on the way back, as I stopped at a set of traffic lights in the middle of the street. Three lads rounded the corner, and for some reason, one of them tapped his mate on the shoulder and they just started laughing. I was very surprised indeed by this reaction, but I didn't have time to wait and consider it as the lights changed and it was then time to move.

Obviously, tonight did not go as smoothly as Sunday night. This is clear to anyone. This WAS only my second mission, but once again, I took the adversity and turned it around, stepped up. I never fell, and this is most important: Never let them/it take you down. Stay standing and make it work for you. Negativity helps no one, and how are you supposed to get anywhere by moping?

The bullies must NEVER win.

Either way, those three scumbags will have told their friends what had happened tonight - told them the name. They'll lay low for a while, too. That's good. I can attend to them later when I've had a little more experience. The name will be spread in fear throughout their punk community too.

However, that's twice I have been caught in the head, and twice I have been disorientated as a result. I have a memory of thinking about a crash helmet with the costume. Why did I let this go? I probably sacrificed it for the good of the costume's effect. Ok, that's fine. I will just have to be more careful of my head in these situations. I'm sure it'll come with practice.

I must admit, all the way home - and while sat here writing this - my thoughts keep going back to the lads at the traffic lights. Why did they laugh? What was funny? Surely not my appearance - the rest of tonight had told me exactly what I knew already, that the costume commands respect - so why did they laugh? I have come to the conclusion that they must have been drunk, really drunk, and their fear came out as laughter. It was their way of dealing with it. Though it makes sense, it's quite sad really. Time for bed now.

Fortieth Entry: Wednesday September 2nd 1998 12:23 PM

Press Report No. 2! Saw it this morning on page 7, column 2 of News In Brief in The Derby Evening Telegraph - looks like someone called it in just in time to catch the morning edition:

Kebab Shop Raid Foiled

Noshers Kebab House was the victim of an attempted raid in the early hours of this morning. A masked man, armed with a can of what is believed to be some kind of personal security spray, attempted to hold up the outlet but was distracted by a customer. They grappled before the thief escaped. No money was stolen, and the police are looking into the incident.

FINE, it says that I was a burglar. That's just what they told the papers, but their scumbag friends will know different. When they see this article, they will fear. I feel good, and the original clipping of this has gone into the collection.

Quick note. Chloe surprised me in aisle F this morning. She reminded me that she was working until eight, and asked if it was still ok to meet after that. I was taken aback by the curtness with which she spoke, but I just said Ok and then she left again. She has a funny habit of that, this arms folded, quick walk-away walk.

I guess that's just the way it is. Back to work.

Forty-First Entry: Thursday, September 3rd 1998 1:23 AM

I have had a terrible, awful evening. I really, really don't feel like writing, but I will because I have made a commitment and breaking a commitment is for fucking cunts.

The hours after work seemed to drag by, like time itself was trying to piss me off. I drove into town and bought a book, partly to pass the time until I met Chloe, and partly because I needed a new book to read anyway. By chance, my eye fell on a copy of Stig Of The Dump, a favourite book from my childhood. It was a magic, magic book as I remembered, and so I promptly bought it. I happily fell into it when I got back to the car, and sat immersed in the chalk pit with Stig and his house with the jam-jar windows and his love of jelly-babies. I read the bit where the bullies come to get Barney and he runs to the chalk pit, and you sit and eagerly wait for Stig to come and trounce them all soundly. Isn't that what we all want really? Don't we all want to beat the fucking bullies? To take them and hurt them back, to shove it right down their fucking throats? To make THEM cry out in pain; to see the fear in their eyes; to feel the sweet, desperately intense satisfaction that would come from finally being able to stand up and knock the fuck out of them; to watch them be cut open to bleed and hurt and be TOLD. That would be right.

Eventually, it was time to drive back to the pub in order to meet Chloe. I gently placed the story in the glove box and set off. I got there just before eight and took a seat in the lounge (there was no way I was going to sit in the bar; that shit would be asking for trouble) waiting patiently. At about ten past eight, she walked in, still in her uniform. I was very pleased to see her.

She saw me pretty much straightaway and came over, taking the seat opposite me across the table. I asked if she wanted a drink, but she shook her head, not looking at me. I waited for her to speak, wondering what to say. I remember looking at her dark hair and thinking how nice it was. Nobody spoke for AGES.

Eventually she looked up and said:

"I owe you an explanation. And a big apology." I waited for her to continue, and she looked back at the table when she spoke next. "Not even my MUM knows about this, Nigel. I've never really had to tell anyone yet. I thought I'd tell people eventually, but it's only a recent thing, and ...well, I'm just saying that this is very, very private stuff, ok?" I didn't actually know what she was talking about, but I thought she'd get round to it.

Stupid bastard. I'm a stupid fucking bastard.

She started playing with her beer mat, and staring at the table top as if she was trying to work out what kind of wood it was made of.

"The other night ...well, I don't know ...I just wasn't SURE, because I'd made my mind up before, but for some reason ...I really liked you. And I had to know." She trailed off for a long time. I was going to say something, but then she spoke again. "And that made me think, you know, obviously, because until then I'd been sure. I'd made my mind up. I mean I was with Sandra and everything, but if I was still wondering about you ...but I just asked you to come out with me. I mean I wanted you to, and I shouldn't have. It wasn't fair to you, and it certainly wasn't to her, and it was stupid anyway, but it was so fucking selfish Nigel. It was utterly selfish and shitty and an awful way to treat BOTH of you." Now she looked up. "I'm sorry. I'm just really sorry. I just don't want you to hate me." She wasn't crying, but her eyes were teary. After another prolonged silence, I assumed I was supposed to say something.

All I could think to say was:

"What for?"

Looking back, I must have looked like an absolute arsehole. I was being honest, that was all. I really didn't know what for. And didn't know how much worse things would get before the end of the night. Fuck FUCKFUCKFUCK

Right, back.

I took a break from writing. Had to. Anyway.

She looked at me for a good minute with those wide blue eyes. Blue eyes and dark hair. Then those eyes narrowed for a second like she was working something out. She eventually spoke - after a deep breath - very slowly, as if realizing just how much of a fucking stupid bastard I am:

"Nigel ...you do know ...you HAVE ...realised ...that I'm gay, haven't you?"

Once again, my stomach did that turn, but much worse than before, and my skin - and I will never forget this - seemed to go cold all over. Chloe was a gay, and it made perfect, perfect sense.

It was blindingly, stupidly obvious.

The girl in the pub, what she was saying afterwards, Chloe's reaction, what she'd just fucking said to me: obvious.

Why hadn't I seen it? Why hadn't I noticed? The way she said it, YOU DO REALISE, meant that she couldn't believe I didn't know. She'd assumed I'd already got it because it was THAT obvious. How often does this happen? What else do I miss? Why the fuck does everybody else get it and not me? What the fuck is wrong with me?

I wasn't going to tell her no, obviously. I swallowed back the sick feeling and said:

"Of course." Then she just looked confused. Eventually she wiped at her eyes and said:

"Well ...I'm just sorry. I'm really sorry. Not for being, you know, but because I had to ...to fucking USE you to find out for certain, and I can't ever change that. I just ...really hope, we can, you know... be friends. I hate to say something so cheesy, and I know I don't deserve it, but it's true." The coldness sank into my gut, like a block of lead, but I just repeated myself:

"Of course," I said, with a funny little tight smile on my lips. I could feel it. A smile of her own flickered across her lips, but was then replaced with a look of concern, like she'd noticed something.

"Are you sure?" she asked cautiously.

"Of course." I said it again. It was like it was all I could say, but for some reason it didn't matter because my thoughts were set on the weight in my stomach. There was a very, very long pause, and the palpitations began to start again as the silence began to take on that suffocating air that I had experienced before. After an eternity, she said:

"Well ...would you like a drink then?"

I heard myself respond with:

"No, thanks ...I have to get back."

"Nigel- "

"Would you like a lift?" I felt strangely, as if I were running on autopilot, that these responses were automatic so I could cut her off.

160

Her mouth worked slightly as if she were going over something in her mind, trying it out on her lips to see how it felt ...but I don't think she decided to say whatever that sentence was.

"Yes ...yes, all right. But listen..."

"Come on then," I said, rising, that funny smile still plastered to my face, and I don't know why that was the case because I didn't feel like smiling at all. Nevertheless, I was heading for the door and my legs felt funny, but then I was out of the pub and walking towards the car park, with Chloe beside or maybe it was just behind me, I can't remember, and that's when we saw the two lads on the other side of the street beating up another lad. It was dark now. The sun had been beginning to drop even when I entered the pub. Even so, the change seemed somehow unusual.

It felt like everything was happening at once and it was confusing me, but I knew I had to do something to help. That much came through, I remember that.

But the funny thing was that I couldn't.

There was no rush like the last two times - none of the wild desperate rush, nothing at all, only a horrible quickening of the pulse and another twist in my gut as my testicles tightened. I could actually feel it. I'd stopped walking, and I'd realised that Chloe was standing next to me as well.

I needed my costume. I needed my stuff, but I didn't have it and there was a presumably innocent fella getting the beating of his life by two TWATS and I couldn't move. I heard Chloe saying something like let's do something come on come on, and inside I was like what the hell is she on about, what's she going to do and the guy on the other side of the street was shouting like they were killing him, really horrible pleading noises, pained, defeated, crying sounds as they landed each kick.

Then I heard her say something like they're killing him and then Chloe was crossing the road at a half-run, shouting at them.

One looked up at her; the other still kicking. Both were wearing expensive looking tracksuits. She was shouting at him, and he was suddenly right in her face, shouting at her to fuck off, fuck off, and I was still on the other side of the road, unable to move, like all thought had detached, and I couldn't string things together, only the instinct to flee. But she was there, a girl, Chloe, with a guy in her face and the other guy starting to pay attention, and now I was drifting over there too, getting closer, but still with every cell in my body desperately wanting to be away. If only I'd had the FUCKING SPRAY, but suddenly the second fella had seen me and he had run over and pushed me shouting yeah, yeah, come on then ya twat, what's your fucking problem, seeming to make as much noise as he possibly could, and I was just sweating and panicking and sweating, shaking my head and making little noises. What the fuck were those little noises? I don't know where they were coming from and then his other mate ran over. and I was suddenly looking the other way and blinking back whiteness as I realised the incredible pain in my jaw and lips and mouth and nose that I had just been punched really hard in the face, and I swung wildly and I got one of them and must have got him good because my hand really hurt, and I felt something give under my fist and the shouting stopped and his head snapped backwards with a little spray of blood. I shut him UP with a great lucky punch so there is THAT. I know I did THAT, but then the other guy must have joined in because I then felt another blow in my gut, and I felt my head smash into the ground and then I was lying in the road as I heard shouting and there was kicking me in the sides, and I was lying in a ball on the ground, but this time it was really HURTING when it became two sets of kicks in my sides as the other one got himself together and came back, and I could hear Chloe screaming, but I was just cowering and hiding - and then they'd gone because a car was coming down the road where we were, beeping its horn for them to get out of the way, and then some guy was asking if I was OK, what happened, but I was still balled up and saying yeah I'm fine, I'm fine, but feeling wet stuff on my face, and I realised it was coming from my nose. They'd broken my nose.

I can't remember exactly what else I said to the car driver, but somehow I was on my feet and walking to my car. Chloe was walking just behind me, and kept saying 'Nigel', sort of shouting it but not too stern, like she wanted to talk to me but also almost like she was scared to get my full attention, but I just wanted to get in the car and go. I sat in the car, shut the door, and waited for her to get in. Eventually she got in beside me. I could feel her looking at me.

"Nigel, please, please, you have - ". But I just cut her off by saying:

"No." I started the car and drove off, wiping my still streaming nose with the back of my hand, wiping off other wet stuff that made me realise I had been crying.

We drove along and the silence was very oppressive, but this time there were no palpitations at all. I really didn't care. She kept staring at me. After a while she said:

"Nigel, please, are you OK?" Her voice sounded a little funny, and maybe she had been crying a bit herself. I nodded, and then it struck me, struck me hard as I realised I was ashamed. I can admit it, fuck it, I was ashamed. She had seen me stand there and do nothing, didn't really DO ANYTHING TO FUCKING HELP HER when some thug was in her face, I'd stood there and done nothing. She was concerned for me, but I knew she looked at me with contempt.

FUCKkhgdkahsfasfkhjafkhjsafkjhafhkfakhlfklhfdhklfdkhj

I just felt it, and as I realised this I felt her contempt grow. I felt it fully, felt just how much she was really looking down at me.

"Nigel," she said for the millionth time and I just said:

"Forget it," and that was it until I dropped her off. She got out of the car and walked to her front door without a word. I drove off.

How is this? I talk of saving people, doing the right thing, of focus and effort and motivation and becoming more than human, and I shit it. Not only do I shit it, but I cry out for them while they laugh and scowl and take pleasure in my pain and fear. We all want to ram it down the bullies' throats, yes, but doing it... doing it, well, that's another fucking thing entirely. Can you? Can you fulfill your imagination or are you just all talk? I CAN'T be all talk. I've done it, I've done it, so why not tonight? I didn't have the costume, didn't have anything, but that seems like such a thin excuse, a shit excuse. But surely it's a good one? A GREAT one? A superhero without his kit? How can he work? Surely it's common sense. It's not my fault Chloe ran over there. Stupid. She should have stayed with me doing the sensible thing. It was sensible. I was being sensible, but I got into a situation that wasn't my fault for being there and it wasn't my fault I took a beating,

Not my fault.

Forty-Second Entry: Thursday September 3rd 1998 3:23 AM

Can't sleep. My nose is pretty much definitely broken. It took ages for the bleeding to stop, and I can see the swelling in the mirror. The thugs have changed my face, affected my body against my will, messed me up. I hope it goes down.

I found myself reading Stig Of The Dump all the way through. What a wonderful book. What a wonderful, innocent time. What a fucking loss.

Tonight is a whirl. Chloe's a lesbian and I've taken a beating. Me, The Night Man. Everybody has secrets, it seems, even the quiet guy on the street corner I'll bet. I'm not going to work tomorrow. I have to sort my face out and I cannot see Chloe. I'm not going to, couldn't do it.

I keep thinking about my father, which is weird as I have spent a lot of my life generally trying not to think about him. For the most part, the memories I do have are very good ones, although I often find nostalgia to be an untrustworthy ally. Up until the age of about ten, I remember him being around almost constantly, working as an accountant from home. He only ever wore glasses in the office, as I recall. That always struck me as funny. I don't know why, but I'd walk in and see him in his glasses and just stand there giggling, and then he'd see me and smile and put his fingers behind his ears, making the glasses jiggle up and down, and that would put me in hysterics. When did everybody become a threat? What the fuck happened to everybody?

He always thought of great games, my Dad. Mum would always be going, 'Michael, be careful with them,' from her armchair – this was in the days when she had a personality - if the games were ever a little rough, or if me and David were helpless with laughter in the middle of a session of 'Upside Down', our heads about to burst both from the blood pressure and the giggles that racked our entire bodies, but Dad was ALWAYS careful. Whenever Mum warned him, she was smiling when she said it. She hasn't smiled like that for quite some time, to be honest. I've seen her do it towards David recently, perhaps, when he emerges from his bedroom with something he's made.

One day stands out in particular, though. Of course it does. Everything changed after that. I certainly did.

David and I were watching Sesame Street on TV – although of course back then David couldn't even speak - off school for the summer holidays, and Mum was on the phone to a friend or something. Suddenly the door flew open and Dad came bursting in. He instantly leaned over and pressed the hook on the phone down. Mum opened her mouth to let fly with an enraged barrage of protest, but Dad just said:

"Don't."

It was completely understandable that Mum shut up. If you'd have seen my father's wild eyes that afternoon, you wouldn't have said anything either.

"The kitchen," he said, turning to leave, and his eyes fell upon me and David. He suddenly came over and hugged us both, painfully tight, so much so that I was literally fighting for breath. I could feel my father's chest heaving, like he was gasping himself. Then he stood up, turning so we couldn't see his face, and headed into the kitchen.

With our child's instinct for avoiding getting caught in an argument, I stayed out of the kitchen, trying to keep David from picking up that anything was wrong. We could only hear the occasional raised voice, and eventually, the sound of anguished wailing. To this day I don't know whether it was my Mother or my Father crying like that.

Later that day, when we felt it safe to venture out of the living room, Dad was nowhere to be seen. When I eventually came across my mother, she was in the kitchen grilling beef steaks, her hair frazzled as always but red in the eyes, the skin below them looking puffy, her face downcast. I asked her where Dad was.

"Having a lie down upstairs," she said, without looking at me. The atmosphere in the room was cold. I could feel it even at ten years old. The kitchen seemed immaculate, far more tidy than usual. My mother had clearly busied herself that afternoon.

"Is he all right?" I remember asking her, tentatively.

"He's fine, Nigel. I'm busy now, son. Go and play with David."

I realised that to ask further questions was to incite trouble and so I left. I didn't see Dad at all for the rest of the day, but I did hear Mum continually disappearing upstairs to see him. The next day, when I came down at my usual crack-of-dawn-it's-the-summer child's time, I came across my Dad at the kitchen table. This was unusual for two reasons: One, he was never up before me ("When I work for anyone other than myself, I'll get up before 9:30. Not before"), and two, when he DID get up, and whenever he worked in the office, he always wore a shirt and tie and was shaven ('If I don't take care of myself and keep things in order, how am I supposed to do the same with anyone's accounts?').

He was always the epitome of personal hygiene and pride, satisfied with knowing that he looked smart, like a professional. Not today.

He was sat there, in his red dressing gown, a lukewarm, skinning-over cup of tea on the table next to him. He had clearly been there for some time. His hair was all over the place, his stubble sat on chin like a cancer telling me there was something worryingly wrong. His bare feet were splayed out in front of him, and he sat with the remote in his hand flicking through all the channels on the kitchen TV. I stood watching him for some time, a horrible creeping feeling in my belly. My father shouldn't look like this. Whipped and broken. It was horrible.

Eventually, he came across a news program on one channel and stopped his flicking. He sat attentively, listening to the headlines. Apparently there was nothing there he was interested in, as once they had all been read he carried on flicking, round and round the four channels.

"Dad?" I asked after a while. He didn't even turn round.

He stayed whipped for weeks. We hardly ever saw him for the first week after that day, as he didn't even go to his office. He would appear intermittently, his ever thickening stubble making me want to cry, to tell him to makes things normal again, but I couldn't. For some reason, I was scared of him looking like that. This current and complete contrast to the smart, organised man that was my dad made him like some sort of wild animal; an unpredictable powder keg that might go off if I stepped too close. Maybe if I had, things could have been different.

I don't like to think about that too much. I have made myself stop thinking about that many times over the years. I often believe that regret, true regret, is the one thing that can truly destroy a person. When you can't stop it, and it constantly crests on the beach of your soul like a tide, that beach erodes like so much salt. I put a lot of effort into not thinking about my father. I still had the blackouts, and I wonder if they maybe came BECAUSE I'd been trying so hard. The counseling certainly never did a thing. Waste of fucking time.

One day, during that first week, I heard a noise coming from the living room; a pained, terrible sound. Curious, yet not wanting to see, I crept up to the doorway, fearful that it might actually be my father. Of course, it was.

Peeking through the crack in the quarter-open door, I saw my father sitting in the middle of the living room floor, the day's newspaper in pieces around him, as if it had been flung and then burst open all over the room. He was crouched down, doubled over, and rocking gently. One sheet of the paper was clutched tightly in his hand, screwed up, and all the while he was making that awful, terrible, pathetic noise.

After the second week, we saw him a little more, but I don't believe he actually saw us; not me and David anyway. He moved around the house like a zombie, shuffling about in his dressing gown and slippers. It was during that week that I found the newspaper article.

I had come across my father's dressing gown lying on the landing, as he, perhaps for the first time during those two weeks was having a bath. The bathroom was silent from outside, not even the movement of water as he shifted in the bath. He must have been lying completely still. I picked it up, perhaps to be helpful, I don't know, when I felt a little round, fairly compact object in his pocket. I reached in and took it out. I was curious and who wouldn't be?

It was a balled up sheet of newspaper. I assume it was the same one he was holding the day I found him on the living room floor, but who knows? Either way, I disappeared into my bedroom and opened it.

LITTLE HARRY'S BODY FOUND the headline read. I remember a horrible, horrible, horrible feeling of cold settle into my shoulders. I was only ten, yet I felt a terrible sensation that something was ending, then and there, and I was filled with dread.

It has been confirmed the body of nine-year-old Harry Geraghton was discovered in a ditch on Cowley Lane during the early hours of Tuesday morning, writes William Rees. A rambler's dog had uncovered Harry in a ditch where he had been covered with six inches of shrubbery and leaves. It appears that he had not been sexually molested in any way, as had initially been feared. Early assessment of his injuries suggest that Harry had in fact been the victim of a hit-and-run accident, and that the driver had buried the body not far from the scene of the supposed collision. It had been thought that Harry had been on his way to play with friends, and family members have said he was more than used to traversing the country lanes near his home on his bicycle. Investigators are trying to piece together a new sequence of Harry's movements before his death, as it appears initial tracking was 'inaccurate,' meaning searches have focused more keenly on other areas until now.

"This was a cowardly act of the highest order," said Chief Inspector Reddy of South Derbyshire District Police. "Whoever has done this - not only to drive away but also to put Harry's family through this week of false hope that their son may be alive - is inhuman. If you know anything about this incident, please come forward so that the Geraghton family can at least have some justice in their time of unimaginable pain." Local farmer Richard Jones said:

And that's it. That's all I can remember. I read that over and over for years, until I buried my dad in my head. But all of that, I can guarantee you, is absolutely word perfect.

At the time, all I felt was that cold feeling and so I decided to deal with it. That was the best way. To reach an understanding that made sense.

The reason that dad was so upset by this story was that he had neglected his children, his wife and his job recently. That was all and that was just fine. That was just fine, everything was fine, Dad would soon be all right, and everything was fine. Everything.

Then I began to feel a bit strange. I went into my room and woke up some time later on the floor. That would then happen regularly over the years, but I got used to it. Things became tougher at school because of it, but I dealt with it.

Another two weeks later, my father left. I didn't see it, but I came down to breakfast, and saw my mother at the kitchen table, pale as a winter sky. She was holding a note in her hand, eyes red, and a look of grim resolve on her face. She had expected this, and to be honest – FUCK it, why not say it - I now believe that she knew the man my father was had died the day that he ran over and buried the body of Harry Geraghton. She was sitting there in HER dressing gown, perhaps now the standard sign of grief in the Carmelite household, staring out of the window with her mouth set in a firm, thin-lipped way. She looked at me, and beckoned me over weakly. I went.

"Your father's gone, Nigel. He's gone away. He's done a bad thing and he's gone away." She paused for a long time after this, and I could hear her composing herself before she then pulled her head back so she could see me.

I started crying, and she did as well, and we sat like that in the kitchen for some time. That was before she went away. Not physically at least, but you know. She came back – she could look after us – but you know. She should have come all the way back. We were kids. She wasn't there. She would smile sometimes and make conversation, but it was hollow. She pretended to be normal. It took me a while to realise, but I figured out that she'd been pretending for years. I got over it.

I don't know where David thinks Dad went. I think he assumes Dad died. He was too young to remember him at the time. I wouldn't be surprised if it was true. I never read the note, I never dared ask, but from my Mother's acceptance of the truth, I wouldn't be surprised if it was suicide. I sometimes wonder if it was, but there is never any worry in that somehow.

You see, though my Father had been a good man, a man I admired - in some way, I still do even now – he made a choice. He chose to run. He chose to conceal a nine-year-old child's body in a ditch as opposed to atoning for his crime. He chose to be un-righteous.

I can't understand this.

How can a good man do this? How can a brave man choose the coward's way out? At what point, despite our very essences, despite our most strongly held beliefs, do we think 'hang on,' and the urge for self-preservation overrides our civilised mind? Yes, we've all heard the stories of bravery in the face of adversity, but every time it's just, 'Well, I don't know what happened, I was just pulling them out of the burning building.' These must be just lucky sods whose subconscious reaction was for some genetically gifted reason, to everybody else's. Why the hell should it be this way? Why the hell did I want to run and leave Chloe to the wolves? Why the fuck couldn't I be the burning building guy?

I can tell myself and tell myself I didn't have my Night Man kit or whatever and all of that shit, but the fact remains that Chloe went over there and I didn't. I stood there and bottled out. What kind of hero am I? What kind of bum? If I don't have the Night Man, if I can't even do this, what the fuck else have I got? What the fuck have I got?

Forty-Third Entry: Thursday September 3rd 1998 5:64 AM

Bullshit. Bullshit. I'll tell you exactly what it was. Common sense. That guy was probably taking a kicking because he was probably a hoodlum just like them. He probably deserved it. I saw this and didn't bother, but Chloe was just too stupid not to see it. I didn't dive in because I didn't want to be injured trying to save ONE hoodlum, and therefore be too injured to go out as The Night Man and save MANY actually innocent people. My father panicked and ran, but I made a rational, correct choice. I didn't like it, but I weighed up the choices. THAT'S what happened. None of that shit earlier. I need to get some sleep now because The Night Man is riding again TONIGHT! Fuck waiting for Saturday. He will be righteous and full of justice and pain to any motherfucker that dares to break the law and terrorise the innocents. Everybody has secrets, but MY secret is a good one. I am a superhero. I am a superhero.

Forty-Forth Entry: Friday, September 4th 1998 12:45 AM

I've been and done it. The Night Man hit the streets again tonight. I'll get straight on with it. My nose is swollen to hell, but no one has noticed. I didn't expect them to. I hid it from Mum and stayed out of David's way.

I was in town from 9:00 PM onwards this time and had only to ride around for a mere hour and a half - out of costume - before I saw some trouble.

As it was still early, I decided that it would be a good idea to patrol some of the residential areas of the town centre, the rather scummy neighbourhoods. No doubt all the fights and violence would be happening in non-residential town later, and while I would be there to clean up, I thought that my time before that would be better spent by going and looking for some burglaries etc., something I had previously not looked into.

Eventually, after riding up and down identical-looking terraced streets and finding these places to be more or less deserted, something happened. I was now beginning to almost reach the edge of the residential area - riding along a back road that would take me into the town centre proper - when I saw a car parked on its own by the side of the road.

This would have been completely unremarkable if not for the figure dressed in scruffy blue jeans and a basketball vest crouching by the door.

Once again, I thanked the heavens that I'd chosen the silent-running Go-Ped.

He wasn't a particularly big fellow. He was quite weaselly-looking in fact. Probably trying to prove himself to the rest of his cronies. Pitiful.

Of course, he was on the side of the car that was furthest away from the road. He must have assumed that this was a good place to attempt this sort of thing, as it was a reasonably quiet street, and not many cars came through on a regular basis.

He couldn't have been that good a thief as he hadn't seen me, so obviously he didn't pay much attention to his surroundings. By the time I had turned around, driven quickly to the closed auto repair shop just a few metres away, squeezed into the gap between the wall of the garage and the shop next door, put on my Night Man kit and arsenal and Pedded back ...he was still there. As I drew closer, I could see he was fiddling with the car door. To be fair, I could see why he thought he was safe. No one would ever come walking along here at this time of night, and if any cars were coming, he'd hear them a mile away. He could simply stand up and start walking nonchalantly or something.

But he hadn't reckoned on The Night Man coming along.

However, when I was getting very close, and just about to jump off the Go-Ped and use the element of surprise, he must have finally heard its very faint whirr. He suddenly spun around with a look of surprise on his face. I saw his fuzzy hair – just like my mother's - bounce on his forehead as he turned. Fortunately, by the time he'd stood up, I was already close enough to spray him and did so. My Man Marker aim had yet to fail me, as I got him square in the face. I wonder what his name was.

Although it had the usual instantaneous reaction as with the other criminals so far, he actually tried to get away, tried to run, now that he knew I was actually attacking him as opposed to just seeing him. The natural cowardly criminal instinct. He knew I had the spray, and he didn't want to get any more of it. He ran, shouting, wiping with his hands and gasping blindly. Looking back, I admire his persistence.

However, he was a crook, a man who was going to take whoever's car that was and steal it, take the thing they'd worked for and probably just rape it around the estates for a bit, not caring if he hit or killed anyone before setting it on fire in a field somewhere just to watch it burn. The rage welled up and as I rode up behind him and struck him across the back of the neck – I hadn't even stepped off the NightCycle yet, I was just so focused for once - and he stumbled and fell.

I was surprised at how easily I brought myself to hit him. It was almost as if I didn't have to think about it at all, as the anger I was feeling surpassed conscious thought and I could simply club away at will. This wasn't like in the Revill Arms car park at all. I decided that this was a good thing. I stopped the Go- Ped and got off.

Once again though, he showed surprising determination as he blindly got up off the ground and tried to continue running, but I was already there. I surprised myself by catching him perfectly across the face as he was rising, and his head snapped backwards beautifully. An arc of crimson fluid jetted slightly upwards as he fell backward. Although I knew that this was particularly good going, and the efficiency with which I was working here was pleasing me greatly, I felt that something was ...different. The nervous rush that usually accompanied my outings was gone, seemingly replaced with a rather clinical anger that was so white-hot I actually felt calm. It was most unusual, but I found myself bringing the nightstick down across his upturned face, and felt a sharp pain in my own mouth as I realised that I had brought my teeth together on my tongue. I winced at the pain, but I still hit him again and again and again - first on his face, then working my way up and down his body, a grim satisfaction welling up with every stroke. Even when my arm became sore, my shoulder aching, it was like a pump working up and down. An almost desperate sensation began to well up in my neck of all places. He eventually stopped struggling, unconscious, but still breathing.

Then the most curious thing happened. Suddenly I was looking at his bleeding face, and the coldness that I had been powered by abruptly left. My legs began to buckle slightly, and I had to sit down in a rush, my heart pounding. But the satisfied feeling, the sated feeling, remained at the back of my mind in some strange comforting way. That's the best way I can describe those moments, to be honest.

I did wonder whether or not I should call the police, tell then where to pick up the perp and that The Night Man was responsible, but I decided against it. I wanted him to wake up and tell his punk friends about the guy that had stopped him. Maybe they might even know the guys from the kebab shop. This was good, and the satisfied feeling grew. After a bit, even the shaking in my legs stopped as well, and I was able to mount the NightCycle once more and return to where I had left my rucksack. For some reason, I decided to return home. I felt I was done for the night.

I feel strange tonight. I feel like I have achieved something, proved a point, and yet I do not feel as comfortable as I have recently. I don't feel as ...assured. That's the word. Perhaps I shouldn't have gone home as early as I did. Perhaps I should have patrolled a while longer, and that would have made me feel better, more complete. But either way, the fact remains that at the time I really felt like I should go home. The evening was still a success, however - a crime aborted and another seed sown, so if you ask me, everything is all right.

Didn't see Chloe at all today. This makes me feel relieved. Perhaps I am more prejudiced than I previously realised. We are who we are.

Forty-Fifth Entry: Friday September 4th 1998 7:11PM

I have been tired all day. This, combined with the muscular pain, is making me think I should just go straight to bed in order to catch up with the sleep lost on these night missions. Or perhaps I should stop working Saturdays and use the weekend daytimes for recuperation. That is perhaps the best idea. I can afford it. I don't spend much, superhero kit aside.

My nose, though broken, does not look so bad now that the swelling has gone down a little. If you looked closely, and if you knew its appearance well before, you would tell by the slight ridge that has formed in the middle, but it has been easy to avoid Mum and David so far.

About ten minutes ago - whilst preparing my Night Man bag for this evening's assault on the criminal underworld of Derby City Centre - David came in, and I was forced to rapidly stuff the bag under the bedclothes. He knew he had caught me once again, but this time he looked scared. He hadn't meant to.

The frightened look on his face brought a wave of saddened compassion for my little brother washing over me, and I smiled broadly to show I had no aggression towards him. If he was prepared not to pursue the issue, I was prepared not to be angry with him. I could tell that he'd learned not to push his luck, and regrettable as the incident had been, I think you'll agree it had to happen. Boundaries have to be reinforced.

He understood the smile and smiled back.

"Mum says dinner's ready," he said, but I noticed his gaze flit to the bedclothes momentarily. He DID want to know what was under there. I let it go because he'd done the same.

"Cheers Davey," I responded, "What we having?"

"White fish!" he said, genuinely disgusted. White fish was the once-every-month-or-so torture that the Carmelite household underwent. A seemingly endless slab of plain cod, in reality perhaps only about five inches by five inches, but one that somehow managed to take about three hours to eat, covered in a stomach-churningly repulsive creamy cheese sauce. It was, quite simply, the worst meal in existence, and both myself and David dreaded its arrival. I pulled an exaggerated grimace and David nodded sagely. This was no laughing matter. This really was going to be a torturous meal. I knew David understood. It's moments like this that make brothers, brothers.

"Is ...your nose all right?" he asked, squinting at it.

"Yeah," I said quickly, "fell over today and banged it! Everyone laughed! We all laughed." He blinked and half-smiled, and I needed to move things on quickly so I added: "Man, white fish. Why do you think she keeps giving it to us?" His face changed, and I knew the emotive subject matter had done its work, nose forgotten.

"Ugh, God knows," he said, using one of Mum's favourite sayings. "Healthy healthy healthy or some rubbish." He turned glumly and walked out of the room, like a condemned man going to meet his death, rather than a five-inch-square block of cod in cheese sauce.

This did highlight a problem. I need to find a very, very good hiding place for my equipment. David has smelled blood in the water, an all-too curious shark, and soon it will get the better of him. I'm going to cut a hole in the floor boards at the bottom of my walk-in cupboard (it used to be my parents room before we had the big switch-around) when Mum takes David to swimming tomorrow. He'll never find it, especially when I put the boards back on top.

But tonight, I'm resting. Fuck it. I need it.

Forty-Sixth Entry: Saturday September 5th 11:12 PM (Important date in The Night Man Saga)

A most eventful and interesting evening tonight. I didn't even go out as The Night Man either. I will explain.

Coming back from the gym (pain almost like an old friend now ...hard to remember days that weren't filled with it constantly), I was even more tired than usual, having spent the morning before my gym trip prepping my 'hidden panel' in the floor. I won't bore you with the DIY details, but it had been quite easy. It didn't have to be too big as David already knew about the Go-Ped and only needed to hide the rucksack. On arrival home, I quickly grabbed a drink of orange juice in the kitchen and bounded up the stairs, keen to get my stuff to proceed with the evening's mission. As I mounted the landing however, I was surprised to notice my bedroom door hanging open. This should not have been so, as I always shut my bedroom door fully. Always. Especially these days.

I continued on up the stairs, deliberately slow, in order to be as quiet as possible. Whoever had opened my bedroom door might still be inside, and if they were, I wanted to catch them in whatever act they were committing. As I got closer, listening carefully, I could hear only very faint sounds, meaning that whoever was in there was trying to be quiet. It had to be David.

I burst in through the doorway, and saw him kneeling by the open cupboard. Lying on the floor next to him was the Go-Ped. His head whipped around and I saw his terrified, ashen face. He was busted and knew he was deep trouble.

I grabbed him and pulled him to his feet. I was absolutely furious, and yet I couldn't scream as to do so would be to bring Mum running and make the situation far worse. Somehow I managed to keep my voice to a fierce hiss as I pulled his face close and said:

"What the hell do you think you're doing, you nosy bastard??" He was speechless, although I don't think this was due to fear alone. He had clearly thought that he would be able to hear anybody coming, and my sudden appearance in the room had shocked him nearly out of his skin. "This is MY room David. What the fuck are you doing nosing around in here??" I knew any minute now I would begin to slap him again, like before, and that I would start very soon and it would be bad. I forced myself to drop him.

Falling back onto his bottom, hard, he looked up at me with tearful eyes. He was stammering slightly, trying to speak.

"What? What?" I said, standing over him, a little frightened of my own fury and yet unable to walk away from him.

"I just ..." he managed.

"WHAT?" I yelled, shouting for the first time, but there was no sound of the living room door opening below.

"The scooter thing," he said, almost crying now, "I just wanted a go on the scooter thing." My anger started to fade as rapidly as it had arrived. He hadn't found the costume rucksack. He'd only wanted a go on the Go-Ped, and I had promised him one after all. I simply hadn't been here to ask, and he wasn't trying to discover anything else. But he HAD been snooping in my room ...my rage was reducing fast, no matter what I thought. I put out my hand to help him stand up, and he looked at me strangely, not sure or not believing he had been forgiven so quickly.

If he had looked inside the Night Man bag, he wouldn't have been.

He took my hand, and I pulled him up.

"I'm sorry," he said sheepishly, looking up at me. I frowned at him. I didn't really know why I was letting him off. He WAS sorry though, I could tell. He's a good lad, still somehow good when everyone in his generation is beginning the inevitable slide into bad, and he had just let his curiosity get the better of him. I found myself feeling that sad feeling again, regret and pity for my brother's future and was going to actually hug him and tell him it was okay, that I didn't mind and he was my brother, when something struck me hard.

It was so OBVIOUS! It's such a simple and clear path that, as I sit here and write, I'm laughing at the fact that I never thought of it before. Not only would it solve all of David's problems for the future - solve the terrible problem of his inevitable slide into young thuggery – and not only would it be of USE to me but it was the way things should have ALWAYS been. Really, my friends, you have probably all thought about this already and are chuckling as well that I didn't spot it before.

I eventually realised that I had been standing in front of David in silence for some time, almost as if I had one of my Moments. As I slowly snapped out of it, I felt as if I were coming up for air, like I was coming into myself from elsewhere. Perhaps that's a little dramatic, but that's the best way to describe it.

David hadn't moved either while I had been 'away', and he was still watching me cautiously with a sheepish expression.

I looked him in the eyes, and after a moment of brief inner confirmation, I said:

"David, I'm not going to hurt you. I'm going to let you in on a secret." His eyebrows furrowed, uncomprehending, but I moved past him into my closet and crouched by the trapdoor. I looked at him over my shoulder. "It's a big secret. Bigger than the scooter thing. Far bigger. But I'm going to tell you all about this one, as I've decided I want you to know." His eyes were wider than perhaps he meant them to be. "BUT ...if you suspect for one second that you can't keep a big secret, if there's any doubt in your mind that you might let it slip, then I want you to tell me now." He shook his head hurriedly. "Seriously David. I mean it. If you tell anyone, we aren't brothers anymore. Never again. Do you understand how important this is?" He swallowed a little, but then said, quietly:

"I can keep it a secret Nigel." I stared at him a moment, then nodded and turned back to the trapdoor, pulling it open.

"Then I want to show you this," I said, and pulled out The Night Man bag.

He was actually a little pale in the face with curiosity and anticipation, and for a moment I really envied his situation; a child's capacity for wonder and magic. I realised that in his eyes this bag could contain ANYTHING, for his mind is free of cynicism and doubt and the negative thoughts that poison everyone once innocence is gone. He was finding out my secret.

Everybody has one. I was choosing to share mine, to reveal my own secret to another human being. This was always going to be a moment to savour. I wished to God I could have been in his shoes to experience this.

I began to undo the straps on the bag as slowly and dramatically as possible.

"You like Batman, don't you, David?" Nod. "How about Robin? What do you think about Robin, David?"

"Uh ... well ...he's okay."

"Just okay?"

"...good, I suppose. Yeah." His lips squeezed together, as he moistened them. I lowered my gaze back to the rucksack as I opened the flap.

"How cool do you think it would be to actually BE Robin, David?" Looking back up, I could see that he really didn't have a clue as to where I was going, but was still hanging on my every word. I imagine he must have been thinking I was making small talk while I was opening the bag up, but he would soon understand. I fixed my eyes on his. "What would you say, then ..." I said, pausing for a moment to let the anticipation hang in the air, "...if I said I could fix it for you to be like Robin?" His eyes instantly narrowed, and a small smile spread across his lips. He thought I was winding him up. I stopped this straightaway by fixing him with a gaze that let him know instantly that I wasn't bullshitting. I let him know how deadly serious I was about being The Night Man. He looked scared. Good, I thought.

"I'm absolutely serious. I swear to you here and now. I've never been more serious about anything in my life. Do you believe me David?" He nodded very slowly, finally realising that this little discussion could be a lot bigger than he had previously guessed. I could almost hear his thoughts: was it really possible that his big brother was offering him the chance to be like Robin? REALLY? I reached into the bag and pulled out the top and bottom halves of the mask. I held them up for him to see.

"This is my mask David. This is what I wear when I go out at night. This is what the scooter is for. This is what the rest of the equipment in this bag is for. At night - for some time now - I have been going out like Batman and stopping criminals. I call myself The Night Man. And I'm offering you the chance to come and help me. To be Robin to my Batman. What do you say?"

It was meant to be an impressive speech, and I think it WAS particularly impressive given that it was off-the-cuff. It had obviously done the job, because my young brother - my kid brother - was speechless, staring at the mask. It was a real moment, a turning point, an epiphany, me holding the mask up to him and offering the kind of adventure that all kids dream about. I know I always did.

"You ...go out like Batman?" he asked, finally taking his eyes off the mask and looking at me. I nodded, sagely. "How?' he asked, his face screwing up a little. Part of me felt a tad offended by this, but I knew it was not the time to be descending to such levels of pettiness.

"I've been training, David, training hard and well for far longer than you'd know. I was training and training until I was good enough to go. I've kept it a secret for a very long time, Davey. I've been planning this for years." This was all true. "I have weapons as well. I have a utility belt of tools that I use to help me." His eyes widened to the size of dinner plates as this revelation set in, and I felt pleased that he was taking this so well. I was proud of my brother's faith in me and of his belief in the fantastic. Even so, if I had told him all this without the cold, hard evidence of the costume, the purchase of the NightCycle, the very fact that I had gone to the trouble of constructing a fucking trapdoor in the floor, then I doubt that things would have flowed together quite so nicely. But here we were, surrounded by the truth, and Davey could not ignore that.

"How long have you been ...out at night?" he asked, looking at me with undisguised awe.

"Not long. A few weeks. But this is just the beginning."

"Every night?"

"Not every night Davey. I wish I could, but there are physical limitations to be taken into account here. I still have to train. I have to rest." This was all so cool sounding that I was getting excited myself.

"And you want me to help?" A smile flickered around the edge of his lips, and I could tell the shock was passing and the buzz was beginning, as I had suspected it would.

"That's right. You want to help me David?"

"Yeah," he answered quickly, with that little dip-and-back-up-again tone that only kids can manage when they are at their most emphatic about something. "What ...do you want me to ...do?"

This stopped me a little - which was annoying as it broke the moment for me slightly - because this was something that I hadn't thought about. I knew there would be SOMETHING he could do, as he was capable and bright, and that there SHOULD be something to do, as he needed this. I decided, therefore, it would not be best to set anything in stone right now.

"Don't worry about that yet Davey," I said, putting the mask back in the bag. His eyes watched it disappear. "You'll be starting small to begin with. You aren't trained like I am." David nodded sagely in agreement, and I was proud again. Most kids would probably whine about this, wanting instant beginnings or results and foolishly wanting to dive in unprepared, but David showed a restraint beyond his years. "But eventually," I continued, "we will be fighting side-by-side. Brothers in arms. Helping people. Fighting crime. Cool, huh?" He smiled then, a wide-eyed smile, but the hugeness of the situation descended again and it faded.

"I can't believe this Nige, I can't believe it. You ...doing this stuff. What ...when you first ...were you scared?" he asked. I nodded again. "Did you get hurt? Did you have to fight anyone? Seriously, you really did this? Really, really honestly? Honestly. I'll never believe anything you say ever again if you're lying." I was strangely calm now, and was simply nodding in a slow, wise fashion. I had to let my brother get it all out of his system, let him accept the idea and his new role. It took him a while. Eventually, I held up my hand to cut him off and he stopped talking.

I then produced my laptop containing this very journal, booted it up, and without telling him what he was about to hear I read to him the story of **The First Sighting**. By the time I reached the end - after a narration set to the sounds of David's heavy breathing, sharp gasps, and the odd excited giggle - he believed me.

We talked into the night then - until Mum called David for bed - him asking me questions about the training, getting me to tell him about other missions, about the weaponry, how I designed the costume. At various points I had to physically grab him and tell him to keep his voice down. This usually seemed to be at points when the conversation drifted towards his costume or a possible name for him. I panicked at one point, when he actually seemed to start gasping for air and I realised he was hyperventilating. This was when he finally got the full perspective of what was going on, which was a shame, as he had handled it all so well up until then. I managed to calm him down with soothing talk and even said that we should stop talking about it, but he became so agitated at the thought of abandoning the issue for the night before his bedtime that I decided to carry on. However, I continued with caution lest he should start gasping again.

I know he won't be sleeping tonight. As for myself, I have to absorb the fact that I have inducted the first recruit into the world of true superheroism. I'm doing it. I'm finally doing it! I'm going to make a DIFFERENCE, and my name will be remembered for years to come. I can't wait to take David out into the heart of the action with me, but of course I must - as even David knows - have restraint. He must be trained, prepared, and tempered. Even so, I can't believe it!

Forty-Seventh Entry: Sunday September 6th 1998 6:53 PM

David is venturing out with me tonight. I've decided that it's best to give him the sights and the taste of being The Night Man's companion, so that he will stay stuck to the task ahead of him when things get tough. As the song goes, "If I hadn't seen such riches, I could live with being poor," and this will go for David. I will show him what it is like - what he will experience - just this once, to make sure he stays hungry throughout the months and years of training that lie ahead.

Now HEAR ME OUT!! Ha ha. OBVIOUSLY, he will not be going into the 'heart of the action', but merely GOING WITH ME whilst I am in CIVILIAN COSTUME. He will see the hunting ground and feel the charged atmosphere of the night. He will merely stay and keep an eye on the bag and its contents should I need to indulge in any action, safely out of harm's way, until I return. I feel this will be an invaluable experience for the forging of David's new soul. When I told him today ...well, let us just say he quite literally had to run to the toilet to stop himself from wetting his pants. He has been buzzing around the house all day, quiet and tense, and keeps whispering to me about what he's going to wear, and how long until we go, and what are we going to tell Mum. I've told him not to worry about those things and that he knows all he needs to know for now. I have tried to get it through his skull that HE won't be getting into any action tonight - that this is merely a taster before we begin his training properly - but he still won't seem to relax.

I have, of course, already planned stage one by now. His costume is not an issue here, because obviously it will be based on mine, and I already know how to get the various pieces of equipment. He will come with me to the next Aikido class to hone his skills. Think about it! He will have years to master the art before he ventures out. I envy him. He will be a formidable ...Night Boy? Night Lad? I will have to ponder this. The gym can come later ...I will wait a while before the Aikido has conditioned his body before he joins me in the gym. His young frame will not be ready for the strains and will not absorb them in the fashion that mine does.

Mum has actually asked me if I have said anything to him to make him act funny, which alarms me somewhat. He will have to learn to suppress his excitement should it continue to arouse suspicion like this. My response to her, of course, was dismissive on this matter.

I can't believe that only yesterday David didn't even know about The Night Man and now he is about to ride out with me. That happy accident yesterday opened my eyes and here we are. This only confirms my suspicions that my mission is fated by some external force. Will, of course, report later.

Forty Eighth Entry: Saturday September 26th 1998 6:22PM

It has been three weeks since my last entry.

Though I have attempted to write several times since then - and failed - I now feel that I can write a descriptive and accurate account of the Sunday night three weeks previous.

This is what occurred.

I remember going into David's room at about 7:30pm. It was just beginning to darken outside. He was standing there, surrounded by thick clothing that he had pulled from his cupboard. He had decided on wearing a black woolly hat, his 'Trek Team 73' jumper, some jeans, and a scarf. He was pulling on his gloves. He turned around and smiled. The look on his face. The admiration and excitement. I will never forget this. It is as clear as a cold blade in my mind. I told him we were leaving and he nodded, without saying a word.

I told my mother that he and I would be going bowling together, and she did her best fake smile in order to seem very pleased about this. I didn't take the Go-Ped with me that night, as I wanted to be able to walk and talk as we patrolled. The plan was - once David was fully trained - to get him his own Go-Ped eventually. We would ride around together.

Excuse me, I have to stop.

Back.

We didn't speak in the car on the way. I was setting myself; David was trying to calm down. He understood the importance of focus. Bright boy.

Back.

Once in town I parked the car in the same car park as before and set off on foot. It was cold and the air was crisp. He had never been in town this late before, apart from when out late-night Christmas shopping with Mum and I. He was wide-eyed with excitement, almost physically vibrating with enthusiasm. Looking back, he was probably also a little scared too, finally being confronted with the realities of The Night Man's environment. I remember asking him if he was okay, and he responded by nodding quickly. He didn't look at me though. We walked on.

He kept asking me questions. We would walk past a row of shops, and he would ask if I had saved anyone there. If we passed a suitable looking hiding place he would ask if I thought I might get changed there. We would pass thuggish-looking people, and he would suggest that we follow them, wanting to help, or to simply see some action. Once, I even agreed that we would follow one such individual, and we did for a good ten minutes, only to discover that he was heading for his car so he could drive out of town. It didn't matter to David, though. To him, the night was alive with possibilities for adventure and heroism. Adventures. Do you remember when you were innocent enough to think about having those all the time? To be constantly, playfully thinking how you could have an adventure, instead of constantly wondering how you could have your next orgasm?

Back.

Eventually, two and a half hours had passed, and I was starting to become bored. David was suffering no such problems at all. He hadn't noticed the idly-wondering eyes of people as they passed, surprised to see a child like David out this late in town on a Sunday evening. I felt proud of him that night. Most kids would have been complaining about the cold by that point, or about their aching legs, but all David had on his mind was the job at hand. The fantasies from a thousand comics were coming true. That said, his eyes were continually darting around and he was walking close to me. Every now and then I would look at him, pat my Night Man bag, and wink. He would then giggle and visibly relax. But not completely.

At this point, I was wishing for a crime to occur. Not out of boredom, but because I did not want David to go home disillusioned. Time was running out, as the bowling excuse would only be good for about another twenty minutes. We were already pushing it as it was. However, I knew my brother, and I knew that if he saw The Night Man - saw ME - fly into action and do some good, then he would commit himself to his new life with concrete, titanium conviction. However, there was a large risk that if we went home without saving someone or stopping a crime, then David would lose a small amount of faith in the project. Perhaps he would stay committed, but the seed of doubt would be sown. I decided an excuse for my mother could be thought up later. I decided to stay in town for an hour longer.

I made the decision.

I'd decided to go the long way round town again - following a route that would allow us to arrive back at the car at the end of the extra hour, and also take us through a few shitty pub areas where trouble was most likely to occur. Half an hour later, we saw the mugging.

It looked like a mugging, or it could have just been four lads beating up one lad. Either way, one person was getting hit by four people. It was enough.

We'd heard them before we saw them. I could hear before the violence started that there was going to be a fight. I could hear someone trying to placate someone else. I could hear another someone talking aggressively back. The sounds were floating out of an access alley to one of the shops, just ahead of us on the left. We were walking along the front of Marks and Spencers. David was on my right. I have to stop again for a moment.

Back.

I put out my hand to stop David, crouched down, and held a finger to my lips. He nodded, wide-eyed again, as I put my hand on his shoulder and turned him so he could see where I was pointing: the entrance to GT Sports across the street. He was trembling. He turned back, and I made small shooing gestures at him, my right hand still pointing at the shop front. He paused for a moment, as if desperately confused - even though what I was saying was perfectly clear - but then the lights came back on in his eyes and he nodded again. He turned and ran quietly to the darkened shop front. Once there, he looked to make sure I hadn't gone anywhere and hesitantly held up his hand. I put a finger to my lips again, and ran back up the road, three shops back, and ducked into a shop entrance of my own. I can't remember which one it was. I only know David was in GT Sports.

I got changed quickly, listening to the escalating aggression further up the road. I remember sticking my head out to check on David as I prepared the costume, but the angle of the street meant I couldn't see into his darkened alcove properly. Once finished, I left the rucksack where it was – realising that I should have changed where David was standing so I could leave him the bag to look after - and slowly sidled out of the doorway. Eventually, I drew level with David on the other side of the road. He was craning his head in a vain attempt to see what was happening in the alley, but he saw me and stopped. I had been expecting a smile or a thumbs up, but there was none. As I looked at him huddled right up in the corner of the alcove, his gloved hands almost to his mouth, I realised that David was terrified. And I had put him there. Instead of turning around, removing the mask, going over to hug him and tell him I would take him straight home, like a good brother, I thought that I would show him there was no need to be frightened. I was The Night Man now, and I would show him that when he was with me there was nothing to fear. I did it I did it I did it.

That was the second wrong decision I made.

I moved on, giving David a thumbs-up of my own to put him at his ease, but he just slowly shook his head at me, not taking his eyes from mine. I kept moving, giving him an OK sign as I walked, trying to let him know that he was wrong and it was fine, but his head kept shaking. I turned away from him then, from his imploring eyes. I had a job to do. I was doing the job, I WAS DOING THE JOB I WAS DOING TH

Back.

There were now loud scuffling sounds coming from the alley, and it was clear that physical violence was occurring. Instantly, the thudding sensation began in my chest; the dry paper-like feeling in my arms. I remember this in particular because of the way it came out of NOWHERE. I was only two or three feet away from the alley as I began to thumb open the pocket on my utility belt containing the Man Marker and the shouts were now very loud. There were bursts of swearing and muffled yells, but the worst sounds were the impacts. Someone was taking a beating, and the soft yet somehow forceful sounds of solid fists and feet against unwilling human flesh and bone, cushioned only by a few thin layers of material ...it seemed evil. This was as clear as day.

I realised I couldn't get the utility belt pocket open.

I couldn't get the Man Marker out. I'd put it in a different pocket than the one I'd used before. The material of the utility belt is made of some sort of denim or canvas; the fastening, a brass button, like the fly on a pair of button-up jeans. Somehow, without me realizing, some of the cheap denim had split and snagged over the button in this particular pocket, creating some kind of double hook. I didn't know this at the time. I hadn't used that one before. I've only found this out since. In my panic, my fucking panic at the time, I only knew I couldn't get the spray out.

I should have checked my gear before I went out. For all my talk of speed and preparation, I hadn't thought of it. How could I? How was I supposed to think of this? I am sorry. I am sorry. It is my fault, and I shall never forget it. Then the sounds in the alley moved several feet closer. They were knocking their victim back up the alley, towards the street, towards me, and I became very, very scared. I was terrified. Like a rabbit. A scared little rabbit. All over again. My fault. All my fault. I had no spray, and they were coming towards me.

I began tugging desperately at the fastening, trying to rip through the material, but I was too weak. I was leaning against the wall, working at the fastening, and I recall a strong stinging in my eyes as some sweat must have run from under the band of my mask, rolling into my eyes. Something shifted in my head then, and I found that I actually couldn't breathe. I began to gasp quietly and my hands flew from the utility belt and pulled down the bottom of my mask so I could gulp in air, as more sweat poured into my eyes - -and I heard the running. Whoever they had set upon had broken away and was running towards my end of the alley. His pursuers were bellowing and it was clear that in about two seconds they would leave the alley and be visible and I would be too.

I had no Man Marker and no crash helmet. Why? Crash helmet. Mask. I could hear little high pitched noises at the end of each of my gasping breaths as - and this is the second most vivid thing that I remember - time seemed to turn into glue, and I suddenly was riding in my own eyes as I felt my hands find the handles of the nightsticks and my grip tighten. Lack of oxygen, perhaps, but all I could feel then was the thudding and the dryness and the confusion that I was elsewhere and still there. I saw them run past me into the middle of the road - a young man about my age followed by four other young men.

He was dressed in a blue shirt and trousers and as he passed me I saw the right hand side of his face was streaked with blood. It was gushing from a cut underneath his right eye. The other lads were all wearing jackets of assorted styles, and I think they were a couple of years older. Two were shouting, one was silent, and I shall never forget the face of the last one in the pack as he sped past. He was smiling, a look of glee on his face. He was laughing in a shallow, breathy fashion, unable to fully express his mirth because of his breathing.

They dashed straight past, so engaged in the thrill of the chase and filled with a thug's bloodlust that they didn't even register my presence. They were faster than the lad who was running away. They hadn't taken a beating, and he was wobbling as he ran, perhaps blinded a little by his own blood. The nearest lad to him booted the back of his ankles and he fell, hard, in the middle of the road. His assailant began to kick him in the head.

The second guy was there instantly, kicking him in the spine, and the third jogged round to the front of where the beaten lad was lying with his body drawn up into a ball in a fruitless attempt to protect his head. He wasn't crying out. The third bent over, staring, and began saying stuff to him. He would draw back his foot and then follow through as hard as he could, seem to ask a question, do it again, talk, question, do it again. The fourth had, by now, jogged to a halt behind the two working on his back and head, and stood watching, taking a pull now and then on the large bottle of Newcastle Brown Ale that he held in his hand. He was still smiling. He seemed familiar. This went on for some time.

I don't think the man on the ground remained conscious for very long. They continued to kick him in the head, and it began to loll from side-to-side with each kick as if he wasn't trying to protect it any more. And the very worst thing of all was that I still hadn't moved away from the wall.

I realized this, and somehow, on shuffling feet, I did. There was that. I did move. Maybe it was because I knew David was watching me. I couldn't look over to where he was.

He saw all this. He saw it all. My God, what was I thinking?

The talker looked up and saw me.

The other two carried on kicking. I was the most terrified I had ever been in my entire life. Coward. Terrible. I had no spray. No spray at all, different, not trained. my fault...

He stared for a moment, then pointed. He shouted at me and was instantly striding in my direction. My heart rushed. Amazement, fear. It was the instant hate from him that struck me. The instant decision and desire to hurt another human being. Anyone. I think I staggered forwards, trying to grip the nightsticks tightly, but I do remember that I couldn't. My hands were wet and slippery, and they seemed to have no power to grip properly. It was like the handles weren't there.

It is genuinely hard to remember now what I was thinking from that point onwards, what motives I had in my head or what thinking helped me move and controlled me. I wish I could. I must have dipped into something in my mind because as he drew within striking distance and shoved me hard in the sternum, I saw my arm come across and strike him with the nightstick, clipping him slightly across the jaw. I don't know how hard it was or how much damage it did but I saw it knocked him off balance. However, the wild blow he had already started to swing with his left hand still connected with my right temple, clumsy but hard. I saw a flash of gold out of the corner of my eye just before it did; a ring, one that cut into me slightly.

This must have happened a lot quicker than I remember. On natural reflex, I assume, I brought both arms up, either to push him back or to protect my head, but I felt the end of the left nightstick come up sharply under his jaw. His head snapped up and he staggered back a few feet, caught off-guard and badly stunned. Again, I am not able to remember my thoughts of the moment, but I know that I ran at him, ran straight towards him, and we collided. Somehow, I found myself grabbing him around his waist tightly, with my head against his chest, just acting I think, just doing, and lifted with all my strength. He went up and I then dropped him, and I think that did him because the collision with the ground must have combined with the two blows from the nightsticks because he went limp on impact.

Then I felt a kick in the back of my knee and my leg suddenly buckled sharply, dropping me to one leg and leaving me unable to move anywhere before someone elbowed me hard in the face and I fell sideways. I was on the ground and whoever had joined in and kicked me in the back of the knee then kicked me in the back of the head, scraping my forehead against the tarmac and making me bleed. They were screaming at me. The Question-Asker appeared and kicked me in the face. One of my bottom front teeth fell onto my tongue. As I grabbed a breath I felt my throat swallow it. The breath burst straight back from my lungs as the Question-Asker's boot slammed into my stomach, then into my groin. There was a horrible sharp sensation in my ribs. Whoever was behind wedged their foot sharply and very, very hard into the base of my neck and I felt something grind. Agony exploded across my shoulders. They were all shouting something, but I couldn't hear it over my own desperate breathing and guttural noises. Another boot in the back of my skull, and something began to relax in my body when the blows stopped and I heard them shouting to someone. My skin became damp, whether through relief or fear I do not know, but I remember it literally seeming to sweep across my whole body, as the shouting remained directed elsewhere, though I again couldn't hear what they were saying as my stomach lurched and I vomited, choking as I tried to get air in my position. My head was bleary, foggy. Then I heard the voice through the shouting, and the dampness washed again.

It was a kid's voice.

I heard one of the lads laughing. The other two joined in. The kid had stopped talking. I heard a moderately hard thud, followed by a little gasp, bitten off, like whoever had been struck was trying not to cry out. I heard another blow, a little harder, and this time there was a surprised, pained cry. A third blow, much harder, and this time whoever had been hit twice had fallen onto the deck, hard. The laughter burst out again, and something clicked through the fogginess like a switchblade in my brain.

The person they were hitting was David.

They hadn't hit him as hard as they'd hit the other guy – I could hear that – but they had hit him and knocked him to the ground. I tried to stand, but the sharp sensation had obviously been one of my ribs breaking. It ground against something and the pain made me cry out and jerk suddenly. I fell back down. I heard running feet and then felt a sharp blow to my stomach. I heard loud, terrible crying begin. Desperate sobs. David was terrified for me. It was obvious what had happened. He'd ran from his hiding place, trying to help me. The shouting had been him trying to get them to stop. My ribs hurt too much. A bigger man would have done it. He would have gone through the pain. He wouldn't have felt it. He would have been like the woman with the kids trapped in the car, the man running into the burning building, and taken it all to stop what was happening. I lay there in the road with blood on my cheeks, making gasping sounds while my eleven-year-old brother lay on the ground a few feet away,

"What the fuck are you supposed to be then?" said whoever was standing over me. I focused my eyes, my mind whirling. It was Bottle Boy. The guy I'd dropped had gotten back to his feet and was standing next to Bottle Boy, but he wasn't talking. He was holding his head with his eyes screwed up, bending over occasionally. He looked like he was in a lot of pain.

I then became dimly aware that the reason Bottle Boy was familiar was that I knew him. I had gone to school with him. I had never spoken to him, but I knew his name.

Jason Marlett.

He kicked me again, and I coughed up a little more vomit.

"Eh? Twat.'" He started grinning and began kicking me again and again, that little excited, breathy laugh ever present. David. David. I was curled into a ball to stop the kicks landing properly. David was wailing now, maybe out of pain, maybe out of fear, maybe out of humiliation. He screamed my name.

When Jason's foot wedged itself into my stomach again. I somehow tightened myself even harder, and caught it between my drawn-up and folded knees.

I want this known. This move was not heroic or planned or clever. I just did it.

I felt Jason try to pull away and found myself tightening up on his foot even more. He shouted something, but I blindly wrapped my arms around his leg so he couldn't move it. He was yelling at me and still trying to kick, but he couldn't draw his leg to swing. If he really swung he would fall over. I pulled up and held him higher, around his knee, my head drawn around the other side of his leg, and he could hit me in the back now, jarring my broken rib. This hurt very much, but I still held on. I don't know why. He was yelling and yelling, and I could hear his friends laughing, and suddenly I pulled again on his leg and he overbalanced. He went down, and I heard his head hit the ground. I dived up on his body and head-butted him in the face, hard.

I opened my mouth to bite him, and I had a split second to see the terrible, terrible sight of my little brother standing slumped against the nearby wall, holding his face with one hand and crying. He'd gotten himself to his feet was looking at me. Then Jason Marlett's friends stopped laughing and I was kicked in the face again. Several hands grabbed me at various places, tightening at my collar and the material covering my shoulders as they pulled me up, punching and kicking. They jostled me back up against the window of the shop behind me, I don't know which, and Jason Marlett was up again. The wind rushed from my lungs and my stomach lurched, but no pain, just nausea and increasing dizziness. David. David. The hands holding me were digging into my flesh now too, pulling it up and tight. Then David was suddenly there and punching Jason Marlett in the back, red in the face, his teeth gritted in a horrible grimace. Crying.

There was no laughter this time. Jason Marlett gave the briefest of brief glances under his armpit towards David, then forcefully drove his elbow backwards into my little brother's chest. Both David and I screamed at the same time.

He staggered backwards into the road. I was screaming, screaming, screaming, screaming, screaming, thrashing at the three. I couldn't move. One of them was actually laughing. The one on my right kicked my legs out from under me, and I fell on my coccyx, my back lancing with pain. My brother, my brother, my brother, hurt and bleeding in the middle of the road. He is eleven. Another tooth went in my mouth.

Then. I am sorry. This. I didn't see. My right eye was shut and there were people in my way who were stopping me. I couldn't. My ribs. People and pain. It happened. I heard. We all heard. A few seconds of engine noise growing, then the horn, then the scrape of desperate tyres, then the worst sound I will ever hear.

Sometimes I think the worst thing was that he drove off. Straightaway. Fear and cowardice and scum and cowardice. But then I remember what the real worst thing was. The worst thing ever. My attackers stopped. They were staring behind their shoulders and I still couldn't see. Of course, I already knew, but there was no feeling. None at all. It was almost at the moment I heard the noise, when I KNEW, but didn't know because I couldn't SEE, that all feeling winked out. Like a switch had been flicked. The sudden fear, the terrible horror of suspicion was so much that my head shut down feeling in response. The thugs looked at each other. One gasped:

"Fuck."

Then another one immediately started to run. The others automatically followed, without once even turning their heads to look.

I saw my brother lying several feet away from the end of a long skid mark on the tarmac. His right arm was bent the wrong way. A pool of blood was spreading from his head. He had always been small. His height. The very worst thing of all was that he was still conscious, and the sound of his desperate, shocked, and pathetic gasps for breath was so loud. This could not have happened. I threw myself towards him, moaning.

I fell onto the ground beside him and looked into a pair of eyes as wide and staring as my still functioning one. His chest was heaving and pitching wildly. There was blood down one of side of his face and something in his side was making his top stick out slightly. His mouth was gaping, and he was trying to speak.

"Nnnn!" he gasped, looking into my face, knowing me. Everything in the entire world stopped and was replaced by this unspeakable nightmare. I held a trembling and spasming hand an inch over his face, scared to touch him, like I would break whatever fragile link was still keeping him here. I could not think. I could not speak. I could not move. All I could do was moan and suck in air. This was the purest horror. "Nnnnnnn!" he said again, as his eyes pinched and he knew what was happening. I cried out a loud, wailing moan, wordless, unable to say his name. He whipped out with his good arm and pulled my wavering hand down onto his face, tight, desperate, where the tears rolled from his eyes and over my fingers. I was gibbering, wailing and screaming guttural noises like a tortured animal, hardly able to breathe as I knelt in the middle of the road and stared into his crying eyes.

"Nnnnnn?!" he gasped, and it was a shocked question. I screamed, my own tears blinding me.

I stopped instantly as I saw his chest begin to heave faster and shallower. I watched his eyes as I began to babble, watching them widen to impossible proportions. They begged me to make it stop, and I grabbed the sides of his face and screamed. I wanted to hug him to me, to hold him tighter than ever, to squeeze my life INTO him, but he was going. I squeezed and madly stroked at the side of his face with my free hand, screaming his name, and his grip on my hand tightened and his mouth widened, then went terribly, horribly slack. It all stopped. David stopped. I stopped.

I slapped him, hard, in the face. His eyes didn't blink. They stayed open. I slapped him again. And again. His mindless head rocked gently from the blows. Then I finally DID hug him to me, pulling his limp and so fucking light body and squeezing hard enough to crush his lifeless chest as I willed him back, screaming and screaming and screaming.

Forty-Ninth Entry: Saturday September 26th 1998 9:30 PM

I had to take a break after that last entry. I am sorry. I have been writing and crying for several hours, and I felt too drained to continue. I have made myself some coffee. I will now continue my account.

Eventually, some form of awareness filled my head. I realized that I had been sitting motionless in the road and holding my younger brother's dead body in my arms for quite some time. I could not say exactly how long. Thoughts began to creep through. People. Discovery. Police. I remember knowing somehow that these were important and that I should be doing something, but no sense of urgency was present in my head. I was not thinking. The tears had stopped and I was holding David's head against my chest, looking at the unlit, darkened windows of Marks and Spencers. Offers on Ready Meals, 3 for 2 Lingerie, new Organic Food range. Young male models in suits and slightly unshaven faces.

My mask had come off. It was lying somewhere in the road, I assumed. I had closed David's eyes. I had often wondered to myself what it would feel like to close a dead person's eyes. Would they fold easily shut - nothing but soft folds of skin - or would it take some effort? David's eyelids offered no resistance and closed easily. They were soft and cold, and I could feel the curve and solidity of his eyeball underneath.

More time passed, and I began to wonder in the same unconscious way what I would tell my mother. This also did not penetrate, but I must have thought it somehow because I remember the thought passing through my head. I don't recall coming to a solution, however.

Suddenly, consciousness kicked back into life when I heard people talking from some distance away. The switch had been flicked again, but to a different setting now. While I was now hyper-aware of my surroundings, there was no conscious thought occurring. I was operating on instinct and that instinct was panicked fear. The approaching people were not far away. And I was sitting with a dead body in my arms.

I saw them from quite far away, coming around the corner at the end of the road. There were five or six people, three women, three men. I don't think they could see me very well from where they were, and I think now that they must have been drunk, as they were singing merrily. I remember it striking me as strange that they were singing. How could they sing? Didn't they get it? But they were coming this way nevertheless.

I was looking around wildly, a strong sensation of time running out pounding against my brain. My eyes fell on the access alley. I looked down at David's body. I pulled him up higher on my lap, rising to my knees, pulling his head fully onto my shoulder and biting my lip down against the screams that wanted to batter their way out of my mouth as my broken rib moved. I staggered up to one knee, wobbling treacherously for a second, then took a deep breath as I pushed up to a standing position.

David had become heavier. Far heavier than he should have been. I told myself it was my own exhaustion, pushing away the knowledge that a dead body is notoriously heavier than a living one due to all of the muscles lying dormant. Rigor mortis would eventually set in.

I thought I would pass out before we made it to the alley. I made it to the alley.

I slid slowly down the wall, lowering myself and David, his body leaning against mine. I had not the strength to properly lay him down. His legs slipped out of my fading grip once they were about three feet from the ground and his Reebok trainers dropped against the concrete with a horrible, terrible, dead-sounding thump.

I sobbed quietly, knowing the shock was still saving me from the very worst of the pain. I sat this way, making little sound, as I heard the group pass by.

I came to about two hours later. I didn't look at my watch, so I don't know for sure. It was still very dark.

I didn't have a single clue what to do.

I didn't know what to do.

I was catatonic, trying to grasp at thought. I nearly just sat there and let them find me, because I really didn't feel capable of doing anything else.

I found myself remembering when David fell off the garage roof when he was younger.

That smashed through the catatonia and the GUILT, the GUILT, the terrible, terrible guilt, and then I knew in a blinding, revelatory instant exactly why my own father had run and why good men do bad things, and then I realised that I had pushed David off me and had left him in the alley behind me and I was running and not feeling the pain, just knowing I had to get to the car and get out of the city centre as quickly as possible; running, running, babbling wordlessly and thinking nothing but the knowledge that will hound me to my grave.

I found myself running to the car park

The instant I heard the familiar sound of the door slamming shut, something clicked again. This was normal. This was safe. Inside the little bubble of my car was a quiet world where nothing bad ever happened. It was a far cry from the cold dark streets that I knew only a little of, where people were scared and hurt. This was SAFE.

Obviously, I knew I could not go home. I was never going home again. Somewhere this registered very sharply and painfully; yet at the same time I found myself realising that this was just a matter of course and logic. I sat there for a little while after that one, alone again, until things started to tick over in my brain once more. Clinical thought continued to creep back in.

Without emotion, I sat in my mother's car and very slowly came up with a plan. Money wouldn't be an issue. I had a fair bit of money in the bank. After all, until recently, what the hell had I been spending it on? Nothing. Nothing. A young man, spending his money on nothing.

I had to get out of the town. As far away as possible. Far, far, far. The rest could come later. That was fine.

Yet as the keys went towards the ignition slot, two very important things clicked in my mind.

The second thing was about good people and choices. My father had chosen to run. Perhaps now I finally understood why, but his choice was not mine. There had been so many times – during the difficulties, shall we say, after my dad had left – that I had sat alone with poison in my mind, trying to fathom it out. I would not do the same. Never. I was not going to run. I was not going to leave David. I would NEVER let

David down, even when it was too late. This was something I knew from the very core of myself.

But the first of those things that I'd realized had been a plan. It was short-term, it was something to move with, and feelings about it could come later. But I knew that it had to be carried out.

I started the car, noticing my rib again as the seat rumbled at the engine's firing up. The rib would soon become a constant agonising throb, every turn of the non-power-assisted wheel aggravating it. I bit down and gritted my teeth through it again as I pulled slowly out of the car park and set off around the one-way system of Derby city centre.

It took about five minutes to get back to the street where I had left David. The nearest place to the alley entrance in which I could park was about five feet away. I knew I would have to be quick. There was no one around, but I stopped and listened anyway as I opened the door. As I got out and walked slowly to the alley, very much not wanting to enter, I had a terrible thought that David would not be there - taken by some pervert for his own needs or by the police or whoever, but as I took the deepest breath of my life and stepped around the corner, I saw the outline of one small Reebok trainer. I nearly broke to my knees again at the sight.

I didn't look at David's face. I couldn't. I saw the clothes he had put on specially when we left, saw the back of his head as it lolled forward on his chest, on his Trek Team 73 jumper, his wooly hat and scarf missing, his little scarffffffjghljgljfkfghkdgkhdl

Back.

I moved around behind his head, with my own turned away, and felt for his armpits. Working my hands in, I felt how cold he was already.

How his flesh felt like recently-defrosted meat. I pushed this thought away and pulled, rib screaming. I couldn't lift him now. I was going to have to drag him. I set off backwards, pulling David out into the darkly-lit street.

I reached the car and hefted David up and into the back seat.

I was going to drive until I was far enough away from Derby to feel right, then find a back street to sleep in the car 'til dawn. That was the first step. There was a blanket in the boot that I used to cover David.

Twenty-four hours, say the police. You hear it on TV all the time. 'I'm sorry. Madam, but we can't report a person missing until they've been gone for at least 24 hours.' I had until 8:00 PM the next day to do everything that I planned to do. I knew it would be enough.

I was correct, as it turned out.

I am too tired to write anymore tonight.

Fiftieth Entry: Sunday September 27th 1998 12:11 PM

I will continue. There is a lot to tell you.

I actually drove as far as Coventry before tiredness became strong enough to force me to find somewhere to stop for the night. I drove into an area of town that - according to signposts - was called Cheylesmore, and I found a quiet street. I would be undisturbed here for at least for a few hours of sleep, and there were enough parked cars that mine would not create unwanted attention. The signpost told me that I was on Cecily Road.

I'd driven all the way there with the window open, letting the rushing noise from outside the car mirror the one inside my own head. Now that exhaustion had finally made it empty, I slept.

I awoke at around 7:30am, a blinding early light streaming in through the windscreen. This was unpleasant - as was the dull but harsh pain in my jaw that I awoke to - yet not as unpleasant as the pain in my rib that flared up when I moved. Even all of that paled into complete nothingness when the sleep-mugginess faded and I remembered where I was and why. I shut that down automatically once more. Switch, click. Gone.

I didn't feel human, but it meant that I could go to work.

I didn't want to look round at the large bundle on the back seat. The blanket in the car boot had been more than enough to cover him, as well as what I had left of my Night Man kit. I had tucked the blanket in tightly around him to avoid it moving or falling away whilst I was travelling. I wanted to sleep some more, and yet I knew it was best to stay up now. I had a lot to do before the police became involved any time after 8:00pm that evening.

First on the list was a wash in a public toilet. Looking as I did, I couldn't interact with anyone without arousing suspicion. A look in the mirror showed the dried blood on my face. Closer inspection showed that a wash would not be enough. I had a long graze on my forehead, cuts on my lips, and some very heavy swelling around both eyes. It was a different face than the one I remembered, but it seemed entirely appropriate. The boy I had been was as dead as my brother. Some cheap sunglasses would be needed to cover my eyes, I realized. It was a bright day outside and no one would see anything unusual about a man wearing shades.

I set off, driving reasonably empty roads. This was good, although I knew in about half an hour they would be very busy indeed. I found a petrol station not far away in which I had my face-wash. The dried blood came off. This was quite difficult as it had congealed very hard and thick, but eventually I got the job done. I then ran my head under the tap for about five minutes, getting the few bits of blood that had dried into my hair. When finished, I squeezed as much water out as possible with my hands, and then stood with my head under the drier for about five minutes. My rib was screaming, and I knew I would have to get some painkillers soon or I would have great difficulty completing the day's tasks. A look in the mirror told me that I had actually made a slight improvement. I certainly looked a hell of a lot more presentable without my face covered in blood.

The cuts on my lips weren't fantastically obvious. The only real problem was the graze on my forehead. If all else failed, I decided, I could just tell people I had been beaten up the night before. I left the toilet and picked up a very cheap pair of dark sunglasses from a stand near the magazines. The girl behind the counter looked at me strangely, seeing the bruising, but not too strangely. This was fine. I asked her where the nearest pharmacy was – one was very close, as it turned out - and I said thank you. She quietly asked me if I was ok. I told her I had been beaten up the night before.

I put the sunglasses on and drove to the pharmacy, where I waited for it to open. I then purchased the much-needed painkillers along with two rolls of surgical tape and a bottle of water. This time there were no strange looks. They saw a man in sunglasses with a graze on his forehead, one who maybe had a black eye and was trying to cover it. This is perhaps a common sight in Coventry pharmacies. Back in the car, the information on the bottle told me to take no more than two tablets on once. I took three. I very gingerly lifted my jumper – I'd taken off the baking trays before I slept - and began to tape up my ribs. I used up a roll and a half. They now felt a bit more supported, at least. It would have to do. I wondered what I would do after I was done with the tasks ahead, but I cut that thought off sharply. Anything coming afterwards? Unthinkable.

Next, I went to the nearest branch of my bank. Fortunately, I had my wallet with me, and so I had enough I.D. to withdraw all the remaining money out of my bank account. This was around £2500. This would be sufficient for the foreseeable future. It would have been nice to be able to sell the car too, but that would just raise too many questions when my name wasn't the one on the documents. The fact that I had withdrawn everything from my account, would, no doubt - once I was reported missing – be noted by the police, but I thought at the same time that it might be a bonus. They might have thought that I was still in Coventry, when very shortly I actually wouldn't be. Very soon I would be back in Derby.

I had things to do and the police were something I would just have to try and work around.

I looked at my watch - surprisingly unbroken, I noted for the first time –to see it was now 9:23 AM. The last thing on my mind was food; indeed, I thought that I may have to force it down my throat, dry heaving and choking. However, I knew that I would have to take some on board if I was going to last the day. I bought a cheap cheese and pickle sandwich and some water from the newsagents. Eating the sandwich was like chewing a lead pillow, with sharp bursts of agony as odd bits of it found themselves being chewed into the jagged stumps of my two broken teeth. Then it was another trip back to the phone box.

I dialed the number for Scoot, and asked them to look up private garages in the area. They gave me a number and a name: Hamlin Garage. I rang them next and an Asian-sounding man answered the phone. I asked what they had for up to £400. They had two cars, a G-reg Sierra for £350, and an F-reg Escort for £400. I said that sounded fine and asked for directions. They were long and complex, but the garage was situated in a winding backstreet of an area called Earlsdon. Still, I eventually managed to find it, parking the Micra about 400 metres up the street from the garage itself. David might have been covered by a blanket, but I didn't know how likely mechanics were to nose around any car that pulled up in their forecourt. Two young lads walked past; they looked hungover to hell, almost as if they could barely stand up. I remember one of them mentioning Don Quixote; for some reason, this hungover oaf somehow talking about the classics, and then I remembered that I didn't give a shit what anyone else was talking about. I got out of the car and walked over to the garage.

I chose the Escort and signed the logbook with a fake name and address. It didn't matter. I would only need the car for a short while. They didn't ask me for any ID. It wasn't that kind of place.

I drove the Escort out of the garage, dimly aware of the fact that at one time I would have been elated to have purchased my own car. I drove the short distance to where I'd left the Micra, pulling up opposite. I transferred my laptop from the passenger footwell of my Mum's car - where it had been since I placed it there before David and I had set out - to the same spot in the Escort. Even then I was conscious of the fact that I did not want to lose it.

Next, David.

I very much did not want to do this in the middle of the day, but I had no choice; I had to get on with things, and I could not have David's body on the back seat.

Making sure his feet were covered, I faced the intense pain and transferred him to the Escort. I thought it might look like I was carrying a roll of carpet, if anyone saw. The street was empty, no curtains stirred, and as I said, I didn't really care either way. Looking back, I think that it looked like the type of street where it was perhaps best to ignore what happened outside. Sometimes, in some homes, the prettiness of your living room is infinitely preferable to the concrete jungle outside. It helps maintain the illusion of comfort and safety.

Once it was done, I took a moment to lean against the car and ride out the yelping pain until it subsided. I decided I would wait an hour and then take another three painkillers.

I locked the Micra and left it there. I don't know what's happened to it since. Maybe it's been found. To be honest, I don't yet know what the police have made of my disappearance, along with my brother's. It doesn't matter anyway. They won't find me. Who knows me to witness me? What friends do I have to see me in the street? None.

Writing is strange. Recalling feelings that seem like they happened to someone else' feeling for the first time in weeks. I have always seemed so able to immerse myself in the past when I write - to recall so much that happened externally and internally - and not surface for hours until I am done. I know when I am done with this account that I shall slowly go back to the other place.

It gets hard to concentrate, sometimes. To focus on anything at all. This journal helps. Helps me focus in some small way.

I have not yet brought you up to speed on my current whereabouts and situation. But I am hungry and will eat now.

I will explain all of that when I'm done and tell you what I did next.

Fifty-First Entry: Sunday September 27th 1998 4:46 PM

I left Coventry at around 3:00pm after purchasing a baseball cap in a sports store. Whether or not this merely succeeded in making me look more suspicious when combined with the shades, I don't know, but if I was going back to Derby, I wanted to cover as much of my face as possible.

It took around an hour to get back to my hometown, and although I found myself feeling increasingly heavy - to the point where I had to pull the car over and vomit onto the pavement - I drove into the city centre.

Back to the alley by Marks And Spencers.

There were no police lines up. There were only a few marks of blood left on the road. Most of it had been washed away by rain in the night.

I saw what I was looking for almost straightaway. It was unnoticeable if you weren't looking, something that would pass straight through your consciousness like the little people you never see.

The two halves of my mask were lying screwed up in the gutter, looking like used black dishrags.

I walked slowly over and picked them up. They were sopping wet and filthy. I knew that I wanted them. I didn't know why. They weren't even really part of the plan. I just knew that I wanted to pick them up. I wanted to make sure I at least had them.

I returned to the car and drove to the nearest petrol station where I bought that day's local paper. Checking the cover, I saw that there was nothing about David and me, but that wasn't what I was buying it for anyway. I went to the back. Rooms to let. Specifically: self-contained one-bedroom flats. Bedsits. There were four, situated in various parts of town, and I promptly made some phone calls to the advertisers.

One of them had already gone, but I made appointments with the three others, and spent the next few hours driving around and looking at these rooms and meeting the relevant landlords. It took until the third landlord/bedsit to hear what I wanted. He was only asking for the number and name of a referee that he could call if he couldn't get hold of me and a month's rent in advance. All rent was to be paid in cash. I said that was fine.

He got me to write my name down in his small registry book, as well as the name of my referee, which I of course made up as much as I had the name I gave for myself. That, as far as the landlord was concerned, was Barry Horowitz, and my referee would be my fictional brother John. He gave me the keys, told me the rent dates for the next three months, and left me a card with his phone number and address on it.

When he was gone, I went to the car to get David. It was about 8:00pm by then and dark. It was a lot safer to move him than it had been earlier.

What felt like a whole hour later, I dropped David heavily onto the bed and collapsed on the floor, moaning loudly. Eventually, I propped myself up and took in my new surroundings once more.

Bed. No duvet. Whitewashed walls – dirty - with a mass produced print of a mountain range hanging on the wall, shot in black and white, encased in a cheap plastic frame. One electric fire in the corner. One sink. One small oven/grill with two hotplates on top. One old, wooden cupboard. One lightbulb hanging from the ceiling. No shade on it. Thin red curtains that would be insufficient at keeping the light out. The bathroom, I knew, was a shared one out in the hall.

Once I'd recovered enough to move, I gently pulled David off the bed and onto the floor. The blanket came away a little, and I tugged it back into place without looking. I flicked the light switch off and gingerly settled onto the bed. I was exhausted, but even then I lay in the darkness for about three hours before I actually slept. When I awoke it was into a world blessedly full of nothing but instinct and dull, steady purpose. I needed to keep doing, keep moving, or like the shark I would drown. The first thing I did was down another three painkillers and then stashed the majority of my money under the mattress.

I drove into town.

I made my way through the busy Monday morning crowds, cap and shades on my head. Perhaps these were pointless, after all. As I have already said, the odds of anyone recognising me were small-to-non-existent, but the news of mine and David's disappearances might have been known to some degree.

I picked up a copy of the telephone directory at the BT shop, after which I retired to a quiet corner with it and found the information that I needed. After that, I made a trip to C+A and purchased a plain white shirt, a black tie, and a pair of black trousers. I also made several purchases at a hardware shop.

I then returned to the car and ran an important errand. This took about an hour. It turned out to be easier than I thought. More on that later. I then bought and forced down some food.

It was after 1:00pm by now, so I knew I had some time to kill, but I didn't have a clue what to do with it. The thought of sitting and doing nothing for 3 hours or so was almost unpleasant enough to break through and scare me. I was still capable of feeling boredom, it seemed. I went to the cinema.

The movie finished at around 3:30pm, and when I left the theatre I thought I would now get to my destination in plenty of time. I did. I got to Sinfin at about 4:00pm, pulling up near the end of Nicholls Close. The phone book had told me this would probably be the right place. I was sure it would just be a matter of waiting. If not today, then sometime soon. I really did have all the time in the world. I had stopped to pick a magazine along the way, and I pulled this out to read while regularly glancing up the road. I waited there until about 5:30pm and then I saw what I had been waiting for.

It was the third car that I'd seen drive onto the street. A red XR3i. I had thought that if I got there early enough, I wouldn't miss him coming home. I knew that he was the sort of lad that would never get a job doing anything other than the standard nine-to-five. I had banked on this being the case in order to be here to catch him mid-arrival.

Jason Marlett got out of the XR3i. I actually felt something click; part anger, part satisfaction. There had only been 5 Marletts in the Derby phone book - not a common surname - and the only one that was based in Sinfin. I knew from my schooldays that was where his family lived. I'd bet that he still lived at his parents' house, and I'd bet right. He didn't look in the slightest bit haunted or guilty. He looked positively relaxed. Coming home from work, end of the day, dressed in his cheap suit and blue shirt, hair done up nice. A different looking fellow all together from the wild-eyed thug that I had seen on a Derby street at night. He didn't look at all like a murderer, but I of all people know that appearances can be deceiving.

Physically shaking with anticipation - a strange, dull excitement, if there can be such a thing - I got out of the car and started to creep towards him. He still hadn't registered my presence, even when I was so close. Why would he? He was on his home street, safe. Where in England do you expect to be attacked on a suburban cul-de-sac, especially in the middle of the afternoon? Even so, I was moving as quietly as possible, going slowly. The sun was still up, but the day was a dull one, and this helped a little; no shadows, not that Marlett would ever notice, Ideally, I wanted to get him before he got into the house, but even if I didn't I was just going to go in there after him. As it was, he hadn't reached the front door by the time I came up behind him. I was parked on the same side of the road, very close to his house. It wasn't too far a distance to cover.

He was at the front door, putting down his small leather briefcase and fumbling with his keys, when I stopped creeping and rushed up behind him, clamping the folded up cotton pad over his mouth.

Getting hold of the chloroform had been fairly easy, as I say. I have always looked younger than my years, just like my brother. It had been a simple matter of getting hold of my old school uniform - a simple dress code of white shirt, black tie, and black trousers - and heading into the school at around dinnertime, when it would be so busy that I could go relatively unnoticed. Even if anyone had seen me, they would have just thought I was a 'new sixth form kid.' Plus, it was near to the start of a new academic year.

The chemistry lab supply office had always been the least secure room in the school, ridiculously. There was supposed to be at least one white-coated lab woman in there at all times, but I knew that there regularly wasn't. I hung around outside for about half an hour, before said white-coated lab woman left to go and jump the dinner queue to pick up her lunch. I'd then simply nipped in as quickly as possible and looked along the shelves of jars that would soon be used in pointless chemistry experiments. I found the one labeled 'chloroform' and pulled the carrier bag - which I had received with my food from the newsagents the day before - out of my pocket. I dropped the sealed jar into it and opened the door a crack to make sure there was no one around that would ask questions. I left quietly and calmly. Normally I would have felt thrilled getting away with it.

Jason didn't struggle all that hard. He was actually a little bigger than me. However, I suppose he was too confused to actually register that he was being attacked, and so was spending half his energy trying to work out what was going on and the other half struggling with whoever had put something over his mouth. Unfortunately for him, his exertions, of course, forced him to breathe harder, and - with his air passages smothered with a chloroform soaked rag - he could breathe nothing but that which promptly rendered him unconscious.

Quickly, I dragged him back to the car and deposited him in the boot. I had other stuff to do with him immediately, but I obviously wanted to get away from his street before I did so. Wonderfully, there was no one about. No curtains twitched. Welcome to suburban England, where no one looks outside of their own fucking world.

I drove for a minute or two until I found the first back street where I would be unlikely to have any would-be witnesses strolling by and pulled into it. I nipped around to the boot, carrying the roll of gaffa tape I had bought at the hardware store. I bound his wrists behind him, bound his feet, shoved another rag in his mouth, and then taped over that as well. I then taped over his eyes. I checked that he could breathe through his nose. He could.

I then set off for Alstein Park. This is an out-of-the-way nature park, far from the city centre, not a public play area like McGlone park. This is pretty much just an enormous wood with a well-worn path through the middle. It was perfect for my needs. It took a good 25 minutes to get there, shops and houses and concrete eventually giving way to narrow, hedge-hemmed roads. Even though it was highly unlikely that anyone would be about at this time of day, I wanted to wait another hour by the side of the road that led up to the park. I wanted it to be darker. Then it would be about 7:30 PM, the perfect middle ground between it being too dark for the nature walkers, and too early for the teenagers to go and get drunk on cider amongst the trees.

I pulled over and watched the sun set. After about five minutes, I could hear Jason's muffled struggling coming from the boot. Occasionally I could faintly hear him trying to speak, sometimes with a pleading tone, the words completely unrecogniseable. Sometimes they would sound angry, sometimes a questioning whine. I think he was beginning to guess what this was about. I think he was amazed anyone had tracked him down. How could they, he was probably thinking. What evidence would link him to the murder? He probably didn't even have a criminal record.

After another hour, I thought that it was time to go. I drove until I reached the gravelled area which was supposed to be the car park. There were no other cars there and it was dark now. Not night, but dark. No visitors for Alstein Park. Soon someone, some groundskeeper, would come to close the car park. I would have to move quickly to be done before then. I stepped out of the car and listened. No sound of people, and sound travelled well here, I knew. Okay to go. I put on the pair of gloves I'd bought.

I opened the boot, and as I did so I saw Jason Marlett's terrified form suddenly freeze in its thrashing. Grabbing his armpits, I gritted my teeth as my rib bleated its usual deafening noise, and heaved him out onto the gravel. He was babbling away, writhing on the ground helplessly, and I took a moment to let the pain in my rib subside.

Once the knife in my side was bearable once more, I pulled his head up by his hair. I kept pulling, and as I hoped, he managed to get his bound feet under him to stand and relieve the pain on his head. He tried to thrash, to club me with his bound hands, but I kicked him in the balls without a word. He dropped to the ground again and I let him recover. When I pulled him up again by his hair, he came along without any trouble, mumbling and whimpering behind the tape as he shuffled along.

I began to pull him along by his hair to keep him hopping along to where I wanted him to go, as he would follow just to relieve the pain on his scalp. He was crying, I saw, and his constant noise - now always pleading in tone – came in choking sobs. I didn't say anything at all to him. We walked slowly along like this for a few moments, heading into the trees, and I was glad I'd taped his eyes. I wanted him to wonder where we were going. At one point he broke free and began to hop blindly – I almost admired his determination - but I tripped him and he fell onto his face. When I pulled him up again he was bleeding from a deep cut above one of his eyes. His muffled babbling was at a fever pitch, and I wondered if he'd suffocate. We began walking again.

Eventually, we came to the spot I'd chosen - the point where there was a fairly steep shrub-covered slope on one side of the path. Me and David always used to scale it as kids. Back then, it seemed like a mountain. I pushed Jason down it, and his surprised and terrified yell continued as he rolled all the way down to the bottom. When his descent finally stopped, his thrashing was greatly reduced. Perhaps he was winded. However, he then seemed to sense that I was not with him for a moment and that maybe he could get free. He'd actually made it to his knees by the time I'd descended the slope and reached him, but I kicked him in the back of the head and he fell forwards, lying still. Confident he wasn't going anywhere in a hurry, I headed back up to the top of the slope and jogged back to the car. I'd left the collapsible deck chair and rucksack - that I'd also bought at the hardware store – on the back seat. I grabbed these, and then stuffed the jar of chloroform and a rag in the rucksack as well.

When I returned Jason was still pretty much where I'd left him, although he'd managed to move a few feet further forward. A wriggling path was grooved into the dirt behind him, showing his caterpillar-like progress. His babbling intensified again as he heard me getting closer. After taking a moment to rip the tape from his mouth and remove the rag, there was a frantic burst of open screaming while I drugged him anew. Once he was out, I set up the deck chair.

After about ten minutes of agonizing struggling - my rib feeling like it would actually pierce my lungs - I had Jason Marlett seated in the chair. I bound him to it by wrapping the tape around his waist several times and around the back of the chair. I then unbound his wrists from each other and, working as quickly as possible, I taped his forearms, palm down, to the armrests. I used almost the entire roll in doing this. I didn't want him going anywhere. I then very carefully bound his fingers so that his hands hooked over the ends of the armrests as if he were gripping them. His knuckles pointed horizontally forward. This was important. I then unbound his ankles from one another and used what was left of the tape both to secure his legs to the chair, as well as re-taping over his mouth after stuffing the rag back inside. I then sat down in front of him and waited.

I was still unable to hate, no matter how much I replayed what he had done in my head. It wasn't that I needed to psyche myself up for the next stage. There was never any question that the job would be done. This was something that HAD to be done. It was just that I wanted - really wanted - the satisfaction. But it didn't actually come in the end.

Eventually he woke up, realising his new position with instant terror. He jerked and jerked and tried to free his forearms, but they were going nowhere. He couldn't even free his lesser-bound ankles. Gaffa tape is very strong stuff. It has been rumoured to hold together light aircraft, you know.

I stood up and pulled the tape off his eyes. He screamed, as I had pulled out some of his eyebrows with it. His face was pure terror. Here he was, at dusk, bound to a chair, with a man standing in front of him wearing a black cap and sunglasses, in the middle of the woods. I could understand, but not sympathise. Well, I couldn't even hate the man that killed my brother, so how could I feel any pity for him?

"You killed my brother," I said. His head rocked back and forth, but I didn't care. That was all I said to him that evening. It was all he needed to know.

I bent down and opened the rucksack. I took out eight bricks. The front two and the back two legs of the deckchair were joined by a horizontal bar; I placed the bricks along these in order to minimize the wobbling that I knew his struggles would cause. I put my hand back into the bag and - slowly, so he could see - I pulled out the large wooden mallet and the small plastic bag of six-inch nails.

His eyes looked like they were going to burst out of his head, and he started screaming so loud that even through the cloth and the tape, it had a lot of volume. It didn't matter. This wouldn't take long.

I squatted down and opened the nail bag, taking one out. Jason became a flurry of movement, thrashing whatever part of him that he could, and the chair wobbled from side-to-side. It wasn't enough to stop me. He was screaming and jerking, but he couldn't get away. If he'd really thought about it he might have been able to get the chair to topple over, but he was too busy panicking; plus, the end result would have been the same, regardless.

I set the point of the first nail between the knuckles of the index and middle finger of his right hand. Like Wolverine, now that I think about it. The nail was very thick. I looked up at Jason's face for a moment. I wanted him to look into my eyes and see what I was doing, but he wouldn't. He was yelling like a wounded tiger. I hadn't even done anything yet. I drew the mallet back and hammered it down forcefully onto the flat head of the nail with a horrible sounding thud.

About a third of the thick nail disappeared into his hand, parting the knuckles with an audible crack. Jason's screams hit a white-hot pitch, and he thrashed his head around like it was full of wasps. Blood erupted around the nail's entry point, and as it went in, a little splashed onto my face. It flowed out of his hand and down the connected armrest and chair leg. I hammered the nail again, and though it was more difficult this time (I had to part more bone as the nail's tip moved further in), the nail disappeared almost all of the way in. I withdrew a second nail, and moved to the second gap between his knuckles. Jason's agonized screams echoed loudly and sharply amongst the trees, but there was no one but me to hear them.

As I moved across the knuckles, it became noticeably more difficult to continue the process. The more I filled his hands with metal, the less room there was for the next nail. Even in the low light I could almost see their dark shapes through the thin skin on the backs of his hands, like the outlines of sharks chewing their way through a lake of flesh. Jason passed out once or twice through pain, but only for a few seconds; that which had made him unconscious almost instantly woke him up again, screaming and screaming. Sometimes he screamed so much that he didn't get enough oxygen through his only breathing point - his nose - and he passed out because of that. Like I say, he was awake again almost straight away.

Eventually, I was finished, and six nails were embedded in between Jason's knuckles. His hands were a mess of blood and flesh. He was unconscious, his body finally pushed to a point of pain so intense that it had shut down. I thought maybe the shock had killed him. I didn't know. But I was following the plan. I took away the bricks and toppled him over backwards in the chair.

Picking up the rucksack, I moved behind him to kneel and place my thighs at either side of his head. I took the nail scissors from the rucksack. Unfortunately, his eyes opened at precisely the wrong time.

If I hadn't had his head between my knees, it would have been impossible to do as I planned, but as it was his head couldn't go anywhere no matter how much he screamed and struggled. I got the idea for what I was going to do from a film, although I'd had to figure out how to actually do it - how to keep his head still without someone else there to hold it. Using my thighs was the obvious solution. I reached down and gripped one of his eyelids – it felt like a foreskin, only slightly thinner – and pulled it outwards, stretching it away from his face. I then snipped it off. I repeated the same with his other eye. Then I stood up to watch him.

Jason's unblinking eyes gazed up at me as his screams became a gargle, a look of permanent amazement on his face as he saw a world that he was unable to stop seeing. His head thrashed back and forth madly, as if doing so would bring his eyelids back and allow him to stop seeing. It didn't work. His body convulsed as if he were having a fit.

After a while, I drove a final nail into his stomach – he barely even seemed to notice, his screaming was so constant – and then I left him there. I knew that he would probably be found in the morning.

Surprisingly tired, I clambered back up the slope and drove back to the bedsit, where I washed the blood from my face and hands and sat for another horrible four hours, awake in the dark.

I knew that the job had to be completed, but now that it had been, the real trouble would begin.

I knew - on the edge of my consciousness - that the terrible, terrible emptiness was looming. My 'great plan' was complete. All that was next was reality, and it would destroy me. I denied it, and continued to deny it, so afraid of it that, incredibly, I actually managed to keep the knowledge at bay.

Denial worked. I know, it's incredible isn't it. If it hadn't been for The Difficulties after my dad left, I doubt it would have been possible, But I'd learned early. Anyway.

I existed. I bought a portable TV - a cheap second hand one that cost £50 – and watched it, absorbing nothing. I didn't eat for four days. I drank water. I watched the ceiling at night.

For the next few weeks I occasionally checked the papers, which soon reported me and David missing. Jason was reported sooner, being found dead the next day. I tried to tell myself that I was surprised, but I wasn't. It was the nail in the stomach. Part of my brain said I hadn't known that would kill him, and part of it said OF COURSE YOU DID. I stopped reading the papers and watching the news. What will come will come.

Because this is all. You have heard everything that has happened up and until now. This is real. There is no denouement. I have done nothing since. Three weeks. Nothing. I have filled the days of the last few weeks with TV and trips to the cinema. The latter has become a previously undiscovered blessing, keeping me going even if I can't really figure out how. The bedsit has started to smell very unpleasant. Inspired by a film I once saw, I have filled the place with air fresheners and made sure I took my rent to the landlord's house in advance in order to prevent him coming round for it. He seems happy for that to be the case.

I got Jason. The plan. Over. Before, I had none of the feeling but all of the purpose. But now I don't even have purpose. I occasionally sit and play with The Night Man Mask, but I never put it on. Obviously, I still have the rest of the costume. My clothes smell. I haven't bought any more since I moved in here.

Being The Night Man got David killed. And yet now it is all I could possibly ever have. But it got David killed. I am restless. I haven't shaved in all of this time. My rib doesn't hurt as much, but I don't think it's healed correctly if it has at all. It hurts when I touch it and doesn't feel right under my fingers.

I have to talk to someone, but there is no one to talk to. But I have to. But there is no one. But I have to. I should find some way of creating income, yet I don't want to do that. I have to talk to someone. It feels like my mind is slowly going, and once that process is complete, there will be nothing here but a shell that moves and eats and shits until I can't even afford my rent and end up on the streets. Is that how you become homeless? Is that how the crazy guy that walks up and down the streets shouting gibberish finds his start in that role? His mind draining until he is left in that state? I have to talk to someone. I can't. I hope I starve soon. They'll find me eventually, I know. I don't care. I just need to talk.

Back.

I have thought about it, and I am going to take a risk. Maybe this will help me get myself together. I can see no way out, and I have to talk. I think I can trust her. She won't give me away. She doesn't know what I have done.

I have to go and talk to Chloe.

Fifty-Second Entry: Monday September 28th 1998 7:01 PM

Oh glorious! I sit with tears streaming down my face as I write, wonderful sensations of elation and sorrow combined in me and coursing through my soul. The pain, the sadness, the joy, I feel it all. I am alive and reborn and FULL. I cannot be long, but I will tell all. Here is your denouement, after all! Fate! FATE!

I went to see Chloe after work. I hoped that I had the right day for the right shift pattern and I did. I got there around 5:30pm and waited in the car park until 6:00pm, watching the staff exit until I saw her. She looked the same as always. It was strange. In my state of detachment I noticed for the first time, in a completely indifferent manner, that she was actually quite beautiful. I got out of the car, wearing my cap and sunglasses. I moved in the same direction as her, moving to intercept. She was walking quite fast, and I had to jog a little to catch up.

I was behind her now, about three feet away, and so I was close enough for her to hear me when I quietly said:

"Chloe."

She turned round quickly, and on seeing me, she looked scared. I suppose it must be frightening for a young woman, alone with her thoughts, to suddenly turn round and see a guy dressed completely in black - wearing sunglasses and a cap - who knew her name. She didn't recognise me. I have a beard now, after all. She looked at me for a moment, and composing herself, said:

"Yes?" in a bold manner.

"It's me," I said, not moving. I didn't even know what I wanted to say. She must have recognized the voice because her face froze. She still wasn't sure though and didn't say anything. She must have seen the papers. Perhaps she thought I was dead. I took off the glasses. She put her hands over her mouth, but didn't come any closer. Neither of us said anything.

"Where ..." she said, and didn't continue. She was in mild shock.

I couldn't think of anything to say, so I just said:

"Hello."

She took a small step forward, faltering a little. It seemed like she didn't dare to come any closer.

"What ...happened to you?"

She didn't mean my bruises and cuts; they had mostly healed, although the pain from the missing teeth had slowly become worse. She meant my appearance. She meant the smell. I must have looked terrible. I still didn't know what to say.

"My brother died," I said, eventually. I couldn't help it.

There was a very, very long pause while she looked me over, wide-eyed. She looked back up at my face, and while she still seemed scared, there was genuine concern in her voice when she said:

"Where have you been?" I wasn't going to tell her where I was living.

"Hiding," I said. She looked really scared then.

She must have known all about it. Bizarre disappearances don't happen a lot in Derby, and the Derby Evening Telegraph would have had a field day, never mind the national media.

"Nigel ...they say you and your brother disappeared."

"Yes."

"They're saying ...they found your mum's car. You took out all your money." Though I hadn't read a paper for a long time, I wasn't surprised because I knew they'd have to find all this out eventually. Fortunately, I'd been unrecognizable from any existing photos of myself when I met my landlord, and he was the kind of guy who was used to conveniently forgetting faces anyway. I'd always dropped the rent off with my cap and shades on as well. "It was on TV again last night," she continued. "It's a big deal, because ...he was so young.' A horrible realisation came to me. I now knew why she had looked so scared when she realized it was me.

"They say ...you might have killed him. "

I had to tell her no. She was the only one I could talk to. I had to talk.

"I didn't," was all I managed. She didn't say anything. I think she wanted to believe me. Maybe not. I had to continue. "I really didn't. He was run over. I was there. Someone ...pushed him." She didn't speak. "He was run over," I said again. She still didn't say anything. "I ran away ...it was my fault he was there. I got a place ...' But that was too much. I stopped. She still stared at me, and I think she knew I wasn't going to hurt her, but I also knew she didn't believe me. "Please, Chloe. I honestly didn't. I loved my brother more than anyone. He's gone. I can't talk to anyone. I need to talk to you. I feel like ...like I'm melting. Please." I took a step towards her and she instantly backed away a step. I felt something soften inside.

"Nigel ..." A pause. "Nigel ...you have to go to the police. Tell them what you just told me. Your family ...they must be ..."

I shook my head.

"No. I can't. I can't."

"But look at you ...Nigel, you have to."

"Chloe--"I stepped towards her again and she actually cried out: "Nigel!"

I knew this wasn't going to help. She was too scared. She had believed the news and the papers and that was it. All I was doing was scaring her. I had no one, nothing, and I had to get out of there. My head dropped.

"I'm sorry," I said. I wanted to say something else, but I turned without looking and walked away, with a strange rushing sound filling my ears and my breathing going funny. She shouted after me, and then I heard her running towards me so I started to run as well, faster than her, and I jumped into my car once I reached the other side of the car park. I started the engine and looked up through the windscreen to see her come to a stop several feet away once she knew it was too late. Then she ran away, crying. For some reason, I put the stereo on very loud before driving away, leaving her standing in the middle of the car park. I kept it on all the way back to the bedsit.

I pulled up on my street and got out of the car very slowly and gingerly, feeling as if I might shatter if I moved too fast, and walked to my front door. I was opening it when I heard a car screech to a halt nearby. A blue Punto. I heard Chloe shout my name. For some reason, I stopped in my tracks when I did so. Maybe it was the pleading tone.

I knew I should have run into the bedsit and slammed the door, maybe waited till she'd left to grab David and find somewhere else to stay, but I was so stunned – and at the same time, relieved - that I didn't move. She came running up and stood before me, panting. I looked at her blankly. Neither of us spoke.

"I passed my test," she said eventually. I wondered what she meant, then realized she had driven here.

"Chloe--"

"You HAVE to go to the police.' she said again, solemnly.

"I didn't know you had a car," I said. Her brow furrowed, and then, in a slow, bewildered voice, she said:

"It's new ...my dad got it for me as a gift when ...anyway, it doesn't matter!" She reached out a hand. "Come on. We'll go together." She placed the hand on my shoulder. 'I'll help you,' she said, looking into my eyes. I didn't move.

"How did you get here?" I asked, surprised at my own calmness.

"I followed you. Shut up and listen. Nigel ...it's for the best. You need ...you need help, and I'll help you get it. Come on. Please."

I stared at her, then shook my head.

"I can't do that, Chloe. This isn't what I came to you for. I won't go. I have to get my things now." Her eyes widened.

"Where are you going?' she asked, sounding nervous. I shrugged. My shoulders felt like lead.

"It doesn't matter, really. Somewhere else." She didn't say anything. "Just away," I continued. She looked at me, finally realizing - I think - that I wasn't going to go with her. What could she do? If she went to the police, I'd be gone before she got back, and she knew it. She tried anyway.

"I'll tell the police then, Nigel. I'll tell them and they'll come and it'll be bad, but if you come now, it'll be fine." She was speaking as if I were a child, and I knew this was an empty threat.

"You won't do that Chloe. You know I won't be here. And there isn't a phone box around here."

"What are you going to do though?" she cried, throwing her arms wide. "What are you going to do now? You can't do anything. Are you going to sit in some hole for the rest of your life? You don't deserve that. Let me help you. It'll be okay. PLEASE." She was desperate now, earnest. The hand again. I shrugged it off.

"I won't. You have to go now." She almost looked like she was going to cry.

"But what are you going to DO?" she shouted, and for the first time in weeks, the question penetrated. What was I going to do? And there was nothing, a blank void ahead that would come as my mind slid further and further downwards. If I went with Chloe, it would only happen in jail. At least if I ran I would be free ...to sit in another bedsit somewhere that might as well be a cell. My brain whirled, the world's edges became tinged with blankness, and I swayed on my feet. I thought I was going to pass out.

No purpose. No motivation.

I felt something shift in my skull and something clicked in my mind.

An idea that actually carried the faintest glimmerings at its edges. Something I had thought was gone forever. Now the question had finally broken through; the automatic process of my mind had found the answer.

I had more motivation than ever before and hadn't even realized.

Here was God showing himself in the details.

I felt something bubbling at the pit of my brain, and I actually began to smile. It must have been a frightening smile because Chloe shrank back a little, but the smile kept growing.

This was a test. A trial. And I had just passed.

Things happen for a reason - I had known this from the start! - and I had known my destiny at the start of all of this. Everyone might have secrets, and I'd been wrong about what my biggest secret would turn out to be, but MY secret would become the biggest help I would ever have. Suddenly, it all came at once, and I KNEW, I KNEW where I was going and what I was going to do, I had known it all along!

Turn it all around my friends. Turn adversity to your advantage. And I had just reframed the biggest adversity imaginable.

It all made perfect sense. It was all completely right! I was amazed I hadn't seen it before, and it all came bubbling up, and I was laughing hysterically, crying tears of joy at my revelation. Chloe looked terrified and that just seemed so funny that I kept laughing and I was FEELING, finally letting the sadness back in but that was OK because I had such good news at the same time, laughing and laughing and laughing.

"I know!" I cried to her, "I know exactly what I'm going to do! I've always known!" She stared at me wide-eyed, and I thought she was about to run, but the laughter and the tears kept coming anyway. "No, no, don't be scared!" I shouted. "You're one of the good guys! I'm one of the good guys! We're on the same side! I've found it, you see? I've had it right under my nose! It's sad, it's the saddest thing, the worst thing, but I know it creates something wonderful! Adapt! Overcome!" She looked more bewildered now than scared, and I realised she didn't understand, and so - still laughing for joy - I unlocked the front door of the terraced house and dragged Chloe towards my bedsit entrance. I unlocked it, delirious.

Chloe didn't enter, and instead, stood in the doorway looking at the air fresheners hanging everywhere. She looked confused but I knew she'd soon understand. I fell to my knees and pulled David out from under the bed, still wrapped up in his bundle.

He had given me the gift. I understood. He will have gone somewhere better for it. So, so, so tragic, but wonderful. My brother. I looked up at Chloe, who just stared at the bundle.

"Nigel ..." she said, and it was a whisper. "Nigel ..." I looked where she was looking. One of David's trainers was poking out from the end of the bundle. I had to explain, I could tell, and then she would get it. Her hand went over her face.

"All this time," I said, "And I never even realized! It was bad, but it's like the Phoenix from the flames, you know the Phoenix? Rising from the ashes. Before I was only PLAYING. The idea was there, but I wasn't COMMITTED enough for the next stage. I wouldn't have been able to start it all properly, you see? But now I can!" The smell was almost unbearable this close, but I kept laughing and laughing. "Don't you see?" I shouted, "A MEMBER OF MY FAMILY HAS BEEN KILLED. What do all the classic comic stories have? What motivates the classic heroes? It's MY motivation!" She wasn't understanding, I could see. "The ultimate motivation!" I bellowed, and then the laughter overtook me.

Chloe said nothing. She just stared at that trainer, her mouth and eyes open. Her breathing became a squeak and she looked at me.

"You ..." she gasped. Her hand went to her chest, and then she stopped breathing altogether. She fell back against the wall, mouth open and frozen, just staring and staring. I was crying more than laughing now – it was all just so EMOTIONAL - as she started breathing again, heavily, rapidly, and then started screaming.

I've have never, ever understood women.

With one last look at me, her mouth and eyes stretched to bursting as she yelled, she ran out of the door. I knew it was a shame, but it didn't really matter that much because I was back in the big picture and that was all that mattered and I was laughing and laughing.

As I collapsed on the floor, my badly healed rib screaming, I realised that this had turned into a wonderful day.

I have to go now, my friends. What more can I write? Any more will be setting your path for you, and this is supposed to only be your STARTING GUIDE. You take it from here! I am the Phoenix. I have been able to lose all my old ties, lose the unimportant sludge, and find the ultimate commitment. My personal life always got in the way, you see. It always would have. Now I am not allowed one! The pain will always be there, but now I embrace it willingly and rejoice for I have found my true calling anew. I knew I was keeping the mask for a reason.

As for my next step, I am uncertain, but I have a glorious goal to follow and I know I shall get there. It's just a matter of planning. As I write, I am in a service station on the way to Manchester. A lot of crime there, a big city. Time to stop pissing about and get on with it. I have cleared all the files from the laptop apart from this very journal. It feels very strange to be leaving it behind. I am going to leave this somewhere prominent for someone to discover and spread the word. Who will find it? Who will share it? It all starts with a single step and that step starts with YOU.

I hope reading this has helped you. I hope you have found inspiration, as I have. Plan, train, and commit, my friends. It's really very simple. Improvise, adapt, overcome.

I believe in you.

***

IF YOU ENJOYED THIS BOOK, PLEASE LEAVE A STAR RATING ON AMAZON; LUKE SMITHERD IS STILL SELF-PUBLISHED AND COULD USE ALL THE HELP HE CAN HE GET ...SO IF YOU FEEL LIKE HELPING OUT (THANK YOU!) YOU CAN DO SO ON THE BOOK'S AMAZON USA PAGE AND THE BOOK'S AMAZON UK PAGE! AND SOME GOOD NEWS; IF YOU DID ENJOY THIS BOOK, YOU MIGHT LIKE TO TRY OF ONE OF LUKE SMITHERD'S OTHER NOVELS, **IN THE DARKNESS, THAT'S WHERE I'LL KNOW YOU** *...READ ON PAST THE AUTHOR'S AFTERWORD FOR THE BEGINNING CHAPTER OF THAT VERY BOOK!*

AND HEY! MORE FREE STUFF! WANT TO GET A ***FREE STORY*** FROM LUKE SMITHERD, AND ALSO FIND OUT ABOUT HIS OTHER AVAILABLE BOOKS AS AND WHEN THEY'RE RELEASED (AND OFTEN GET *THOSE* FOR FREE AS WELL?)? THEN VISIT WWW.LUKESMITHERD.COM AND SIGN UP FOR THE ***SPAM-FREE BOOK RELEASE NEWSLETTER***, AFTER WHICH YOU'LL IMMEDIATELY BE SENT A FREE COPY OF LUKE SMITHERD'S STORY ***THE JESUS LOOPHOLE***. AND IF YOU'RE THE SOCIAL MEDIA TYPE, FOLLOW ME ON TWITTER @LUKESMITHERD OR LIKE MY FACEBOOK PAGE "LUKE SMITHERD BOOK STUFF"!

Author's Afterword:

(Note: at the time of writing, any comments made in this afterword about the number of other available books written by me are all true. However, since writing this, many more books might be out!)

This is my fifth novel, and yet it's also my very first. I haven't written the book's blurb yet, but I'll no doubt mention that fact in there so you'll perhaps already know this. Revisiting it has been a strange experience, but you might be wondering why the hell it wasn't self-published before now, especially when I've said in the past that this book would never see the light of day.

But before we get to *that* ...hello! If you're a new reader, I really hope you enjoyed this book. If you *did,* then welcome to the Smithereen collective; it's kind of a hive mind that unfortunately hasn't quite figured out what day it is. Imagine, in fact, a hive mind that's gone to Vegas for a week and is now trying to figure out how it ended up wearing a tiger costume and surrounded by empty packets of cheese. *My* kind of people.

If you *didn't* enjoy the book, then I'm genuinely sorry. It's certainly my biggest gamble, I think; if my other books are my versions of movies made by big studios, this is my cult independent movie. This book is ragged and violent and more than a little crazy. True, my other books could be described as 'crazy', but at least it was *organised* craziness. This book is my most chaotic, that's for certain, but for me that is part of its charm. If that didn't pay off for you - or you just thought that it was plain bad - then at least please accept my sincere 'thank you' for trying my work.

So ...why hasn't this book been released before now?

I'd started to write an earlier version of it many, many years ago, back when it was called *The Superhero* and I as a writer was actually a few years younger than Nigel himself. That got forgotten about and abandoned after only a few thousand words, but the idea never went away. I picked it up again a few years later and started from scratch, finally finishing it (despite the 1998 setting) in 2001. I gave it a cursory redraft and started sending – at great expense – an absolutely terrible and huge bundle of sample chapters out to various publishers and agents. It weighed a ton and cost a fortune to post. In hindsight, knowing the 'quality' of that bundle, I am utterly amazed to think of how disappointed I was to get an endless series of rejection letters ...but even so, it was enough for me to completely abandon any hopes of becoming a writer. It wasn't until 2008/2009 that I discovered that it was possible to bypass that process entirely and self-publish onto the Kindle store. No Kindle store, no writing career; I'm not sure that I would have ever bothered writing another book again. I found the rejection really devastating if I'm honest. I did have, as I've mentioned in the past, a life-changing meeting with someone the same age as me who'd managed to get a book published, making me determined to do the same ...but would I have stuck it out through another series of rejections? I don't know. I hope so.

So anyway: I wrote my second novel (which a lot of people know as being my first) and fired it onto the Kindle store in 2011. Not a lot happened with it but I still went ahead and followed that with *The Stone Man* anyway ...and the rest is history.

But again: why didn't I release this book as my second/third novel?

Another big problem was that it was *missing.*

I had a printed and bound copy that I'd covered with marker pen notes for a future rewrite, and I knew that at least one friend had another physical copy but they wouldn't know where it was ... but I didn't have a digital copy of it anymore. No Word file, no PDF, nothing. Lost somewhere in the course of moving house twelve times in fifteen years.

I hunted high and low for the original digital file, hoping that maybe I'd emailed myself a copy (I do that a lot these days) at some point in the past, but to no avail. Then the *biggest* problem happened.

The movie *Kick Ass* was released.

Most of you will have already made the *Kick Ass* comparison – young man tries to become a real-life vigilante, complete with nightsticks – and I obviously made the same connection myself. As soon as I heard about it – despite the fact that the comic the movie was based on began publication seven years *after* I'd written *my* book – that was it. *The Diary of Nigel Carmelite* (original title) was consigned to be nothing but a paperweight on my parents' bookshelf. I didn't want people claiming I'd ripped something off when I'd actually written mine first (and by a good margin at that.)

Then earlier this year, I had a very clear thought:

"Fuck *Kick Ass.*"

It's a very different type of storyline; what happens to Kick Ass himself is exactly what Nigel only *imagines* happening; fame and notoriety and real villains to fight. An actual superhero career, over-the-top and cartoonish yet still based in a 'real' world. Mine went the other way; *hyper*-real in the sheer mundane nature of its surroundings, zero colour, and a career doomed to tragedy and failure. I've no doubt a lot of you are thinking *yeah, and Kick Ass was a lot better for it!* You might well be right; I don't know; I liked the film myself. But this book is - despite being a similar *concept* – a very different execution. Plus, there's a million fucking zombie books out there and no one complains about that so basically fuck offRAAAAAAAAAAAAAA

Ahem. Sorry. So: I decided to extensively redraft Carmelite and then publish. The problem was only having my own note-riddled physical copy, and no *digital* copy. It turned out that two other friends also still had a physical copy, but one of those was in storage in Geneva (the copy, not the friend) and the other guy kept forgetting to look for his. I decided that I'd have to try and do something with my existing copy and hope the handwritten notes weren't a problem. I was even considering just retyping the whole thing. Ugh.

Then I discovered that - if I could get the whole book scanned page by page, which amazingly only cost £50 - I could pay someone online to scan the digitised images with OCR technology (software that recognises letters on a page) and then manually correct some of the gobbledygook that would come up (i.e.: the words 'hello I'm Nigel' with my notes over the top saying 'edit this out' would translate via OCR to be 'he3%$; m Nigel'.) Amazingly, that only cost about £80. Now I had a workable digital copy of my fifteen-year-old story back. Yeah, I love the future too.

As I say, it's been strange going back through the text; not only seeing the mentality I and other people had at the time (the character using phone booths, the idea of buying something online being a novel concept) but how I'd used a lot of the surnames of my friends as the names of roads and pubs and places. Most of those friends are still a part of my life; some of them are acquaintances, and some were names that I can't even place at all anymore. That last group of names were changed for this edition.

More strange than that are some of the coincidences I found; by chance, I used a real Coventry street name for the road that Nigel sleeps on when he drives there after David's death (a friend of mine's parents lived there): Cecily Road. I didn't know that, two years later, I would meet a girl and move back to Coventry, living for two years with her and her parents on ...yep. Cecily Road. I still wince very much when I remember how I never paid any rent and ate their food. Christ, if any of you are reading this, I am sincerely and deeply sorry about that.

I had Nigel buy his car in Earlsdon, a part of Coventry that, at the time of writing, I never ever visited. I didn't know that Earlsdon would, nearly ten years later, become my home for five years.

The real capper – one I'd completely forgotten – is that Nigel is heading for Manchester at the end of the story. And have a guess where – by sheer coincidence – I ended up staying while I redrafted the book, and where I'm writing these very words right now?

Many of you will know that Coventry is the setting for pretty much all of my stories. Hey, if King can do Maine ...after many years of off-and-on living there, I've finally moved out of good ol' Cov and don't see myself moving back. It's not that I don't like the place. I do. In my own way, I love it. But I feel funny when I visit now; there's a lot of warmth and memories tied to the place, and this makes it feel like visiting an old life that I'm not a part of anymore. Like visiting a childhood home and finding another family living there. It's not a nice feeling. It's been a strange twelve months or so since I last wrote one of these afterwords; some shocking and heart breaking stuff has happened that I'd never thought I'd experience ...yet a *lot* of exciting adventures and new people. The future is exciting, and I'm heading towards that with open arms.

It's also funny to see how certain themes and ideas were written here first before popping up in other books; Nigel uses the cinema and TV to stave off madness (*The Physics of the Dead*) and wonders where his bravery was (*The Stone Man,* and *Kill Someone. Anyone,* coming soon in 2016! Or already out if you're reading this in 2017 or later!).

The biggest thing of all is looking back to see, after five years (fifteen if you include the first version of this book) how much my career has changed. To have gone from a young idiot wondering why his not-even-spellchecked manuscript kept being returned with a standard response cover letter, to making a full-time living as a writer and having signed a contract with Audible.com for them to publish and market my next audiobook. That's right folks, I can stop adding "Oh, but, like ...self-published" when I tell people what I do for a living. Audiobooks have been a very unexpected and surprising avenue for me, bringing in a lot of new readers and even my first award nomination (Audiobook of the Year 2015 for *The Stone Man.*) It's very humbling, and I'm very grateful every day that all the work is starting to pay off.

But it was *you* guys that made all this happen, those of you who left your star ratings (more on that, of course, very shortly ...you know the craven-review-begging drill by now) and even better, those of you who spread the word. Thank you *so* much. I know I always say it, but I hope you understand that I mean it.

I *really* hope you liked it. I was a younger man when I wrote this novel, and if you think that this book was dark and violent, you should have seen a lot of the stuff that I chopped out.

If you can leave a star rating for this book on Amazon, that would be amazing. I still need as many as I can get. And if you do it before *Kill Someone. Anyone.* gets released, YOUR name will go into the Acknowledgements section of that book! Y'know ...if you could do it now before you forget, I'd really appreciate it. Acknowledgements for the *last* book are, of course, coming up at the back of this one if you missed it at the start.

Normally I tell people to follow me on Facebook (Luke Smitherd Book Stuff) and Twitter (@lukesmitherd) and you can of course do that, but I've recently learned just how much stuff Facebook doesn't actually show to a page's followers. If you really want to make sure you don't miss a release, sign up to the Spam Free Book Release Newsletter at lukesmitherd.com as well.

Plus! You might have noticed a list of 'Smithereens With Titles' in the acknowledgements section. Would you like one? You would? (For the love of God ...*why??*) Well then, all you gotta do is drop me an email saying what title you'd like, and for where, and by golly it will be yours and will appear in the next acknowledgements section. I've had to introduce a few restrictions though seeing as *some* Smithereens have gone power mad and claimed entire freakin' states ...I like their big thinking, but from now on, you can't have: States, counties, or countries. Think *specifics.* Yes, for example, rule of the whole Massachusetts might be already taken (looking at *you*, President Morgan!) but hey! What's wrong with being, say, Mayor Smithereen of ...uh ...(googlegooglegoogle) Lexington? Or even just Robber Baron Smithereen of the office photocopier? You get the idea. Drop me a line at luke@lukesmitherd.com.

Thanks as ever folks. You've stuck with me this far, and I *really* hope I still haven't let you down. See you for *Kill Someone. Anyone.* later this year.

Stay Hungry,

Luke Smitherd
Northern Quarter
Manchester
July 20th 2016

And now for the beginning of one of Luke Smitherd's other books, IN THE DARKNESS, THAT'S WHERE I'LL KNOW YOU, available on Amazon!

IN THE DARKNESS, THAT'S WHERE I'LL KNOW YOU

By Luke Smitherd

Chapter One: An Unexpected Point of View, Proof That You Can Never Go Home Again, and The Importance of the Work/Life Balance
***

Charlie opened his eyes and was immediately confused. A quick reassessment of the view, however, confirmed that he was right; he suddenly had breasts. Not very noticeable ones, perhaps, but when he'd spent over thirty years without them, even the appearance of a couple of A-cups was a real attention grabber. As he continued to look down, the very next thing to come to his attention was the material covering them; a purple, stretchy cotton fabric, something he had never worn, nor had he ever harboured any plans to do so. As he watched his hands adjust the top, he came to the most alarming realisation of all; those weren't his hands doing the adjusting. The giveaway wasn't in the slenderness of the fingers, or the medium-length (if a little ragged) fingernails upon their tips, or even in the complete lack of any physical sensation as he watched the digits tug and pull the purple top into position. It was the fact that, while they were clearly stuck to the end of arms that were attached to his shoulders (or at least, the painfully skinny shoulders that he could see either side of his head's peripheral vision; his shoulders were bigger than that, surely?) they were moving entirely of their own accord.

He was so stunned that he almost felt calm. The bizarreness of the situation had already passed straight through *this is crazy* and out the other side into the utterly incomprehensible. Charlie stared dumbly for several seconds as his mind got caught in a feeble loop, trying and failing to get its bearings (*What ... sorry, what ... sorry, WHAT ...*) While, in that moment, he never really came any closer to coming to terms with the situation, his mind did at least manage to reach the next inevitable conclusion: this wasn't his body.

The loop got louder as these unthinkable, too-big-for-conscious-process thoughts instantly doubled in size, but got nowhere (*WHAT ... WHAT ... WHAT THE FUCK*). All Charlie was capable of doing was staring at the view in front of him as it moved from a downward angle, swinging upwards to reveal a door being opened onto a narrow hallway. A second doorway was then passed through, and now Charlie found himself in a bathroom. He wanted to look down again, to see the feet that were carrying him forward, to help understand that he wasn't doing the walking, to aid him in *any* kind of conscious comprehension of his situation ... but he quickly realised that he couldn't affect the line of sight in any way. The viewing angle was completely out of his control. Instinctively, he tried to commandeer the limbs that were attached to him, to move the arms like he would have done on any other minute of any other day since his birth, but there was no response. There was only the *illusion* of control; the moment when one of the hands reached for the door handle at the same time that he would have intended them to, as he reflexively thought of performing the motion simultaneously. What the fuck was going on? *What the fuck was going on?*

The crazy, unthinkable answer came again, despite his crashed mind, even in a moment of sheer madness—what other conclusion was there to reach?—as he saw the feminine hands reach for a toothbrush on the sink: he was in someone else's body—a woman's body—and he was not in control.

Incapable of speech, Charlie watched as the view swung up from the sink to look into the plastic-framed bathroom mirror, and while he began to notice the detail in his surroundings properly—tiny bathroom, cheap fittings, slightly grubby tiles, and candles, candles everywhere—the main focus of his concern was the face looking back at him.

The eyes he was looking through belonged to a woman of hard-to-place age; she looked to be in her mid- to late-twenties, but even to Charlie's goggling, shell-shocked point of view, there was clearly darkness both under and inside her green eyes (physically and metaphorically speaking) that made her look older. Her skin was pale, and the tight, bouncy, but frazzled curls of her shoulder-length black hair all added to the haunted manner that the woman possessed.

All of which Charlie didn't give a flying shit about, of course; thoughts were beginning to come together, and his mind was already rallying and coming back online. While Charlie would never describe himself as a practical man, having spent most of his life more concerned with where the next laugh was coming from rather than the next paycheque, he had always been resourceful, capable of taking an objective step backwards in a tight spot and saying *Okay, let's have a look at this.* While he was beyond that now—had he been in his own body, that body would have been hyperventilating—he was now aware enough to at least think more clearly. As the woman continued to brush her teeth, Charlie watched, and thought the one thing to himself that instantly made everything else easier:

This is probably a dream. This is fucking mental, so it's got to be a dream. So there's nothing to worry about, is there?

While he didn't fully believe that—the view was too real, the surroundings too complete and detailed, the grit and grime too fleshed out and realised—it enabled him to take the necessary mental step back, and put his foot on the brake of his runaway mind a little.

Okay. Think. Think. This can't actually be happening. It can't. It's a lucid dream, that's what it is. Calm down. Calm down. That means you can decide what happens, right? You're supposed to be able to control a lucid dream, aren't you? So let's make ... the wall turn purple. That'll do. Wall. Turn purple ... now.

The wall remained exactly the same, and the view shifted downward briefly to reveal an emerging spray of water and foaming toothpaste. The woman had just spat.

Right. Maybe it's not quite one of those dreams then, maybe it's just a very, very realistic one. Don't panic. You can prove this. Think back. Think back through your day, think what you'd been doing, and you'll remember going to bed. What were you last doing?

He'd met the boys, gone for a drink—excited about the prospect of one turning into many—the first night out for a little while. Clint's mate Jack had been over from London too, which was both a good excuse and good news for the quality of the night. They had ended up on a heavy pub crawl, and somebody had said something about going back to their place ... Neil. That guy Neil had said it. And they'd gone to Neil's, and then ...

Nothing. Nothing from there on in. And now he was here. As he felt hysteria start to rise, escalating from the panic that he already felt, Charlie frantically tried to put a lid on it before it got badly out of control.

You passed out. You had some more to drink and you passed out. That's why you can't remember what happened at Neil's, and this is the resultant booze-induced crazy dream. So wake up. Wake your ass up. Slap yourself in the face and wake the fuck up.

Charlie did so, his hand slamming into the side of his head with the force of fear behind it, and as the ringing sting rocked him, he became aware that he suddenly had a physical presence of his own. If he had a hand to swing and a head to hit, then he now had a body of his own. A body inside this woman's body? Where the hell had that come from?

There'd been nothing before, no response from anything when he'd tried to move the woman's arms earlier. He'd been a disembodied mind, a ghost inside this woman's head, but now when he looked down he saw his own torso, naked and standing in a space consisting of nothing but blackness. Looking around himself to confirm it, seeing the darkness stretching away around him in all directions and now having a body to respond to his emotion, Charlie collapsed onto an unseen floor and lay gasping and whooping in lungfuls of nonexistent air, his body trembling.

His wide, terrified eyes stared straight ahead, the view that had previously seemed to be his own vision now appearing suspended in the air, a vast image the size of a cinema screen with edges that faded away into the inky-black space around him. Its glow was ethereal, like nothing he'd ever seen before. How had he thought that had been his own-eye view? It had clearly been there all along, hanging there in the darkness. Had he just been standing too close? Had something changed? Either way, there was no mistake now; there was just him, the enormous screen showing the woman's point of view, and the black room in which he lay.

Charlie pulled his knees up into a ball and watched the screen as he lay there whimpering. That slap had hurt badly, and instead of waking him, it had added another frightening new dimension to the situation. He was terrified; he lay for a moment in mental and physical shock, and for now, at least, everything was beyond him. The words that he feebly tried to repeat to himself fell on deaf ears—*it's a dream it's a dream it's a dream*—and so he lay there for a while, doing nothing but watch and tremble as the woman made a sandwich, checked her e-mails on her phone, and moved to sit in front of her TV. She flicked through channels, thumbed through her Facebook feed. As this time passed—and Charlie still watched, incapable of anything else for the time being—he came back to himself a little more. He noticed that, while he was naked, he wasn't cold. He wasn't warm either, however; in fact, the concept of either sensation seemed hard to comprehend, like trying to understand what the colour red sounded like. Thoughts crept in again.

You can't actually be in her head. You can't actually be INSIDE her head. People don't have screens behind their eyes or huge holes where their brain should be. You know that. You haven't been shrunk and stuffed in here, as that's not possible. So this ... HAS ... to be a dream. Right? You have a voice, don't you? You can speak, can't you? Can you get your breath long enough to speak?

Charlie opened his mouth, and found that speech was almost outside of his capabilities. A strange, strangled squeak came out of his throat, barely audible, and he felt no breath come from his lungs. He tried several more times, shaping his mouth around the sound in an attempt to form words, but got nowhere.

Focus, you fucking arsehole. Focus.

Eventually, he managed to squeak out a word that sounded a bit like *hey* and, encouraged by that success, he tried to repeat it. He managed to say it again on the third try, then kept going, the word getting slightly louder each time until something gave way and the bass came into his voice.

"Hey ..."

With that, the ability to speak dropped into place, even if getting the hang of it again took a real physical effort. He at least knew *how* to do it

262

now, his mind remembering the logistics of speech like a dancer going through a long-abandoned but previously well-rehearsed routine. He looked out through the screen with sudden purpose, determined to find out if she could hear him.

"Hey ... *hey* ..." he gasped, his lips feeling loose and clumsy, as if they were new to his face. Charlie sat up, hoping to get more volume behind it, more projection. He thought he had to at least be as loud as the TV for her to hear him, if she was capable of doing so at all.

"*HEY*," he managed, but there was no external response. Charlie's heart sank, and he almost abandoned the whole attempt. After all, it was easier and more reassuring to resign himself to the only real hope that he had; that this truly *was* a dream, and thus something he could hopefully wait out until his alarm clock broke the spell and returned him to blessed normality. Things might have turned out very differently if he had, but instead Charlie found the strength to kneel upright and produce something approaching a scream.

"*HEY!!*" he squawked, and fell back onto his behind, exhausted. Staring at the glowing screen before him, dejected, Charlie then saw a hand come up into view, holding the remote control. A finger hit the mute button.

Charlie froze.

The image on the screen swung upwards, showing the white ceiling with its faint yellowing patches marking it here and there, and hung in that direction for a second or two. It then travelled back to the TV screen, and as the hand holding the remote came up again, Charlie realised what was happening and felt a fresh jolt of panic. Without thinking, he blurted out a noise, desperately needing to cause any kind of sound in an attempt to be heard, like a fallen and undiscovered climber hearing the rescue party beginning to move on.

"*BAARGH! BA BA BAAA!*" Charlie screeched, falling forwards as he almost dove towards the screen in his clumsy response to the images upon it. The hand hesitated, and then the view was getting up and travelling across the living room and down the hallway. It looked like the woman was going to look through the spyhole in her front door, and as she did so, the fish-eye effect of the glass on the huge screen made Charlie's stomach lurch. He still saw the fairly dirty-looking stairwell outside, however, and realised that the woman was inside some sort of apartment block.

Charlie stared, trying desperately to pull himself together, and assessed the situation. She could hear him then; but she certainly didn't seem to be aware that he was there. So she could be as unwilling in all of this as he was?

It'sadreamitdoesn'tmatteranywayit'salladreamsowhocares—

He didn't believe that though. He just couldn't. There had to be some sort of explanation, and he couldn't be physically *in* her head, so this was ... an out of body experience? Some sort of psychic link?

Charlie surprised himself with his own thoughts. Where the hell had all of that come from, all of those sudden, rational thoughts? True, he'd been confronted with something so impossible that he didn't really have much choice but to look at the available options, but ... was he suddenly adjusting again? When this all started, he didn't even have a body, but one quickly appeared. Was his mind following suit? He was still trembling, his shoulders still rising and falling dramatically with each rapid, shallow in-breath of nothing, but his mind was at work now;

the shock had seemingly been absorbed and moved past far more quickly than it should have been, he was sure. Would he be this rational already if he were in his own body? Whatever was going on, being here was ... different. He felt his mental equilibrium returning, his awareness and presence of mind growing. He was scared, and he was confused, but he was getting enough of a grip to at least function.

You have her attention. Don't lose it.

He opened his mouth again, got nowhere, reset himself, then tried again.

"Lady?"

The view jerked round, then everything in sight became slightly farther away, very quickly; she'd spun around, and fallen backwards against the apartment's front door. The view then swung sharply left and right to either side of the hallway, looking to the bathroom doorway and then to the doorway of another, unspecified room. Charlie assumed it was a bedroom. He tried again.

"Can ... can you hear me?"

The view jerked violently. She'd clearly just jumped out of her skin, her fresh adrenaline putting all of her physical flight reflexes on full alert. It was a dumb question to ask—she obviously could—but even with his growing sense of control, Charlie's mind was still racing, his incredulity at the situation now combining with the excitement of finding that he could communicate with his unsuspecting host.

It was clear that she was terrified, and Charlie realised that he couldn't blame her. She was hearing a voice within the safety of her home when she'd thought that she was by herself, and Charlie could only guess what it sounded like to this woman. Did his voice sound as if he were right behind her, or was she hearing it actually coming from the inside of her head? Charlie couldn't decide which would be worse.

Get a grip, man. Of course she's going to shit herself when you start talking to her. Just ... try and think, okay? Think straight. You have to get out of this. You need her to talk to you; you need her if you're ever going to get this sorted out. Get a grip, get control, and think smart.

"Please, it's—" He didn't get any further as the jump came again, this time with a little scream; it was a brief squeal, clipped short as if she were trying to avoid drawing attention to herself. Charlie jumped with her this time, startled a little himself, but pressed on. "Please, *please* don't be scared. I'm shitting myself here too. Please. Please calm down—" The second half of this sentence was lost, however, disappearing under a fresh scream from the woman. This time it was a hysterical, lengthy one that travelled with her as she ran the length of the hallway into the living room, slamming the door behind her. Charlie heard her crying and panting, and watched her thin hands grab one end of the small sofa and begin to drag it in front of the door. The scream trailed off as she did so, and once the job was done, the view backed away from the door, bobbing slightly in time with the woman's whimpering tears and gasping breath.

Charlie was hesitant to speak again; he knew that he simply had to, but what could he actually say without sending her off into fresh hysterics? The answer was immediate; nothing. There was no way to do it easily. She would have to realise that she was *physically* alone at least—and safe with it—and the only way to help her do that was to keep talking until she accepted that there was no intruder in her home.

Not on the outside, anyway.

"I need your help," he tried, wincing as the view leapt almost a foot upwards and then spun on the spot, accompanied by fresh wails. "Please, lady, you're safe—" The cries increased in volume, to the point where he had to raise his voice to be heard. In doing so, Charlie realised that he now had his voice under complete control. And wasn't the blackness around him a fraction less dark now, too? "Look, just calm down, all right? If you just listen for two seconds, you'll find that—"

"*Fuck oooooffff!!*" she screamed, the volume of it at a deafening level from Charlie's perspective. He clapped his hands to the side of his head, wincing and crouching from the sheer force of it. It was like being in the centre of a sonic hurricane. "*Get out of my flat! Get out of my flaaaaaaat!!!*"

"Please!! Please don't do that!" Charlie shouted, trying to be heard over the woman's yelling. "Look, just shut up for a second, I don't *want* to be here, I just want to—"

"*Get out! Where are you? Get out!! Get oooouuuuuttt!!*"she yelled, ignoring him, and as the view dropped to the floor and shot backwards—the living room walls now framing either side of the screen—Charlie realised that she'd dropped onto her ass and scooted backwards into the corner, backing into the space where the sofa had previously been. Frustrated, terrified, in pain and pushed to his limit (it had been one hell of an intense five minutes, after all) Charlie let fly with a scream of his own, hands balled into fists over his throbbing ears.

"*JUST SHUT THE FUCK UP FOR A SECOND!!*" he screamed, and whether it was from using some volume of his own, or because her own screams were already about to descend into hysterical, terrified and silent tears, the only sound after Charlie's shout was that of the woman's whimpers. The view still darted around the room though, trying to find the source of the sound, a source well beyond her sight.

Charlie seized his moment. At the very least he could be heard, and *that* hopefully meant he could start talking her down. She was more terrified than him—of course she was, at least he'd had time to get used to the situation whereas she'd just discovered an apparently invisible intruder in her home—but he had to get through to her while she was at least quiet enough to hear him. Hysterical or not, she had ears, even if he appeared to be currently standing somewhere in between them.

"Look, I'm sorry for shouting like that, I just need you to listen for a second, okay? Just listen," Charlie said, as soothingly as his own panicking mind would allow. "I'm not going to hurt you, okay? Okay? It's fine, you're, uh … you're not in any danger, all right?"

"Where … where are you? *Where are you?*" the woman's voice sobbed breathlessly, small and scared. Her thinking was clear from the confusion in her voice; she was finally realising that she should be able to see the person talking to her, that there was nowhere in the room that they could be hiding. Charlie thought quickly, and decided that it was best to leave that one for a minute. He'd only just got her onside, and didn't want to push her over the edge.

"I'll tell you in a second. I'm, uh … I'm not actually in the room, you see. You're alone in the flat, and you're safe. You're fine. Okay?" She didn't reply at first. The sobs continued helplessly, but Charlie thought that they might have been slightly lessened, if only due to confusion.

"Wha … what?" she stammered, the view swinging wildly around the room now. "Your voice … what the fuck … *what the fuck is going onnnnnn* …." And then she was off again, the hysterical screaming coming back at fever pitch. Charlie stood in front of the strange, glowing screen, his hands at his ears again while she bawled, blinking rapidly as his mind worked. After a moment or two, his shoulders slumped and he sat down. There was nothing he could do but wait, and let her adjust. His own breathing was beginning to slow further, and he was finding acceptance of his situation to still be an easier task than he thought; while it was no less mind boggling, his panic was dropping fast, and unusually so.

It's being in here that's doing it. It has to be.

Either way, he let her have a minute or two to calm down. Eventually, he stood and began to pace back and forth in the darkness— illuminated dimly by the unusual light of the screen—while he decided what to say next. His frantic mind kept trying to wander, to seize and wrestle all the aspects of the situation into submission, and failed every time.

You don't like the dark. You don't like the dark! Don't think about it, don't think about it … think about … wait … there's no breeze in here, no echo. It really is a room of sorts then, a space with walls on all sides?

He looked out into the darkness, looking for walls, and saw none; there was only seemingly endless blackness. Charlie thought it would be best not to go exploring *just* yet. Instead, he tried to control his breathing, and quickly ran through a mental list, double checking his actions and decisions of the previous few days before his night out:

Went to work. Did the late shift. Argued about sci-fi films with Clint. Helped Steve throw the drunk arsehole out that had started slapping his girlfriend. Went home, stayed up and watched a film because I had the Wednesday off. Met Chris in town—

And so it went on. By the time he'd finished a few minutes later—while he was no clearer about what had led him to be inside this woman's head—he told himself that he really *did* feel more capable of beginning to deal with things, and less frightened; in the absolute worst case, even though he didn't believe this to be the *actual* case, this situation was real, and had to be resolved. If he'd got in, then he could get out, and if this was the *best*—and more likely—scenario, where this was all just a dream, then he would wake up and all would be well.

Yeah. And if I had wheels, I'd be a wagon.

Charlie took a deep breath, and decided to speak again.

"Are you okay?" he said. The view jumped again, along with a fresh scream.

For fuck's sake.

"Look, we're not going to get anywhere if you keep doing that," Charlie said, not being able to keep the frustration out of his voice. "I'm sure you're a smart person really, so just knock the screaming and shit on the head and we can work together to sort this all out, right? For crying out loud, if I'm not *there*, I can't exactly do anything to you, can I? I know you're scared, and I know this must have been a hell of a shock, but I'm not exactly a million dollars myself right this minute. So, please ... come on. Just ... have a minute, sort yourself out, and then we'll ... then we'll carry on," he finished, shrugging his shoulders in annoyed impotence. He knew that he was perhaps being a little harsh, but he couldn't help thinking that he had a bit of a flake on his hands here. Being scared was one thing, but a complete collapse like this was another.

Don't be a dick, Charlie, he reprimanded himself. *You don't know what she's been through before now. You might be squatting in her head, but you don't know anything about her.*

It was a fair point. She seemed to respond better to his last outburst though, and the sobbing was now drying up into skipping little breaths. She wasn't responding to his annoyance, Charlie thought, but it might have been the honest approach that got through. Sometimes people just appreciated it.

"Your voice ..." she said, and her own was steadier, but uncertain. "Where—" She hesitated, seeming to try and find a different question to ask, something else to say that would stop her from repeating herself. She gave up. "Where are you? Where ... where *are* you?"

She's not going to drop that one. Would you, in her shoes?

Again, a fair point, and Charlie decided that the honest approach had seemed to work before.

"Look ... okay, I'll tell you," he said, trying to find words to describe the impossible, "and I don't understand it in the slightest myself, but it's ... it's pretty heavy shit, okay? I mean, well, I don't mean heavy as in serious, as I've no idea what *it* really is, but I mean heavy as in ... hard to get your head around. It's ... *weird.* And we can't be having any of the freaking out stuff you were doing earlier, okay? I need you to work with me. Okay?"

Silence.

"Okay?"

Another pause, and then the view nodded quickly; a rapid, brief up and down motion that would have been barely noticeable to an outside observer, but seemed to Charlie as if her flat had been caught in an earthquake.

"Okay," she replied quietly, her voice breathy and small.

"Right …" said Charlie, speaking slowly and trying to prepare each word carefully. "I don't know how this has happened, or why, but the last thing I remember is being on a night out with my mates, we were out in … wait … hang on, where is this? Where do you live?"

"Huh?"

"Which city? Which city are you in right now?"

"Coventry."

"Jesus! That's where I live!"

"… okay."

In the brief pause that followed while she waited for him to continue, his mind grabbed the thought and filed it away for later. It might be relevant. Maybe they'd been somewhere in the city, been *through* something, something that caused a connection …

It's a dream, remember? This is down to cheese and too many pints, or a bad kebab.

He dragged his wandering thoughts back on track, and continued.

"Anyway, *anyway*, we were out in Cov, and then we went back to someone's house, and then, I don't know, I must have fallen asleep or drank too much or whatever, but somehow … *some*how …"

He stumbled, tripping at the vital hurdle.

"What?" she asked, the view still scanning around the room, as if hoping to find the answers there.

"Ah … ah *fuck* it, look, I, I, I woke up or whatever and here I am, in your fucking head. I don't know how I got here, and hell, I might be gone in the next five minutes for all I know, but I'm here, I'm in your head, here I am. That's it."

Silence again. Then:

"You're ... you're what?"

"I'm in your head. I'm standing here, in front of this, this ..." He waved his hands in front of the immense, ethereal screen before him, taking it in as yet another rapid flicker shivered across it. These had been happening constantly; later he would realise that this effect was due to her blinking. "This screen thing, okay, and everywhere else in here it's just black, and I'm stood here, completely ..." he trailed off, looking down at his genitals and deciding that it would probably be best not to mention the nakedness to a scared woman who is stuck in a flat on her own, "... completely without any idea as to what's going on."

Silence again. Then:

"A screen ... there's a screen in my head?" she asked. "What ... what screen, what the hell are you talking about?"

Charlie rubbed at his face, angry now, both with himself and her. Of course she didn't get it, it was un-gettable, but she wasn't even coming *close* to understanding and he was doing a lousy job of explaining it. He needed to get the important facts across if they were ever going to move on, and spare her the more intricate details. He needed a different approach.

"Look, don't worry about that, forget it, forget it. Listen. Right, okay, I'll start again. My name is Charlie. Charlie Wilkes. What's yours?"

There was a long, uncertain silence.

"Minnie," she replied, her voice shaking again. She was about to go any second, he could tell.

Talk her down.

"Are you scared to talk to me?" asked Charlie, as tenderly as he could manage. "You don't have to be. Talk to me. What's your surname?"

THE STORY CONTINUES IN '*IN THE DARKNESS, THAT'S WHERE I'LL KNOW YOU*' AVAILABLE *NOW* ON AMAZON!

Also By Luke Smitherd:

WEIRD. DARK.

PRAISE FOR *WEIRD. DARK.:*

"WEIRD and DARK, yes, but more importantly ... exciting and imaginative. Whether you've read his novels and are already a fan or these short stories are your first introduction to Smitherd's work, you'll be blown away by the abundance of ideas that can be expressed in a small number of pages." - Ain't It Cool News.com

Luke Smitherd is bringing his unique brand of strange storytelling once again, delivered here in an omnibus edition that collects four of his weirdest and darkest tales:

MY NAME IS MISTER GRIEF: what if you could get rid of your pain immediately? What price would you be prepared to pay?

HOLD ON UNTIL YOUR FINGERS BREAK: a hangover, a forgotten night out, old men screaming in the street, and a mystery with a terrible, terrible answer ...

THE MAN ON TABLE TEN: he has a story to tell you. One that he has kept secret for decades. But now, the man on table ten can take no more, and the knowledge - as well as the burden - is now yours.

EXCLUSIVE story, THE CRASH: if you put a dent in someone's car, the consequences can be far greater - and more strange - than you expect.

Available in both paperback and Kindle formats on Amazon and as an audiobook on Audible.

Also By Luke Smitherd:

The Stone Man

The #1 Amazon Horror Bestseller

Two-bit reporter Andy Pointer had always been unsuccessful (and antisocial) until he got the scoop of his career; the day a man made of stone appeared in the middle of his city.

This is his account of everything that came afterwards and what it all cost him, along with the rest of his country.

The destruction, the visions ... the dying.

Available in both paperback and Kindle formats on Amazon and as an audiobook on Audible.

Also By Luke Smitherd:

The Physics of the Dead

What do the dead do when they can't leave ... and don't know why?

The afterlife doesn't come with a manual. In fact, Hart and Bowler (two ordinary, but dead men) have had to work out the rules of their new existence for themselves. It's that fact—along with being unable to leave the boundaries of their city centre, unable to communicate with the other lost souls, unable to rest in case The Beast should catch up to them, unable to even sleep—that makes getting out of their situation a priority.

But Hart and Bowler don't know why they're there in the first place, and if they ever want to leave, they will have to find all the answers in order to understand the physics of the dead: What are the strange, glowing objects that pass across the sky? Who are the living people surrounded by a blue glow? What are their physical limitations in that place, and have they fully explored the possibilities of what they can do?

Time is running out; their afterlife was never supposed to be this way, and if they don't make it out soon, they're destined to end up like the others.

Insane, and alone forever ...

Also By Luke Smitherd:

IN THE DARKNESS, THAT'S WHERE I'LL KNOW YOU

What Is The Black Room?

There are hangovers, there are bad hangovers, and then there's waking up someone else's head. Thirty-something bartender Charlie Wilkes is faced with this exact dilemma when he wakes to find finds himself trapped inside The Black Room; a space consisting of impenetrable darkness and a huge, ethereal screen floating in its centre. Through this screen he is shown the world of his female host, Minnie.

How did he get there? What has happened to his life? And how can he exist inside the mind of a troubled, fragile, but beautiful woman with secrets of her own? Uncertain whether he's even real or if he is just a figment of his host's imagination, Charlie must enlist Minnie's help if he is to find a way out of The Black Room, a place where even the light of the screen goes out every time Minnie closes her eyes...

Previously released in four parts as, "The Black Room" series, all four parts are combined in this edition. In The Darkness, That's Where I'll Know You starts with a bang and doesn't let go. Each answer only leads to another mystery in a story guaranteed to keep the reader on the edge of their seat.

THE BLACK ROOM SERIES, FOUR SERIAL NOVELLAS THAT UNRAVEL THE PUZZLE PIECE BY PIECE, NOW AVAILABLE IN ONE COLLECTED EDITION:

IN THE DARKNESS, THAT'S WHERE I'LL KNOW YOU

Available in both paperback and Kindle formats on Amazon and as an audiobook on Audible.

Also By Luke Smitherd:

A HEAD FULL OF KNIVES

Martin Hogan is being watched all the time. He just doesn't know it yet. It started a long time ago too, even before his wife died. Before he started walking every day.

Before the walks became an attempt to find a release from the whirlwind that his brain has become. He never walks alone, of course, although his 18-month old son and his faithful dog, Scoffer, aren't the greatest conversationalists.

Then the walks become longer. Then the *other* dog starts showing up. The big white one, with the funny looking head. The one that sits and watches Martin and his family as they walk away.

All over the world, the first attacks begin. The Brotherhood of the Raid make their existence known; a leaderless group who randomly and inexplicably assault both strangers and loved ones without explanation.

Martin and the surviving members of his family are about to find that these events are connected. Caught at the center of the world as it changes beyond recognition, Martin will be faced with a series of impossible choices ... but how can an ordinary and broken man figure out the unthinkable? What can he possibly do with a head full of knives?

Luke Smitherd (author of the Amazon bestseller THE STONE MAN and IN THE DARKNESS, THAT'S WHERE I'LL KNOW YOU) asks you once again to consider what you would do in his unusual and original novel. A HEAD FULL OF KNIVES is a supernatural mystery that will not only change the way you look at your pets forever, but will force you to decide the fate of the world when it lies in your hands.

Available now in both paperback, Kindle, and audiobook formats.

Also By Luke Smitherd:

Do Anything:

Tales of the Unusual

In *DO ANYTHING*, Luke Smitherd brings you two more Tales Of The Unusual

Choices Have Consequences

In *CLOSURE*, Gary's wife Carla is kidnapped by a wild-eyed version of...himself. Now he must decide whether to use the strange device left behind by his unknown twin to open a gateway to...somewhere in hopes of finding his wife.

In *YOUR NAME IS IN THE BOOK*, eleven-year-old John finds a book that contains thousands of names, accompanied by a one-digit number assigned to each. John doesn't know what the numbers mean, nor does he know that the decisions he makes from that point forward will determine his final number and, ultimately, whether he lives or dies.

Available now in the Amazon Kindle Store

Also By Luke Smitherd:

He Waits – A Book of Strange and Disturbing Horror

Praise for HE WAITS:

"In the horror genre, familiarity absolutely does breed contempt, and Smitherd obviously knows this. Why else would he be so talented at expertly crafting stories that defy expectations? For me there is no greater joy than seeing an artist excel at his craft." - *Aintitcoolnews.com*

In *HE WAITS*, Luke Smitherd brings you two more Tales Of The Unusual ...

Quite literally, no escape. Because he's always with you. And in the real world - the world of you, the reader - HE WAITS will stay in your mind in a way that you won't expect ...

PLUS THE SECOND STORY, 'KEEP YOUR CHILDREN CLOSE':
A campsite. A family holiday. A broken down car. And an approaching breakdown truck that is just the start of Shelley's nightmare. By the time the sun sets, someone in that field will be dead, and Shelley must somehow make sure it isn't one of her children ... KEEP YOUR CHILDREN CLOSE is a story that you will find impossible to predict.

Available now in the Amazon Kindle Store

Made in the USA
Middletown, DE
25 April 2018